To Hannah

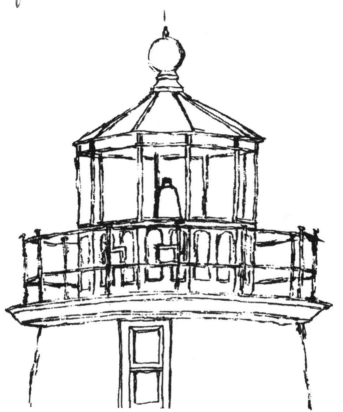

Distress Signal
Jack Comeau

DISTRESS SIGNAL
Copyright 2012 Jack Comeau
All Rights Reserved

Interior: Ellen C Maze, The Author's Mentor,
www.theauthorsmentor.com
Cover Design, Cover Art: Neil Borrell, www.borrellcompany.com

www.jackcomeau.com

PRINT ISBN-13: 978-1475116755
ISBN-10: 1475116756
Also available in eBook

10 9 8 7 6 5 4 3 2 1

PUBLISHED IN THE UNITED STATES OF AMERICA

To my wife, Terry, for all of her loving patience, and to our combined children. Lastly to all those who still labor upon uncertain seas in search of their dreams big and small.

Part
One

ONE

Lightning splinters the night sky, glaring off black, windswept waves that roll as high as hills. Displaced screams mix with the sounds of splitting wood and ride on the back of the wind's howl...

That's how they always started. Not the same images, but always fleeting—like half-remembered dreams, wisps of memory. George's doctor called them panic attacks and had prescribed Xanax, but George resisted taking it. He couldn't get past the feeling that these flashes were more than some brain chemical secretion. Maybe they were things from which pills would be a coward's retreat?

They swirled through George's head as he stood looking down on Boston's gray November waterfront from a high office window. They vanished as quickly as they came, leaving George with that all-too-familiar fear that fluttered across his face, accompanied by a warm, tingling flush, like syrup was being poured over his head. His heart raced. Then it was done.

He watched stray snowflakes drift against the office window to die before his dimly reflected, despondent face. At barely thirty-five, he could al-

1

ready see the ravages of worry-filled time upon his features. A few strands of early gray were beginning to streak through his sandy brown hair. Crow's feet were starting from the corners of his kind eyes. He shifted focus to the city below—ravages there, too. A thick blanket of gray sky felt like endless dusk.

Time is a thief, George thought, as he looked from the Harbor, along the roofs of the three narrow buildings that made up Quincy Market, to Faneuil Hall, the seat of the American Revolution, dubbed "The Cradle of Liberty." In that hall, Sam Adams and Paul Revere had once given rousing speeches to ignite the flames of rebellion. Now, modernization had rendered Boston's rich history little more than a footnote, a wallpaper backdrop to yuppie bars and tourist spots. He felt lost in the present, far from home, as if behind enemy lines.

Beyond Faneuil Hall's grasshopper-topped cupola, he spied Boston's new City Hall, a sight that added to his general default mood of depression. In the 1960s, a whole neighborhood was decimated in the euphemistic name of urban redevelopment—then-Mayor Kevin White's "New Boston" to be exact. The old neighborhood was called Scollay Square, a hotbed of bars, brothels, and burlesque houses that had long been a welcome harbor for sailors home from sea. George thought about those work-hardened men who once walked Scollay Square's crowded scramble of crooked, cobblestone pathways and alleys—men who had forged honest lives from unforgiving seas. Most people George's age didn't even know about Scollay Square.

The voice of his co-worker, Jim, shattered George's introspective moment. "You finally grow a set?"

George spun quickly from the window, surprised that he was not alone.

Jim continued, "If Sheehan catches you in here—"

"It's the day before Thanksgiving. He's not coming back from lunch."

"Still pretty ballsy. What if he forgot his hat or something?"

"That's me—'Danger' is my middle name," George said.

With a chuckle, Jim turned to lead George from the office. Around the same age as George, Jim commanded more confidence and youth-like vitality. George followed Jim from the rich, oak-paneled office to a huge, windowless, white-walled space, packed with a maze of chest-high, gray-fabric-walled cubicles. It was a hive, buzzing with activity. Soft clicks of so many fingers on computer keyboards were multiplied to a din. George's eyes deadened as he looked across it all.

Jim asked, "What was the big attraction in there?"

"Windows."

"They don't open. It's not like you can jump."

"Don't worry," George assured him. "I'm a survivor. Even if it kills me."

George left Jim and trudged along to his own cubicle like there were cinderblocks on his feet. Jim strutted to the coffee station in the corner. Ray was there, filling his *Doctor Who* coffee mug.

Jim said, "When I see that cup, I think Abbott and Costello."

Ray covered his anger, trying to roll with the joke. "That's 'cause you don't appreciate shows with a message." Ray felt compelled to defend his objects of fandom as if actual members of his family were being attacked. "I saw you come out of Sheehan's office with George. You tell him?"

Jim shook his head. "I couldn't. It's Thanksgiving, for Christ's sake. Fucking Sheehan. Couldn't wait until the New Year. Who's going to hire the guy over Christmas?"

"He's got to know. You might even be doing him a favor."

Jim's face tightened. "That's what they say when they put your dog to sleep." After a brief silence, he added, "If he'd stood up to Sheehan just once ..."

George arrived at the opening to his cave-like cubicle and slid into his seat as if it were the electric chair. He slowly looked around at the clutter that had nearly buried his desk. The fabric walls were shingled with thumbtacked memos and Post-it notes. In all of the mess, there were very few personal items. A calendar on the cubicle wall featured Nantucket scenes. This month's scene was a sunset photo of Brant Point Lighthouse.

Jim popped his head up over the cubical top, rescuing George from his thoughts.

"Why don't you come by for Thanksgiving? Wendy and I'd love to have you."

George pushed himself back from his desk. "A pity invite?"

Jim gulped from his Red Sox coffee mug and said, "I always root for the underdog—" Referring down to his mug, "—like these guys."

"They're heroes."

"Underdogs will do that sometimes."

George let out a long breath. "Thanks for asking, but I'm set. Janie's coming by."

Jim said, "Oh, another chance at—"

They finished the sentence simultaneously, but with different words:

George, "—working things out."

Jim, "—self-flagellation."

After a short, uncomfortable silence, Jim changed the subject. "Hey, come on out for drinks with Ray and me. Everything looks better after a few belts."

TWO

Quincy Market glistened in the rain-slicked blue of evening. Twinkle lights, strung in the trees, glowed warmly, finding their reflections in the puddled granite stones of the promenade. Well-dressed yuppies from the nearby offices of government and finance hurried along, dancing around the deeper pools of water on their way to the subway, or more likely, to a few drinks with co-workers, celebrating the start of Thanksgiving weekend. Their upscale tone was contrasted by the musical strains of a nearby Salvation Army band getting a jump on the imminent Christmas Holiday season.

George trailed slightly behind Jim and Ray as they made their way to a dugout basement bar in the main market building. The wooden sign over the doorway proclaimed it The One If By Land Pub. Jim and Ray quickly descended the steps in search of the warmth inside.

George lagged back, staring around for a moment. With sad wistfulness in his eyes, he pondered the hard-bitten history of this once rough waterfront strip. He thought back to stories he'd been told of when the crowds were made of ships' crews fresh off schooners, brigs, and barks. Eager for the taste of one night's shore leave, they'd seek it out in the bars and brothels that once laced these stone and brick facades.

He took in the Salvation Army band. The poignancy of their sad music and faces was a sharp contrast to the rush of joyous yuppies on the way to their first drink of the weekend. Something deep within George connected with those solemn, joyless, band faces. He identified with them but also wanted to save them from their solitude. He searched his pockets for change to give them—none. He dug out his wallet and opened it—only one twenty from the ATM. In this world of plastic, George wondered if the forlorn-faced army ever made a dime for their trouble. Helpless to change their fate, he descended the stairs to join his friends.

The packed bar room blasted of noise and color. Men chatted up women half their age in the delusional hopes of reclaiming lost virility. Females clung in packs of easy and loud drunkenness— safety in numbers. Sports memorabilia shared bar space with knick-knacks that flaunted a half-assed historical or nautical motif. Most of them were jokes—humor only the humorless could embrace, the kind found in souvenir and trinket shops. A thick, wooden-beamed, two-hundred-year-old ceiling hung low overhead, the only hint left of the room's grand history. A large, flat screen TV over the back bar corner played FOX News. Ann Coulter spewed silently from the screen.

George quickly squeezed in with Ray and Jim at the overcrowded bar. Three beers had been ordered by Jim and were already being served when George arrived.

Ray continuously talked at Jim, who prayed to be saved. "First, they cancel *X-Files*, then *Pretender*—it's like a plot. Keep real science from the people. Years ago, there was a great show called *Sliders* about wormholes and shit like that— cancelled!"

Jim could barely feign interest. "Wormholes?"

Ray took the ball and ran. "Wormholes are real! Even *NOVA* did a thing on them. That's PBS. No bullshit there. One day you're waiting for a bus and BAM! You're in a whole other time in history or another universe!"

Jim said, "That's why I don't take the bus."

Jim quickly twisted to George as if he was changing channels from Ray. "Where've you been? Saving mankind?"

"No, just mourning over it, I guess," George answered.

"Lots of women in here. You just have to walk up and say hello."

George reddened slightly with embarrassment and a touch of anger. "Yeah, right. They can't wait to be hassled by nut-jobs like me."

Jim said, "Real positive attitude."

Ray added, "Hey, if the buzz bonnet fits ..."

Jim shot dagger-eyes at Ray. He turned to George. "George, you're not your father."

"The apple doesn't fall far from the tree," George said.

Jim snapped back, "That's a loser's cop-out. We're not slaves to our history." Jim stared at the TV. Ann Coulter was still pontificating. "Maybe *that's* your dream girl."

George stared into his drink. "Oh yeah—'Bitch of the Universe.' "

"Maybe that's your type? After Janie ..."

George said, "Janie's on the other side of the political fence."

"That doesn't matter. Politics aren't the point. The real product is bitch."

"That's a very enlightened outlook," George replied, as he undid his tie, letting the ends dangle down his chest.

"I call it as I see it. How did you two ever stay together?"

George thought a bit before answering. "I made her laugh."

"At you or with you?"

That one stung George. "Is there a difference?"

Ray jumped in. "When George Carlin made some politically or socially astute observation, people laughed with him. If he'd hit himself in the head with a rubber chicken, they would've laughed at him."

"Ray, sometimes you amaze me," Jim said.

"Can I get rubber chickens on eBay?" George asked.

"Need to stock up for tomorrow?"

"You got Janie all wrong."

"You're in denial," Jim said. "You're a glutton for punishment. Best thing you could do is blow her off. Get out of Dodge."

"Leave town? Sheehan would love that. I'd have no job to come back to."

Guilt fluttered across Jim's face as he remembered what George didn't know—the thing Jim was supposed to tell him about his job status. As Jim looked over at poor George, he knew he couldn't tell him tonight. He'd at least wait until after the holiday.

Instead, Jim said, "Fuck your job! Fuck Sheehan! Stand up to him for once. Live balls to the wall. Be the star in your own movie."

Ray chimed in. "Yeah, be the hero!"

Jim added, "Star in your own fucking life!"

George pulled out his tie and snapped it like a whip. "I could tame lions on the weekends."

After a slight chuckle, George returned to staring at his beer, twisting the tie through his fingers, lost in thought.

Finally, he looked over at Jim and said, "Life's not movie-hero bullshit. It's waiting in line at the bank or the supermarket checkout. It's over-packed subway cars and rush hour on the Expressway."

"Not if you take charge," Jim said. "Tell Sheehan to fuck himself. He'll respect you for it. Take a vacation. There must be someplace that you've always wanted to go."

George continued to twist his tie as he listened and then replied, "Nantucket."

Jim was aghast. "Nantucket? That's not even out of state. It's like ninety miles away or something."

"I've always wanted to go to Nantucket."

"Why?"

"I don't know. Who knows why they want things?"

"Nantucket is bullshit. I'm talking adventure here, danger."

George told him, "There are no dragons to slay, no princesses to save ... no magic."

Ray joined back in. "Magic? Yeah, magic. Jim said you do magic."

Jim frowned. "Rope tricks, I said."

Ray was like a kid at a birthday party. "Rope tricks are magic. Do one! Do one ...come *on* ...""

George wanted to escape. "Where am I going to find a rope?"

It occurred to Jim that this might be the perfect distraction. "That tie in your hands will work. Come on—show Ray."

Reluctantly, George wrapped his tie twice around his right hand and then made a large loop that stuck out from between his thumb and index finger. With his left hand, he lifted the dangling end and stretched it out until it was just taut.

George went into his spiel. A new confidence trickled into him. "Keep your eyes on the loop and on the line because—before your eyes—I'll make that loop magically pass through the line and attach itself."

Ray shouted, "Bullshit! It's a trick tie, right?"

Jim said, "Right, Ray. He wore a trick tie all day just in case you asked him to do this."

George said, "Watch now, don't miss it. One ... two ... three ..."

Suddenly the loop did magically dip down and seem to pass through the solid line, attaching itself.

Ray practically exploded. "Shit! *SHIT!* How'd you do that? Do it again!"

To Ray's amazement, George repeated the entire trick right in front of him. It looked just as convincing the second time.

Ray's eyes were still bulging. "Where did you learn that?"

"I always had a thing for ropes."

Jim said, "Yeah, he's a real Boy Scout."

"I'm probably pretty good with a noose, too," George said.

Jim said, "Don't even joke about that!"

"Don't worry. I'm not checking out. I stay to the end of bad movies, too."

"It's Thanksgiving. Four days when you couldn't come in to work if you wanted to. It's now or never. Time to step up to the plate."

George said, "Got any more clichéd platitudes in there?"

"Four days! If I don't get a call or postcard from some cool ass place that you found the balls to go to, I'll lose all my respect for you."

George stared ahead at the glistening bottles of the back bar. The warm, distorted faces of the crowd reflected in every bottle, along with thousands of tiny lights. The din of conversation swirled in his head. He focused on a white Boston Bruins plaque leaning against the back bar mirror. It featured a hockey puck in the center. As George dwelt on that black circle against the field of white, panic

percolated up and rippled through his words.
"What if I can't?"

THREE

George sat in the corner of a nearly empty late-night subway train. The roar of its wheels rattled through the walls. Tunnel lights screamed by at what looked like jet speed. The fluorescent tubes inside the car shone down harshly from above, making caves and craters from facial features that daylight might have stroked forgivingly. Whatever lift George had gotten from the beers was now drained from his body, leaving a dull, heavy fatigue and depression.

He looked over at a young girl of maybe fourteen sitting alone on a bench seat across the aisle. The train window vibrated behind her, making all of its reflections shimmer. Her holiday party was now puke on the front of her fake fur and leather, black and gray jacket. Tears must have accompanied part of the night because her mascara had made raccoon lines run down from her eyes to her cheeks, where they'd long since dried. She held the string of a bright metallic balloon that had somewhere squandered some of its helium and now drifted lazily around her, not sure whether to float or sink. The girl's eyes were vacant, like a shell-shocked soldier. Fourteen and already she'd seen too much, cared too little.

George ached for her. He felt her pain as if it

were his own, but more painful still was his lack of any power to help her. He thought about trying to befriend her, but it would just look like an older guy trying to hit on her, the last impression he wanted to leave. Sensing that life had already exploited her and probably often, he didn't want to add to that list. Still, he chastised himself for doing nothing.

Finally, he reached into his pocket and dug out a few sticks of gum. He reached across the aisle and offered them to her. At least they'd lessen the puke taste that must have still been in her mouth. She eyed him suspiciously but did take the gum and tentatively slid two sticks into her mouth. As they started to do their work, a small flicker of gratitude lightened her face. It warmed George ever so slightly to have been at least some help.

George looked further down the subway car. The only other human was a frail man of seventy-something. George studied him. He wasn't the homeless type. Though his clothes weren't new—in fact they showed much wear—they were neat and clean. This was a man who dressed with pride each morning. Long past retirement, George knew he wasn't coming home from working some night shift.

What brought this man here alone so late? Was he widowed, divorced? Maybe he'd just failed to ever connect? Whatever the reason, loneliness bore the same features of quiet desperation.

George watched the man pull a loosely wrapped McDonald's burger from his pocket. It was something small and sparse, from the Dollar Menu. The man unwrapped it with careful reverence. Each bite he took was slow and deliberate, full of sad appreciation for even this small comfort. On a fixed income, scraping and scrounging like a student, what had his years of work bought him? What would his tomorrow, his Thanksgiving, be like?

George peered into the nebulous blackness of his own future. Would it be any better? Would he end up like that man? What did any of it mean? What was the point? He shook himself free of that growing ember of self-pity and refocused on that poor old man's plight.

George knew that there had to be a way for him to make a difference in the world, but how? Why did it concern him so much? Most people didn't make a difference in the world, and they didn't lose sleep over it.

His subway ride had connected to a lonely bus that now screeched to a stop at the bottom of his Somerville hill. Its air brakes shattered the night's quiet stillness. Its windows blazed blue against the darkness like a Star Wars spaceship. The doors squeaked as they accordioned open. George stepped off alone and started to drag himself up that hill. He was on automatic pilot for most of it. He knew every crack, every bad patch-up job of the sidewalk on this incline. He could navigate blind over every spot where a tree root had lifted or broken a cement slab. It had been his route night after night, morning after morning, year after year. Sometimes he'd secretly wished for a major earthquake or even a terrorist attack just to shake things up and break the monotony. Then it would be easy to be that movie hero who he fantasized about being. People would all be ripe for the saving.

Perhaps that's where the romance of things like war came from? he thought. *War was bigger than you were. It minimized your personal problems, gave you permission to forget whether your marriage was bad or your kids hated you or you'd failed at work or you were just ... alone. You no longer had to think of any of that. You were free to live in the moment, not regretting a past or fearing a future. The sheer enormity of it forced you to be in the present.*

As George walked, he thought back fondly to living through Boston's more benign version of this, the *"Nor'easter."* Every couple of years, one of these winter storms would drop a few feet of snow on the city, stopping all normal business and giving everybody something bigger than their own lives to dwell on. George remembered how strangers would become friends because the storm gave them sudden common ground. He wished there could be a storm like that every day.

The houses that George passed were all pretty much the same, all like his own. They were hundred-year-old, triple-decker, three-family houses, graced with sagging, white-railed front porches that were stacked on top of each other. In the moonlight, they looked like wilting wedding cakes.

George no longer noticed the abundance of Virgin Mary and Jesus lawn ornaments. They used to inspire jokes and commentaries when Janie was with him. Those were the days when his wit was at the ready.

Slightly out of breath, he reached the hilltop and dragged himself up the front stoop of his house. His cold, stiff hands fumbled with his keys. He was home.

Thanksgiving

George watched through his kitchen window as the cloud-patched sun dipped below the black-tarred rooftops. The last of the day was sliding away.

Where was Janie? Was this just the final insult? The final "fuck you"? He walked into his tiny dining area and looked over the table set for two. Two long candles, lit in anticipation of a timely arrival, were now burning low. Two poured glasses of white wine sat, waiting to be consumed. A drying turkey sat in the middle of the table, waiting to be carved. Anger built and mixed with self-pity as George took a seat at the table, the whole time staring at the ticking clock.

He said to himself, "Time means nothing anymore."

He leaned over and blew out the once-romantic candles, watching their ugly smoke trails twist up towards the ceiling. He lifted both of the dinner plates and brought them into the kitchen.

Just as George came through the door, he caught his tabby cat, Garfield, stabbing his paw in through the bars of the birdcage, terrorizing the parakeet inside. George placed the dishes on the counter and lifted the cat.

"Hey, hey, come on, no homicides on the holiday. Okay?"

Garfield glared at him with "fuck you" eyes.

George continued, "You want a bird? Come with me."

He carried Garfield into the dining room and sat with him at the barren table. He ripped off a chunk of the turkey and fed it to the cat. "You know, Petie Bird is like your brother. You should be nice to him."

The cat's face said, "Shut up and feed me."

George complied.

As he kept the food coming, George said to the cat, "You better be careful. What goes around comes around ..."

Suddenly George was caught by a rogue wave of pain. His voice fluttered as he tried to keep from crying. "No, scratch that, nothing comes around. You send out kindness. It just keeps going. It never comes back."

His eyes turned glassy. A knock came at the door. "Great. Oh, just great. Good timing."

George dabbed at his eyes with the heels of his hands as he walked over to open the door.

There, finally, was Janie. About thirty years old, she did have those Ann Coulter-like hard, angular features, but her hair was short and brown.

George's anger bubbled up. "I'm sorry. I should've specified Eastern time, so you'd know I didn't mean California time." Stealing a look at the clock, he snarled, "Or Guam time!"

Janie was unfazed as she walked in past him. "Don't get pissy. I'm here."

After an uncomfortably silent dinner of cold turkey, mashed potatoes, and stuffing, they drifted back to the kitchen. Janie was all business. Eat and leave was her agenda. George's illusions of having a chance to re-spark romance had long since evaporated, but still, his heart was breaking over it. He replayed in his mind a past when at least he thought they were happy. He watched her as she crushed her cigarette out on a tea saucer and took out her lipstick for a quick touch-up, using the toaster side as a mirror while she talked.

Janie said in quick, clipped tones, "I can't stay long. Tomorrow's the biggest shopping day of the year. We're getting our table set up at Downtown Crossing."

Downtown Crossing was the epicenter of Boston's busiest shopping district. Janie had always been active in women's issues. Her group would never miss the chance to set up a table at the most strategic spot for the year's busiest shopping day.

Her involvement didn't intimidate George or anger him like it might some men. He'd long identified with society's victims and saw women's struggles in that light. He was very intimidated by Janie, though. For somebody who could champion the plight of the victim, George was always such a willing one. Some people, Janie included, just couldn't resist the temptation to take advantage of that. It was like shooting fish in a barrel.

George responded to her, "Is that the Women's Action Committee?"

Janie looked up from the toaster with a sour face. "You say that like there's a shit turd in your mouth. Typical. Men never understand."

"I understand. I always did. I support ..."

"I don't need your support."

She tossed her lipstick on the counter. Garfield jumped up to chase it. Janie continued, beginning one of her standard diatribes. "Do you know that every ten seconds a woman in this country has a baby?"

"That woman should be found and stopped."

Janie reigned in her rage to one tight word. "Typical."

She turned to leave. George moved to stop her. "I thought we could talk about us."

"There is no 'us'—not anymore."

George searched his mind frantically for something to keep her in the room. "I'm getting in good with Sheehan down at work. If I get a promotion, we could—"

"You're a joke down there! Don't you know that?"

Seeing the hurt she'd inflicted, Janie softened a bit. "You're just not the corporate type, that's all."

"How do you know?"

"Your whole body rebels against it. Shoes untie themselves on your feet."

"But I'm good with knots."

"Tell that to your shoes. Your shirt can't stay tucked for five minutes. Christ! You get your hair cut at Sears."

"It's their Craftsman haircut, very dependable."

"You're hopeless."

Easing her way toward the door, she said, "Look, I don't want to do this. We just hurt each other back and forth. There's no point."

George said, "I don't see hurt going out in your direction."

Janie's eyes turned to steel. "Oh, right, I'm the bitch. It's always me. How convenient for you."

She was at the door now.

George started to respond, "When my father—"

"Your father was a nut." Janie's words cut through him like knives. Once again, seeing this softened her a little. "Look, I want to be nice ..."

"NICE!" George screamed.

Janie continued, "Why do you think I came up here? You had nobody for Thanksgiving. I was trying to be ... well ... nice."

"Well, you *failed.*"

George flung the door open, took her arm, and pushed her out. He then slammed the door on her as she fumed in angry protest. He locked it triumphantly.

With this bold act of personal maintenance, he reclaimed a piece of his self-respect that he thought had been gone forever. He walked back into his kitchen with a new bounce of confidence in his step.

On the kitchen counter, Garfield was still batting around Janie's lipstick tube. George lifted the cat and looked straight into his eyes. "You're next on my list."

George dropped Garfield on the floor and picked up the lipstick tube. He wasn't sure what to do with it. After a little thought, he shoved it in the pocket of his coat hanging on a nearby wall hook.

With a sudden burst of energy, he strutted to the kitchen window and flung it open. He spun to what was left of the turkey, grabbed it and brought it to the window, leaning out with it. He spied an open, blue Dumpster in the next-door alley, beyond a stockade fence. Could he make it?

After careful aim, he flung the turkey, landing it square in the Dumpster. "Score!" he shouted. He spun to the still-disinterested Garfield. "Tonight the old George gets a Viking funeral. Tomorrow I re-boot!

FOUR

Black Friday

A mixture of fear and excitement greeted George as he ascended the gangplank of the Nantucket ferry. If Jim could only see him now—he might still give him shit about it only being Nantucket, but inside George would know that it was a big step outside of his comfort zone. Would he be that movie-hero version of himself that he'd pictured from the safety of home, or would he be the small, scared, lonely guy who had become his true day-to-day persona? Would he be able to live in the moment or be lost in the jungle of chatter that festered in his head?

George dropped his duffle bag on the deck and stepped to the starboard rail, looking over the still-sleeping town of Hyannis. A new determination had seized upon him the night before. He'd gotten up at four a.m. in order to catch the Plymouth and Brockton bus out of South Station and to get to Cape Cod in time to catch the first ferry of the day. He planned to cram in as much enjoyment, introspection, and perhaps, real adventure as the three days could hold. He'd have stories to tell Jim and Ray, but more importantly, he was determined to find answers as to why his whole life had fluctuated between despair and numbness.

Numb was as good as it got. Joy had always eluded him. Last night, he'd decided to end this for good, no matter what it took. This trip would be do or die. While quickly packing, he'd grabbed the bottle of Xanax and tossed it in his bag. Rethinking it, he'd taken the bottle back out and left it on the counter. He'd be working without a net on this trip.

Doubts began to creep in. Maybe the jungle of chatter would win out? The whole bus ride from Boston had been one long mental rehash of last night and a torturous recounting of his relationship with Janie. He'd called up all the old wounds and rubbed them raw enough to hurt freshly again. He'd remembered all the times he'd taken the initiative to try to fix things, all the hours spent in the "Self Help" aisles of bookstores.

One time, he'd brought home a book titled *Healing Your Toxic Past*. Before George even had the chance to crack it open, Janie had gotten a hold of it. She had gone through the whole book with a pink highlighter. When George opened it up almost every page had something highlighted. With a pen, she'd scribbled in the margins alongside the pink smears, writing things like *THIS IS YOU, THIS ONE'S REALLY YOU!!* and *THIS, TOO!!!* On and on it went. Talk about your preemptive strikes. Just thinking about it now curdled George's soul with anger so all-consuming that the world around him was mere wallpaper.

The ferryboat cast off and drifted away from the dock. The whole vessel shuddered as the engine roared into forward gear.

No turning back now.

George watched Hyannis' stately summer homes slowly pass by. As they cleared the inner harbor, the white clapboard houses of the Kennedy Compound came into view. Just watching it gave George a new feeling of hope, a thought that dreams might be possible. As they moved further into Nantucket Sound, the wind picked up, batting around the wisps of hair that usually lay across his forehead, making them dance. The original surge of self-confidence that George had felt after last night started to flow back into his bloodstream.

George had a strong urge to explore the boat. He looked at his duffle bag. Should he carry it? He glanced around the deck. It was as empty as that late night subway had been on Wednesday. The few people scattered about were older, hardened, crusty sorts, all men. There went George's hopes of meeting his soul mate. He realized that the duffle bag question was silly. Was one of these few old coots going to steal it and jump ship? He'd let it sit there. The new George would take risks. No more "worst-case scenarios."

He made his way toward the bow. As the boat ventured further from Cape Cod's protected shore, it started to roll with the bigger ocean swells. George stumbled along in the strange landlubber dance that those without their sea legs always did. For a fleeting second, it panicked him, but then it made him smile. Soon the ferry's rolling fit him like a glove, like he'd always known it. Confidence trickled into his soul. The wind now plastered his hair straight back across his head. He liked it. Years of self-doubt seemed to melt away. Every time those thoughts started to make George giddy, he caught himself, reined himself back in. How could such a small thing bring on so great a change? He couldn't trust it.

Looking ahead, George saw a few wisps of fog dancing across the swells. Before he knew it, the cold gray broth enveloped the boat. From the bow, George could barely see the waves below. Behind him, the wheelhouse was but a soft, chalky impression against the gray infinity. The rhythmic wail of the boat's foghorn pierced the emptiness. George heard other vessels respond, their horns curiously displaced and muted by the thick, opaque air. It all had a haunting quality that gave George a tingling chill on the back of his neck.

George straightened up at the bow, forcing a new confidence to flow through him. Finally, the fog lifted. It was like pulling back a curtain on the world. Suddenly, right before George, was Nantucket.

It didn't slowly creep up from over the horizon like he'd expected it to. It snuck in, hidden under the fog's thick blanket. It wasn't close enough yet to make out fine detail. Through the remaining haze, it looked like a gray desolate spit of land, very much the way Melville first described it in *Moby Dick*.

As they drew near, the morning sun burst through ragged holes in the cloud cover, creating heavenly rays. George watched Brant Point Light House drift by, bathed in the sidelight of orange morning sunshine. He saw a woman, bundled up against the cold, traveling the long wooden-planked walkway to the light. She stopped to watch the ferry as it cleared the Point. George waved to her. After a short hesitation, she waved back. George was thrilled by this first contact with an Islander.

As George continued to lean on the bow rail, watching Nantucket town twist into view, he noticed an old man standing alongside him. Every life trauma and hardship had left its mark on the old man's face. They made eye contact.

The man asked, "You an Islander?"

"No, just taking a short vacation," George said.

"November ain't the time for tourists. Nothing to do, no one to do it with."

"I like the solitude. It'll give me time to think some things out."

"Well," the old man said, "see that you don't go stir crazy."

The fat ferry drifted into Nantucket's Steamboat Wharf and folded down its truck-sized door like a huge tongue, creating its own ramp. Mammoth eighteen-wheelers inside the boat's belly revved up their mighty engines and snorted black smoke from their stacks.

From the top deck bow, George surveyed the scene, filling with excitement. He turned and ran for his duffle bag, brushing away the nagging fear that it wouldn't be there.

There it is! he thought, adding, *Take that, you stupid fear. One for me!"*

He departed the boat with a new bounce in his step. He made friendly, comic faces at a young kid sitting on his father's shoulders watching the passengers disembark.

As George walked along the edge of the wharf, he spotted a gaggle of seagulls in a feeding frenzy over something that floated in the water. He eased his way toward the commotion for a closer look. A dead tabby cat was the object of the frenzy. George recoiled, but still he watched as the gulls pecked at and ripped apart the former cat. It looked like Garfield. George thought back to Garfield stabbing his paws in at the parakeet. He remembered the last words that he spoke to him: *What goes around, comes around.*

Foreboding flooded across him. Was he through the looking glass here? He felt like a small child who had lost his mother in the supermarket. He wondered if he'd ever make it back. He looked at the ferry on the far end of the wharf. It was already lifting its ramp and sliding away from the dock.

No escaping now.

FIVE

Not sure of where he was going, George took a left towards Main Street. On a narrow road that wound along the waterfront, he passed gray, weathered, wood-shingled fishing shacks that stood on stilts in the water. At one time, they'd functioned as such, but now they were cute little cottages, the subject of many a postcard and probably cost a pretty penny to rent.

As he looked around, it was easy to see that the town was built to accommodate a lot of people. At one time, when it was the whaling capital of the world, there were lots. Now, as a summer vacation and tourist spot, these streets still swelled to full capacity for two months a year.

Standing here in windswept, late November, it was nearly a ghost town. Buildings and pathways that were photogenic and quaint in July had now shed their summer masks and reveled in the history that bore them. Absent the people and the cars, there was little to tell George that this wasn't the Nantucket of Melville's time.

It was a Nantucket the summer folks couldn't know. They could learn about it at the Whaling Museum or at the Atheneum. They could harbor nostalgic fantasies for what it must have been like. But they couldn't feel it in their bones.

If they could, it wouldn't be the quaint vision they might expect. They wouldn't feel romantic nostalgia for a simpler time gone by. They'd feel hardship and loss and fear, wrapped in cold and loneliness. They'd feel the pain of a tiny isolated island whose men went to sea for years at a time, often not returning, an island of women left to fend for themselves against cold, poverty, and disease.

Sometimes these women were done in by just loneliness itself. Children, if they survived that long, might see their fathers for the first time at age three or four as their mothers brought them down to meet their returning whale ships. Part-time husbands and wives would barely recognize each other as they tentatively studied the faces each had last seen with three or four years less hardship, wear, and age upon them.

This true Nantucket slept through today's summers, a reverse hibernation of sorts. As George would discover, the empty season of winter was when true Nantucket reclaimed its soul.

When George reached the cobblestones of Main Street, he stopped. He playfully stretched a foot out to test the street as if it were a sheet of ice. George had seen cobblestones before. Boston was full of them, but not like these. George was used to the flat-topped, brick-like stones that graced parts of Quincy Market and still dwelt in some little-traveled North End and Beacon Hill back alleyways. These Nantucket cobblestones were something else again.

Some were round as a grapefruit, others jagged or square, appearing in every size, shape, and color. They seemed to have sprung up naturally through the dirt like some unkempt garden. Most were of the round variety and stood ready to cast off any foot that tried to negotiate them. Their surfaces were smooth as polished pearls. These stones had been ballast. They had been dug from European soil and tossed into the holds of empty ships. Their weight held the ships down so they wouldn't capsize on their way to the New World.

George forced down those worst-case scenario fears that warned *What if I twist and break my ankle? What if I slip and fall from a big round stone, and my head hits a jagged one and splits open?*

This time he laughed at that old-lady voice in his head. He dropped his duffle bag on the brick sidewalk and stepped out onto the cobblestone street, spreading his arms for balance the way a tightrope walker might. As he gained confidence, he began to hop across on the big ones as if they were stepping-stones in a wild river. With his ego full of accomplishment, he skipped back for his duffle.

As he lifted it, he saw an elaborate poster attached to the side of a clapboard building. It read:

TRISTRAM BOLGERS THE FOURTH
A name from the past
with a vision for the future.
Come hear for yourself.
Saturday morning, ten o'clock,
in front of the Pacific National Bank.

George's face twisted in confusion as he reread the sign. *Pacific* National Bank? He heard the clop of hoofs and the squeak of wagon wheels on the cobblestones. He turned but saw nothing. With a shrug, he lifted his duffle.

SIX

The Quahog Bed and Breakfast was on Centre Street on the outskirts of town, just after the street twisted up past the famed Jared Coffin House, Nantucket's most famous old dwelling, now a very upscale hotel. While no Jared Coffin House, The Quahog was classic Nantucket: weathered shingles, white trim, black shutters, and a red door, with an ornate, brass, pineapple-shaped doorknocker.

George was shown to his room up an old, narrow, steep flight of wooden stairs that creaked in protest with every step. He listened to the creaks as he went. They stirred some distant memory that he couldn't define. He felt guilty each time he put his weight on a stair plank, as if the creaks were groans of actual pain that he was inflicting on them.

His room was standard Victorian. The bed was anchored by intricately carved oak columns at each corner. A matching oak armoire, bureau, and writing table also graced the room. Sheer Irish lace curtains adorned the window. The bathroom featured an old-fashioned, claw-footed bathtub.

George inspected the room with a nagging sense of apprehension. He stepped to the closet and opened the door. There, on a small, roll-around table, was a TV with a long cable connected to the back.

Thank God! George thought. He started to pull out the TV.

Suddenly he stopped. What was he doing? Did he come here to hide in his room and watch TV? This was to be his journey of self-discovery; his mission was to confront and conquer his demons by stepping out of his "comfort zone." He eased the TV back into the closet and shut the door.

On the writing table, he found a short stack of postcards depicting the Quahog B&B in a pen and ink drawing. George settled into the spindle-back desk chair to write a postcard to Jim. He would prove to him that he could take charge of his life.

He got through the "Dear Jim" part.

What next? "Having a wonderful time?"

"That's stupid," he said to himself. "I'm not having any kind of time yet. I'm just hiding in here writing letters. Writing letters and talking to myself like a goddamned nut."

As he tried to think of something else to write, his attention was grabbed by something outside the window.

On the second floor porch of the next house over, George watched a young, raven-haired woman in a long, black, Victorian dress. The sight drew him from his chair to the window for a closer look. When he pushed back the sheers and gazed out though the glass, there was no woman. Panic ran through him as he wondered what he had seen. He quickly reasoned that the web of bare tree branches between him and the empty porch could have been mistaken for a person through the mesh of the sheer lace curtains. He looked down to the alleyway. A couple of kids were hanging around a Vespa and a moped down there.

"I bet they didn't see anything either," George said to himself. "Great! Now I'm seeing things *and* talking to myself."

George stepped away from the window and headed for the desk. "I'm already going stir-crazy, like that old guy on the boat said." Again, this was aloud to himself.

"Stop talking to yourself!"

"Okay! I will!" Now he was answering himself.

He sat down at the desk again to continue the postcard. Again, he thought out loud about what to say. "I'm here in Nantucket and ... I'm just sitting here in Nantucket and ... and talking to myself like a FUCKING NUT!"

Fear crept across George's face as he sat there rubbing his eyes. "Maybe the apple doesn't fall far from the tree?"

George stood up and went for his coat. "I've got to get out of here!"

"STOP TALKING TO YOURSELF!"

SEVEN

George sat at the edge of the pier watching boats slip through the velvety folds of the inner harbor water. What a world away he was from his day-to-day. Maybe this would be the weekend he'd start to reclaim parts of himself he'd lost somewhere along the way? He could feel old, long-ignored joys and strengths calling to him. Should he just allow them in or stop to analyze where they'd been and why? Is that the real work from which true healing would come?

George opted for letting it flow in. Instead of sitting, he'd explore.

Though less of an adventure than the cobblestone street, the brick sidewalks of Main Street held their own challenges. A few hundred years of storms, ice patches, and tree root surges had turned them into an obstacle course. George barely noticed as he let himself enjoy the charm of the shops. Though the buildings reeked of history, many of the shops inside them catered to the upscale New York sensibilities of Nantucket's summer residents, and most were closed at this time of year. The places that remained open were geared more to the rustic, year-round crowd. This helped the old Nantucket come alive in George's heart. He felt rejuvenated.

At the far end of town heading away from the water, where Main Street narrowed, a building jutted out, half into the middle of the street. It was red brick with a small, half-circle grouping of white columns around the front door. This was the Pacific National Bank. In front of it, a crowd of about thirty had gathered to hear a speaker, orating from the steps.

As George got closer, he could see the speaker more clearly. He was a portly man of around sixty, a dichotomy of sorts. He was pudgy in a way that said life had been easy for him. He'd over-consumed, over-indulged, and had little in the way of hard work to challenge him. But living within that soft exterior was a fierceness, a determination that informed you at once about his potential ruthlessness when fighting to get his way. This was Tristram Bolgers the Fourth, Nantucket's current mayor. The look of those listening ran the gamut from skeptical to supportive.

George caught part of Bolgers' speech. "—The early 1800s saw Nantucket as the whaling capital of the world. Our wealth was envied by the mainland, by the whole country for that matter. It was hard, then, to conceive of lean times occurring. But this island finished out that century in poverty and despair."

George heard muttering remarks from some of the listeners. One man said, "We'll get worse when you're done with us."

Bolgers continued to pontificate. "Then we enjoyed success again, thanks to the vision of a few men. They saw the potential for summer tourism and so we bounced back from the brink. Now it's time for a new vision so we can continue through this new century with growing prosperity. Nantucket must keep in step with the times or founder on the rocks of a new and changing world."

A man from the crowd shouted, "Go back to Boston, you coof!"

With that, Bolgers bristled. "Coof! I'm more Islander than most of you, not only as your Mayor, but also because of my history here. You all walk by this memorial every day."

As he said this, he spread his arm dramatically towards a round, copper plaque set in a granite block behind him. On the plaque was a relief portrait of a stronger-looking, bearded version of himself. The portrait was nearly full profile, as if it were on a coin. This was Tristram Bolgers the First—the original Bolgers. Even in the crudely sculpted relief portrait, it was easy to see that the first Bolgers was no man to trifle with. He was a man of commanding presence who knew what it was to fight for his life against the elements and other men. Though the resemblance was strong, there was nothing soft about the first Bolgers. He could've had this pudgy, pontificating, present namesake for breakfast.

Fear raced through George's heart as he stared at the plaque. That warm, tingling, syrup feeling began to flow over his head. His thoughts mocked him about it. *Oh, great! Now I'm afraid of a giant penny,* he told himself.

A black void in his brain opened, revealing all of humanity's hardships, loss, and loneliness. As soon as it came, it was gone. This was an especially bad one. He nearly regretted leaving that Xanax at home.

George kept studying the plaque as Bolgers the Fourth continued to drone on about his illustrious family history. Beneath the copper engraving was a legend chiseled into the stone. It read TRISTRAM BOLGERS, 1815 to 1881, PIONEER OF THE SURFSIDE LIFESAVING STATION.

George focused harder to read the brief history etched in script below the banner. It read:

*Without the courage, strength, and kind humanity
of Nantucket's own Tristram Bolgers, many a soul
would have perished on our treacherous shoals.
We thank him for putting the sanctity of
human life ahead of personal safety and profit.*

George felt a wave of revulsion rise within him
as he read. More panic attack? Then he thought
about how pale his life was in comparison, how dim
and worthless. Reading about Bolgers somehow
forced him to ponder, even wallow in, his own failure.

Before he knew it, the present Bolgers was finished. He was asking for questions and looking
around at the faces in the crowd.

George wished he were invisible. It was that
same feeling he'd always had in school, the terror of
being picked, of the secret being laid bare that he
hadn't done the assignment, or worse, couldn't,
didn't understand it, was too stupid. For George,
getting picked was always a precursor to getting
picked on. He decided he'd go a hundred and eighty
degrees from his inclinations and raise his hand.

Bolgers was delighted to have someone take an
interest.

"What about you, young man?" Bolgers said to
George as if there were other hands raised, too.

This was it—show time! Part of George wished
he'd never left Boston, but that part was not in the
driver's seat, not today. "Why do you have the
wrong ocean on your bank?" he asked.

The onslaught of laughter mortified George.

Bolgers shouted to the crowd, pointing at
George, "There's your coof!"

The group burst into laughter.

George sank further. He could feel the warm
heat of shame dance up his back and fill his
cheeks.

Bolgers surveyed the crowd, drinking in the change of group dynamics. Thanks to this silly little nerd, he was winning the group over. It was always so easy to unite an audience by focusing their contempt on a single person, group, or issue. Bolgers knew this theory was as old as history itself. It always worked. Politicians had used it for centuries. "Romans, focus your hate on the Christians!" "Germans, focus your hate on the Jews!" "Christians, focus your hate on the gays!" "Americans, focus your hate on the blacks or the Mexicans or the poor!"

George pondered this at the same time Bolgers did. George thought back to what Jim had said about Ann Coulter and Janie: "Politics don't matter. The product is bitch."

The pudgy orator, Nantucket's shining mayor, looked down upon poor wretched George with false pity. "My dear boy, did you just get off the boat?"

Amid a light flurry of more laughs, Bolgers went on to explain. "While it is true that Nantucket is situated on the Atlantic, our money and our world prominence came from our whaling in the Pacific."

Bolgers wrapped it all in a romantic cloak of risked lives and hardships endured by Nantucket men sailing around Cape Horn. He had the crowd in the palm of his hand. He had them there thanks to George, and he knew it. Perhaps there was a small kernel of resulting guilt. Why else would he turn back to George and speak to him so kindly?

Bolgers said, "Young man, I'm sorry if I kidded you before. Coof is a word and an attitude of the past. You are precisely the kind of person we need more of on this island. Newcomers who are not afraid to explore new adventures, bring new ideas."

To George, this was like water to a sun-baked man lost in the desert. He drank it all in, forgetting whatever wounds came before it. He listened openly as Bolgers continued.

"As Mayor, I'll make sure that the best of Nantucket's charms are open to you. That's not only for your sake, but for our sake, too. You'll go home to Boston or New York, or wherever you may hail from, and tell your friends about your wonderful time here. You may bring them for a visit. When you send kindness out, it comes back to you."

George saw the irony in those last words. It had never worked that way for him.

As Bolgers redirected his attention to the group, George drifted to the rear of the crowd and finally departed, walking down Centre Street towards The Jared Coffin House and the bend that would lead back to The Quahog B & B.

EIGHT

George hadn't gone very far on Centre Street before he came to a red clapboard house on the corner of Centre and Quince Street. The bottom floor had been made into a tourist store and was closed for the season. A strange, ominous feeling came over him, a darkness that he couldn't understand. It was different from his normal panic attacks. It scared him. Needing to turn away from the house, he spun his head to look across the street. There he spotted a man in an overgrown field sitting on a crate, hammering away at what looked like a long, overturned rowboat.

George headed over there. As he got closer, he could better make out the features of the worker. He looked to be in his twenties, but at the same time much older. Already, work had hardened and aged his body.

When George arrived in front of him, the man looked up. His eyes were pools of sadness. George surveyed the surroundings. Nothing was from the current century. The world within his view was completely one of the mid-1800s. Had he walked through some kind of time warp, perhaps through some cosmic or supernatural door? Was he cracking up like his father had done? He couldn't let himself ponder any of it.

He spoke in nervous denial to this poor worker. "Is this an historical reenactment?"

The man looked at him with quizzical suspicion.

George continued, "Like Plymouth Plantation?"

The man answered without much emotion, "Plymouth? Do I look like a bleeding Round Head? Hand me that chisel."

Feeling honored to be included in the action, George scanned the battered, wooden, handmade toolbox at his feet. The tools themselves looked homemade.

Realistic detail, George dared himself to think. He lifted a heavy, rough-hewn, iron chisel and handed it down to the man.

"Building a rowboat?" George ventured.

"Whaleboat!" the man barked back as if insulted by the very question.

The man's reaction brought automatic panic to George, as authority figures often did. Still, the man's answer confused him, and he'd respect himself even less if he backed down. He asked his follow-up question as if he were treading through a minefield. "But ... I just found out that whaling was in the Pacific ... How could men get all the way to the Pacific in this?"

The man tossed his hammer and chisel onto the boat's overturned hull with the exasperation of a father whose son had failed to mow the lawn right. The tools made an echo inside the hollow boat.

Reeling in his patience, the man explained, "A whaleBOAT's what rides in a whaleSHIP to the Pacific grounds. Are you some kind of a coof?"

George grabbed for a rare strand of courage to answer back, "I'm getting tired of that word. What the hell's a coof?"

The man replied, "Them's that don't know the word can't help but be one."

"Enlighten me," George said, keeping a lid on his

meekness.

"Off-Islanders," the man said. "Them's that's ignorant of our ways."

George was bound to continue standing his ground. He also still assumed that this was some kind of historical reenactment.

"So," George stated, "I'm a tourist. I admit it. Isn't it your job to teach us instead of yelling at us?"

The man put his anger into silent chiseling. George tried to keep up conversation. "You guys worked so hard in the olden days. TV kills my incentive."

In shock, the man dropped his tools again. "You have T.B.?"

"TV ... Television ..." George said.

"Oh, teleVISION. 'Doc' Coffin has spectacles to fix that."

George started to relax as things seemed to grow more friendly.

"Help me flip this over," the man demanded.

George took an end, and they turned the boat on its keel. George stared into the boat, noting all of the strange designs inside. He dared not push this guy any further by asking what they were. There was a leg brace of some kind at the bow and a big, square, open box in the middle. At the very back was a thick post that George thought might have been for tying up the boat, but it seemed like a poor design for that purpose.

"Sorry if I disturbed your work. I was across the street, and that house just gave me the creeps so—"

The man cut him off. "Creepy house. Bad place. A cannibal lives there."

"Cannibal?" George's fear and shock were tempered by his certain knowledge that this was all a show of some kind.

The man continued, "Yep, ate his own cousin."

Half smiling, George turned to look at the house. His smile quickly faded. The house was no longer red, but covered in weathered shingles. The store was gone. The road between them was now rutted dirt. George turned pale as the reality of frightening possibilities started to invade his brain. *Was this The Twilight Zone or just good old, mundane mental collapse?*

He turned back to the boatman. He and his boat were gone. In panic, George spun his head away. He was slightly relieved to see that The Jared Coffin House was still standing there on the corner of Centre and Broad, but in front of The Coffin House stood that same gorgeous woman in the dark Victorian dress. She looked straight at him, motioning to him. Beckoning him.

Even at this distance and even in that dress, she was the most beautiful woman George had ever seen. She radiated every quality George had ever dreamt of, but more than that, there was a strange pull drawing him toward her. It was an unexplainable combination of comfort and fear, wrapped in excitement of every sort. The kind of excitement you'd feel cresting the first drop of a roller coaster was nestled right beside the kind of excitement held in one's first romantic touch. These thoughts tumbled around in George's brain as he walked toward her. His steps were trance-like, as if he were in her spell.

Just as he got to the edge of the street, a horse-drawn milk wagon passed by, forcing him to stop and obscuring his view of her. When the wagon had nearly gone by, it was met by a modern SUV that passed in the opposite direction, further obscuring George's view. When the way was finally clear, the woman was gone. George also realized that his surroundings were now back to normal modern-day life.

Cars lined the street. Mopeds sped by. That house was red again with the same closed store at the bottom of it. Far down at the other end of Centre Street, Bolgers still pontificated in front of the bank.

George quickly spun back to The Jared Coffin House. Everything was still modern. In the very spot where the woman had stood was now the old man he'd met on the ferry, the one who'd warned him about going stir-crazy. He was dancing and talking wildly to the sky, obviously crazier than he had warned George about becoming.

George said quietly to himself, "I need a drink."

The Brotherhood of Thieves was crowded for this time of year. Undoubtedly, George thought, more people than he realized had decided to celebrate the Thanksgiving weekend on Nantucket. More likely, the few who did come over were mostly in here.

The Brotherhood was a bar/restaurant that had long been a Nantucket institution. It was a place that even infrequent visitors—even coofs—knew to head for straight off the ferry. Their chowder, as well as their fish and chips, had few equals. Their reputation for landlubber bar-food like burgers and curly fries drew in its share of twenty-something visitors as well. It was a curious mix of authentic Nantucket history and modern accommodations.

The name came from a charge made by Stephen Foster in 1844, denouncing all those who would band together in support of slavery. Nantucket was one of the very first spots to support abolition. They were also far ahead of the curve on women's rights, making waves about it a full century before Betty Friedan or Gloria Steinem set foot on the planet.

The Brotherhood was in the basement of a house that dated back centuries. The ceiling was low, with sagging, thick, dark, wooden beams. Between the beams was roughly troweled, horsehair plaster. Candle-powered lanterns glistened from the polished brick walls.

George felt comforted by the crowd. It seemed that modern reality had returned to embrace him. He worked toward the bar for that drink that would make it all seem better.

Unfortunately, on his way to the bar, he spied that woman again. She was sitting at a corner table on the far side of the crowded room. He had to talk with her. She must know what's happening, be part of it. He turned from the bar and waded through the mass of humanity, catching only fleeting glimpses of her between passing patrons as he negotiated his way around tray-burdened waitresses as well as drinkers on their way to or from the bathrooms.

Finally, he broke through to her table and started to speak. "Excuse me, I've been watching you from across the room and—"

He stopped short. Sitting in her place was now a two hundred and fifty pound guy billowing out of a football jersey. He had the close-cropped hair of an Army sergeant and a tough, unfriendly face. George opened his mouth and closed it again. The man's face reddened. Testosterone oozed from his eyes.

"This ain't Brokeback Mountain," the guy said.

NINE

Not even a full day into his adventure and already George was spent. His footsteps were heavy on the narrow stairs up to his room at The Quahog. Each plank complained extra loudly.

You again! they seemed to say to George as he carried himself up with a mind full of questions and fears about what he'd experienced.

He swung open his door, ready to walk in and fall across the bed, but instead stopped in his tracks. There, sitting at the writing table, was the beautiful Victorian woman. On the desk, a stack of ragged parchment had replaced the postcards that George had been toiling over before. She was more than classically beautiful. She radiated a depth, a soulfulness, a gravity of spirit, that reached straight into George's heart and squeezed it like a ripe fruit.

George had never believed in "love at first sight." Recently he'd stopped believing in any kind of love at all. Still, he had his dreams, dark corners of his psyche where embers of hope could still smolder. In those rare and blissful dreams that his waking brain could scarcely remember, she must have been there. Perhaps she was their author?

On several of those special, dream-fringed mornings, he'd woken up with the same feelings that she now radiated to him. Unfortunately, back then, the bliss always dissipated once his feet hit the floor. One day, he'd often promised himself, he'd wake up with that non-specific tingling joy and not put his feet on the floor. He'd cheat the world of its chance to pummel him that day. He'd stay in bed.

As soon as he'd think this, another voice would take over, stern and parental. *Don't do it! Get up!* He'd ponder the reality of a life spent in bedridden retreat and see all of its ugly features.

A cold sweat broke out across George as he stood there watching this vision of perfection. Time stood still. The inner voice that tried to reel him back to sanity was losing its grip. It couldn't compete with what his eyes and senses were treating him to.

She had hair as black as caviar. It flowed halfway down her back. Her alabaster skin had a translucence that made George feel as if he could see down into her. Twisting delicately toward him, she said, "Can you write it?"

George was taken aback. "Write it?"

After all, she was sitting at the writing table. As he pondered this, she faded from view. Terror raced through George's heart. Was all that bliss just the dawning of insanity? George bolted for the bathroom. He flicked on the cold water and splashed it to his face. He stared at himself in the mirror, still shaking with fear.

"Something I ate," he said to his reflection. "That's it. Last night! I let the turkey stay out too long."

He splashed more water on his frantic face. He looked back up to the mirror. There she was again, behind him, in the reflection!

"Can you write it?" she asked.

He spun from the mirror to face her, but she was gone again. "This must be the TRIP part of tryptophan."

He walked nervously back into the bedroom. There she was by the bed! He froze. Their eyes connected. With a quivering voice, George asked, "Who are you?"

"Can you write it?" the woman repeated.

George's words spilled out like a torture-induced confession. "I can't write it. I'm not a writer. I can't write. I can't ..." His words trailed off.

"Can you WRITE it?" she said.

"Who are you?" George repeated in a thin, dry voice.

She moved closer. His heart raced with terror and lust. She seemed to illuminate the room around her. Now she was almost against him. A tingling warmth rippled through his body. His breath quickened. She slowly reached out to him. At first, he flinched, but his desire overcame his fear, and he nearly turned to liquid as he gave himself in to her. She wrapped her delicate hand around the back of his neck and looked straight into his eyes. The world went silent. Nothing existed for George but the bottomless pools of her pupils.

It was as if she were seeing past him and through him at the same time, drilling straight through to his soul. Not a word was exchanged between them, but volumes of emotion were traded. She released her hand from his neck, drawing it back slowly, letting her fingers run along his cheek, ending on his lips. He'd never felt this height of sexual arousal before.

She slipped past him, heading for the door. He turned to follow her, but she was already gone. On the desk, lying across the parchment was a single red rose. With complete reverence, George lifted the rose to his face. Pressing it gently against his nostrils, he breathed in the scent, closing his eyes to better remember her. Suddenly a name drifted into his brain—*Rebecca.*

Her name?

Yes! It was like a strong thought and like a voice, but at the same time, it was neither. He couldn't define the exact specifics or parameters. It was like trying to recall a dream. He just knew that, somehow, the cosmos had told him her name.

When he opened his eyes, the rose was gone. The B&B postcards had once again replaced the parchment. George's heart broke as he looked around the room. Was any of it real?

"I should've eaten more of that turkey."

TEN

Next Morning

Tristram Bolgers dressed quickly for a Saturday, resenting it the whole way. *Who does business on a Saturday?* he thought, as his tired fingers struggled with the challenge of a Windsor knot.

He studied his face in the pristine mirror. *Not bad,* he thought as he gave his tie a final pull. *Some men are finished by my age, ready for the home. I'm as vital as ever, a babe-magnet to boot.* Fantasies caressed his brain as he pulled on his pants.

Bolgers pranced through the kitchen as his wife, Betty, quickly stirred up a breakfast of eggs, ham, and muffins. God how he loved that smell, all mixed with the sea air and brewing coffee.

"No time for breakfast, honey. Just coffee," he said.

"Sit yourself down. You need a good breakfast, and I got up special to make it."

"But, mother—" he started to protest.

"You just sit right down," she ordered.

Like a reluctant child, Bolgers took a seat. Secretly, he loved the pampering his wife gave him. Secretly, she knew it. It was her unspoken job, their unspoken pact. His dire need for her had coalesced into a solid, quiet kind of love.

Unfortunately for Betty, it wasn't a love he thought much about whenever he was lucky enough to bag the odd young woman at a political or social function.

Not at big functions, mind you. They were reserved for his wife, standing loyally at his side, always the cornerstone, the anchor of his "family values" image. His indiscretions happened at those smaller functions that he told Betty wives weren't invited to. That was when the randy Tristram—the bad boy—took over.

"Call me Trist," the bad boy would say. Tristram was too old and stodgy, too "historical" sounding. Never Tris—that was too feminine. Sometimes he thought about using Ram. He couldn't decide whether that was extra macho or extra gay.

Other women weren't frequent. His age, girth, and pomposity were far greater negatives than his political power and money could balance out—usually. This, of course, was a secret he kept from himself.

Betty Bolgers saw the flip side of that. At times, she'd watch him flirting with some young thing. She'd comfort herself with the security that no one else would have him. She saw him more accurately than he saw himself—a big, overgrown kid who got what he wanted in the world by throwing a tantrum for it. Unfortunately, the world usually capitulated. He never really learned the lesson of those actions not working.

As she watched him eagerly wolf down the meal he had said he had no time for, she thought, as she often did, about how she ended up here. She wondered again whether the love she felt for him was just the comfort of familiarity. He'd never really swept her off her feet, even when they were young.

Betty thought back to the days when she was pretty, and Tristram was but one of a handful of suitors. Back then, she lived in Louisburg Square, the crowning jewel at the top of Boston's Beacon Hill. Her family name was Winthrop, which carried with it high style and Boston Brahmin stature. Her future was a wide-open wonderland of possibilities. She could barely funnel her girlish excitement into the narrow container of social decorum expected of a young lady on Beacon Hill. Coming from old money, she was a good catch for any of the numerous gentlemen who lingered at the wrought iron fence in front of her brick townhouse, hoping for a chance meeting.

For reasons that had faded from her memory, Tristram stood out. He hadn't come courting to the house. He was outside the circle of Beacon Hill society. She'd met him in a coffee shop across from The State House and from Boston Common, at the corner of Beacon and Park Streets. He came from old money, too, but different money—Nantucket money—money that not long ago had meant working for a living. In those days, he was rich, but not idle—anything but idle.

Not quite making the grade for Harvard Law School, he'd settled for Suffolk, right there on the Hill. He said he was ready to shake the sand from that tiny island off his shoes and take the world by storm. He had his eyes set on a State Senate seat. His fallback position was one in the House of Representatives.

There was something rakish about him, something dangerous. Betty didn't see her future there, but she sure did see a fun ride, one that would turn heads and put frowns on her stuffed-shirt parents. It was still before the days of a generation gap, but adolescence did present small isolated fires of rebellion. She liked to see herself as one of those fires.

As the priest had told her, "God demands a high payment for your sins." Once she became pregnant, her wide-open wonderland of future possibilities shrunk and dimmed to a few ugly alternatives. In those days, in Catholic Boston, you might as well kill the President or the Pope as mention abortion.

She married Tristram.

It wouldn't be so bad. His wagon was ripe for the hitching. The marriage had to be fast, before she showed. There was little time to think.

The baby was stillborn, a boy. Their hopes for the future evaporated. Divorce was almost as bad to mention as abortion. God really did extract vengeance for even a little bit of fun, a little bit of sin. Sin and fun were interchangeable three-letter words in her world. Trying to distinguish between them was also a sin.

Her life narrowed down more. At first, Tristram rode high. He achieved his early goals. Unfortunately, the raging ego that was unleashed by his small successes slowly did away with the possibilities of future good fortunes.

He never did get a Senate or House seat. Ten years of trying told him he'd have to settle for being a small fish in Boston's big pond. He'd spent his twenties dreaming of the day he'd look back from Washington, thinking of Boston as the small pond. Now, Boston was the ocean that would swallow him. His ego couldn't take it. He had to be the big fish wherever he could. Nantucket was the obvious choice. His family already had near-star status there thanks to his great, great-grandfather. That's where he'd go.

Betty had little to say about it. Her life got smaller and narrower still. They never even tried for another child. As the years progressed, Tristram became her child, her mission of maintenance. At last, he was the big fish, able to bully his way to power, able to get things done.

"Meeting on a goddamned Saturday!" Bolgers

said, startling Betty from her reverie.

"It's bullshit! If there wasn't so much money at stake, I'd blow it off."

ELEVEN

Harry Beal sat in the tiny coffee joint near Young's Bicycle Shop at the bottom of Steamboat Wharf. As police chief, it was his job to stay closer to the action than this, but he didn't give a rat's ass. It was a stupid rule made by a more stupid man—the man who had hired him: Tristram Bolgers the Fourth.

The place was big on cappuccinos, lattes, and all kinds of froufrou drinks that had already killed the self-respect of places like L.A. and Harvard Square. For the past few years, they'd been encroaching upon Nantucket. Harry bemoaned the fact that he had to take the boat all the way to Hyannis to get his beloved coffee regular ("regulla") at Dunkin' Donuts. Other than that, he was happy to see chain franchises kept off the Island, a thing that Bolgers was in a hurry to change. Bolgers was willing to sell off every piece of Nantucket's charm, originality, and history if he could turn it into something he could pocket.

The most maddening part was that Bolgers used that very same history and charm, exploited it, when all the time he planned to kill it. Thinking about that made Harry fume, made him feel impotent or worse—a sellout, an ass kisser, a brown-noser. Harry Beal had no shortage of phrases he could condemn himself with when he thought of his relationship with Bolgers, but the plain truth was that he had little choice. Bolgers owned his ass.

Harry took a sip from his steaming, defiantly plain coffee and chuckled as he watched some coof through the window fumbling with a moped he must've just rented from Young's. He had no clue how to use it. He was terrified of it.

The coof was George.

"What's a coof like that doing here in November?" Beal said.

His second-in-command, his deputy, a scrawny, big-toothed kid named Sam, with an Adam's apple more like a grapefruit, leaned over the table to size George up.

"Looks like a geek."

"He's lucky we're all so friendly and open-hearted here," Harry said.

Harry quickly lost his grin as he saw Bolgers strutting across the street toward him. Pete Coffin was in tow. Both were much too well-dressed for a Saturday. A cowbell clanged as Bolgers and Coffin came through the door, bringing with them a cold blast of early winter. Bolgers immediately bristled at Harry lounging there.

Sam sat up at attention. Harry made no change.

"Jesus Christ! Can't you at least drink your coffee up on Main Street where people can see you?" Bolgers said.

"That's the whole point," Harry explained. "Here, I'm undercover, ready to spring unexpectedly on the criminal element."

Was Bolgers too stupid to get the sarcasm? "What criminal element?" he said.

"Terrorists could pile off the next ferry. I'm right here to foil their plot," Beal said.

"What about Barney Fife? Why can't he go?" Bolgers' eyes shifted to Sam with derision. Sam showed a childlike hurt at the remark.

"Sam's my backup," Harry said proudly.

Sam absorbed that pride and nodded in agreement.

"Besides," Beal added, "we've got Millie in our nerve center. If an asteroid hits, she'll call on the radio."

Bolgers shook his head. "Honest to God, sometimes I don't know what I'm paying you for."

"You don't pay me—Nantucket does," Harry said.

"I am Nantucket!" Bolgers blustered.

"Yeah," Pete Coffin said.

Harry smirked at both of them. "You two dressed for a funeral?"

Bolgers looked out through the window. Out past Steamboat Wharf, in the small patch of ocean between Brant Point and Great Neck, he could see the approaching ferry. It was still a white dot near the horizon.

"Damn boat's late!" Bolgers barked. "Still a half-hour out."

"Got a hot date?" Harry asked.

Bolgers kept a lid on his rising anger. "If you must know, I'm waiting on a car. A limo, to be exact."

"Wife won't give you the keys to her Plymouth anymore?"

Bolgers was ready to burst. "It so happens that doing business demands a certain image. I'm meeting contractors and investors at my building site to talk over runway expansion."

"You own the airport now?" Harry asked.

"My site adjoins it. Updated runways will benefit us all."

"What's Pete dolled up for?"

"He's to be my chauffer," Bolgers bragged.

"Driver!" Pete protested.

Bolgers had Pete get two coffees from the kid behind the counter. No payment was asked for, and none was offered. They headed for the door as Bolgers talked authoritatively to Pete, "Come on. We best be at the dock when the ferry arrives."

Harry said, "The dock's a whole fifty feet away. Perhaps you should take the chopper?"

Bolgers sneered at him as he backed through the door, Pete trailing behind him.

Harry shook off the new blast of cold that blew through the open door and said to Sam with great satisfaction, "Kramden and Norton." He sipped more plain coffee.

"Us or them?" Sam asked.

Harry smirked, ready with a comeback, but then he realized with one look at Sam's face that the question was an innocent one. He sincerely didn't know.

Harry said reassuringly, "It's never us."

TWELVE

Why did he rent a moped on such a cold day? That question rolled around in George's mind as he drove it against the wind on the road out toward Seaside.

It was an ominous journey. George hadn't seen land like this anywhere else in the state, anywhere else on the planet. The frozen ground was fractured into tufts, topped with long grass that folded over in one direction from the constant blow of wind. In other spots, gnarly underbrush covered the ground. The thick, twisted trunks looked like something out of J.R.R. Tolkien. They were more miniature trees than bushes. It was impossible to judge how far down the ground was beneath their dense tops, or if there was any ground at all. There was the haunting feeling that a person could step into that stuff and sink to the center of the Earth, never to be heard of again.

The small, worst-case-scenario fears that were George's constant companion had not left him. As he got further and further from town, they tumbled around in his brain like hot clothes in a dryer.

What if this thing runs out of gas? What if it breaks down? What if I fall off it, and I'm hurt? Who will ever find me?

Luckily for him, a new voice was starting to

make itself heard. The voice said, *Fuck it!*
His old voice would never use such language.
Fuck it!
"Fuck it" was liberating.
Don't worry about it. Fuck it! You can handle it. Don't worry about it. Fuck worrying about it! Fuck it!! The new voice was getting stronger. The new voice could beat the shit out of the old voice.

Shit—another good liberating word for his mental toolbox. *Fuck that shit!*
He could use it lots of ways.
FUCK that shit!
Fuck THAT shit!
Fuck that SHIT!
It worked for all occasions. It was a shield against the old voice. *Fuck that shit* was a good friend.

This was a good day! Just as *Fuck that shit* was fighting back his timid fearful voice, the unceasing roll of obsession that kept him replaying Janie in his mind was dying, killed off by the rolling obsession called Rebecca.

The Rebecca voice was nothing like the Janie voice. The Rebecca voice was sweet, enticing, a place he could live. It still bothered him, scared him that the Rebecca voice might not be real, but it bothered him less and less. *Fuck it! Fuck that shit!*

Wait a minute. The fact that it didn't bother him bothered him. Another voice tumbled into the mix: his father's. *Fuck it* sounded smaller and smaller against that voice. *Fuck it ... Fuck it ...*

Fearing that thoughts of his father's craziness would drive him crazy, George had to get off the road. The change of scenery would help give *Fuck it* a boost.

He saw the ocean spreading out before him. He was at Seaside. As he dismounted, he felt a stiff pain in his butt and groin that had been hiding itself while he stayed on the seat. Now he knew how cowboys felt. George worried to himself, *How am I going to get on that stupid moped with this pain and ride it all the way back to town?*

Suddenly, there it was again.

Fuck it! Fuck that shit!

It was back! George felt strength, courage, and self-love trickle back into his veins.

He rolled his moped to the edge of the cliff and flipped down the kickstand. He bravely sat on the cliff's edge and breathed in the fresh sea air as he gazed upon the huge sand beach and the wild ocean beyond it. His hair was blown flat back across his head like the high grass he'd passed on the way out. He found a piece of driftwood and started poking it around in the sand as he let his thoughts drift to Rebecca.

Far over to his left, the beach was scarred by what looked like major construction. George noticed that a long black limo was down there. Five men were standing near it, all wearing suits.

Bolgers hated getting sand on his shoes. Not only was it uncomfortable, spilling over the tops and finding its way under the soles of his feet just to taunt him, but it also left a fine dust on his newly polished leather that was hard to get off. It needed to come off before the next polishing or it would become part of the damned shoe! That kind of thing was Betty's job anyway, but what kind of guy would he be if he didn't worry about how hard she'd have to work?

He thought well of himself for considering this. What other men would have such consideration for their wives? *I'm a prince among men,* he thought as he listened to the contactor drone on and on about bullshit.

Bullshit! Bolgers thought. *What a good word, a liberating word, a word that freed you from the ... well ... bullshit. You can't get into Harvard Law with a 2.6 GPA—bullshit! You can't practice law if you can't pass the bar—BULLSHIT! Most people who make a successful run for the state senate are lawyers—DOUBLE BULLSHIT!!*

Now he'd have to stop daydreaming and respond to this guy's bullshit. The contractor was giving Bolgers a bunch of crap about not being able to build him a big enough runway.

"Don't give me that bullshit!" Bolgers barked. "We got the space to build a runway that could land a 747!"

The contractor said, "You may have the distance, but the ground won't take the weight. You're building it on sand. And there is a high water table."

Bolgers shouted, "Don't give me that crap! It's a goddamned plane. It flies in the air. If air can take the weight, my goddamned runway can."

The contractor blinked incredulously at that but decided to leave grade-school aerodynamics alone. "It's not Logan Airport we're building."

Bolgers blew up. "It damned well better be! I want people flying in from all over the world."

The contractor tried to ease things. "They can fly into Logan or even Kennedy or La Guardia and take a Nantucket flight from there."

Tantrum time was coming. Bolgers blasted, "Those puddle jumpers! They might as well be riding fucking donkeys!"

The moneymen and Pete watched this like a

tennis match.

The contractor said, "Let them fly in to Hyannis, then. It was good enough for the Kennedys."

"The Kennedys LIVED in fucking Hyannis!" Bolgers bellowed.

Just then, Bolgers caught a glimpse of something far off, up on the cliff—a man watching them. When Bolgers was in the grip of anger, paranoia was never far behind. It was a good defense mechanism. It helped him be ruthless.

Bolgers pointed at the cliff. "Who's that? Who THE FUCK'S that? You got spies watching us? Is that a goddamned spy?"

Seeing Bolgers' paranoia on the rise, one of the suits tried to calm him. "Relax, you're among friends here."

"No such thing in business," Bolgers blurted out. "You moneymen from Boston would love to exclude me from my own project and keep all the profits."

"And how would putting some guy up on that cliff help us do that?"

Another suit added in, "Maybe it's Lee Harvey Oswald?"

They all chuckled at Bolgers' expense.

George was still digging with the stick, like a small boy with a plastic pail and shovel. He marveled at the smoothness of the wood, at how time had smoothed and perfected something rough and jagged. He hit something in the sand.

It wasn't something hard like a rock. It was just under the surface. He reached in and pulled it out.

It was a sand-encrusted, closed-up rose. Like ice water had been poured over George on the hottest day, that strange mix of shock, relief, and pleasure flooded in upon him. This rose wasn't a thought in his head. It wasn't some wispy dream or delusion. It was real, tangible. Rebecca was there— somewhere. She existed. They shared a life on whatever plane of existence that might be.

As soon as George thought this, he challenged it. Some kid probably gave that rose to his date, and things went bad. She had tossed it in the sand.

George pondered again that Rebecca might just be something he conjured up to focus on instead of his own problems that he came here to fix.

A loud crunch of tires on the nearby gravel shocked George out of his turmoil. He turned to see a long black limo roll to a stop. Bolgers spilled out of the back while Pete stepped out from the driver's seat. Bolgers slowed his charge as he recognized George.

"Why it's you ... our newcomer," Bolgers said.

"Coof, you mean." George was still smarting from that exchange.

The politician in Bolgers re-emerged. "That's an unfortunate word, meant to shut out people rather than welcome them. It's part of the old Nantucket, not the new."

With a broad, gregarious stroke, Bolgers motioned towards his limo. "Can I offer you a ride back to town?" he said.

George looked at his moped and at the rose. Bolgers could see the doubtful look on his face.

"I think I'd better stay," George said.

"Come on. We can put that rented toy in the trunk."

Remembering his painful crotch, George got up and took the ride. He dropped the rose back to the sand. Pete was ordered to put the moped in the

trunk. He obeyed with simmering, secret resentment.

The limo ride back to town was much shorter
and smoother than the moped journey had been.
George sat in the plush back with Bolgers while
Pete drove.

This was a limo made for partying. An elegant
bar stretched across one whole side, sporting crystal decanters filled with an assortment of several
brown, several clear, and a couple of yellow liquids.
Matching crystal glasses were well-secured in their
own little cubbies, kept safe from sharp turns and
quick stops. A flat screen TV with a built-in Blu-ray
player was perched on the top front of the com-
partment.

Bolgers pontificated brilliantly, spewing like a
fountain of friendship. He told George about his
grand plans for the Island. He told him how glad he
was that George was here visiting Nantucket and
how he'd personally make sure the trip was a
memorable one. He practically gave George the keys
to the damned city as the limo floated over the
wilds of Nantucket's moors.

George wasn't sure what to think. Bolgers intimidated him, but there was a magnetic charm to
the man as well. It was the same with most figures
of authority in his life, the same with Sheehan at
work. Sheehan was never this nice, though.

George started to warm up to Bolgers like a father figure—the father he never had, the father who
wasn't crazy. Just as George was thinking this, as if
he were reading his mind, Bolgers said, "I should
take you under my wing ... I had a son who
would've been about your age now."

"What happened?" George asked gently, with
reverence.

For an instant, George saw through the shield of
Bolgers' exterior, saw inside of him—saw his pain

and regret, maybe his fear. In that moment, Bolgers became real to him and whole. As he watched Bolgers search for the right words, he felt compassion for him.

Finally, Bolgers said in a dry, near whisper, "That's a story for another time."

Suddenly they were in front of the Quahog B&B. Pete pulled the trunk latch and hopped out to remove the moped. George said good-bye and thank you as he got out of the car and shut the door. Pete quickly handed off the moped and hopped back in to drive. George waved as the limo pulled away.

Inside the limo, Bolgers spoke through the little hole in the Plexiglas partition to Pete as he drove. "Who comes to Nantucket in November? Why would he follow me all the way out to Surfside in that little contraption? He's no tourist. He's probably a spy."

"Spy for who?" Pete asked.

"Don't question. Drive. I don't like spies. Check him out." With that, Bolgers settled back quietly in his soft seat, letting the comfort of power wash over him.

THIRTEEN

George watched the sun set behind naked trees from his window at the Quahog.

This second island day had been pretty full. So was the first one. What will the next one hold?

These thoughts invaded George's brain as he saw the last of Saturday's sun dip below the rooftops and head for California. The bare trees were now silhouetted against cold blue winter twilight. They looked like black arthritic fingers wagging painfully in the gentle wind. They brought on scary, lonely thoughts for George.

He peeled himself away from the window and went for the comfort of the TV. As he lay on the bed, channel surfing, he provided his own sound track.

Some vacation, he thought. *Ghosts! Who's going to believe that? Maybe I'll see a UFO, too? At least Ray will still talk to me. I must be cracking up! I need sleep.*

He clicked off the TV and the room light. It was dark now, and the moonlight was but a pale blue/gray suggestion across the wall. George thought about what apparitions might be waiting in the wings to jump out at him.

Things got scary for him very quickly. He jumped up and flicked on the lights. He retreated

back to bed, curling up with his pillow.
 Maybe I should change rooms? he thought.

FOURTEEN

Sunday

The morning found George in pretty much the same position that he had fallen asleep in, still clinging to the pillow as if it were a life raft. His eyes popped open from the strident screeching of a crowing rooster. The sound rippled through him like an electric shock. Quickly after the shock came confusion.

Who the hell had a rooster? Why didn't he hear it yesterday?

He noticed that the TV was gone. Stolen?

Then he saw that the postcards were once again replaced by parchment. A cold chill seized upon him. He scrambled for his pants. With shaky fingers, he pulled out his wallet and opened it. Relief spread across him as he found his driver's license. He read it to himself aloud and finished with a pep talk.

"You're George Cooper. You live in 2012. You're just ... you're just ... you're just talking to yourself and going out of your freaking mind!"

He mustered up the courage to go the window. What he saw was no Nantucket he'd ever seen before. The harbor was a forest of sailing ship masts.

Fleet week? he thought. *Yeah—fleet from what*

century?

He saw no streetlights, no traffic signs, no cars.

With a deep breath of resignation, he said to himself, "Like 'dear old' Dad. Maybe I should just accept it? Enjoy it until they catch me?"

Just then, a velvety, woman's voice came to him. It was far away, as if calling over a strong wind.

The voice said, "Can you write it?"

Rebecca!

He could barely get his pants on fast enough. He threw on a shirt and pulled on his coat. Whatever was happening to him, it was going to happen outside.

He bolted down the stairs of the B&B to find another world, the world of the 1840s. Horse-drawn wagons rattled past him. As George walked the bricks, he realized it was warm—too warm for that heavy coat. He took it off and slung it over his shoulder. He realized that this different time-period was also a different season—late spring, maybe, or early summer.

As he walked, he kept trying to talk himself into it all. *Give in to it, George. What else do you have? Go with the flow. That's what crazy people do, right? Enjoy the ride. So what if you're nuts—fuck it!*

Fuck that shit!

Fuck it wasn't working as well for him this time, but he told himself to have faith in it.

As he turned onto Broad Street, it was a maze of activity. Street hawkers barked at him, touting their wares. Stray dogs weaved their way between multitudes of dusty men's legs. The street was dirt. Only Main Street had cobblestones at this point. Many of the buildings were the same ones he'd seen in 2012, but each of them was very different. Nothing had been prettied up for tourists or the idle rich who, besides the locals, were the only ones to afford the Nantucket of today. This old Nantucket was a working town.

George jumped from the path of horse-drawn wagons and dodged between hawkers, beggars, sailors, and businessmen. This was a bustling place.

Just as he was learning to go with the flow, he stepped off the curb into a river of horse urine.

He tried his saving words again to himself. *Fuck it! Fuck that ... piss!*

It was working. A small piece of him felt like a star in his own movie, a man who could contend with adversity. He headed for the water to wash off his pants.

FIFTEEN

There it was! Nantucket Harbor in all of its 1840s' glory—ships of every description, whalers, schooners, packets, brigs, barks—it was endless. Urine-soaked pants and all, George was giddy with excitement. This was the Nantucket he'd dreamed about in that tiny little gray cubicle back in Boston.

Suddenly it dawned on him. *It's Sunday! I'm supposed to be at work tomorrow.*

Just as quickly, he excused himself from the worry.

What tomorrow? Maybe that's thousands of tomorrows from now? Maybe a million?

George couldn't do the math, but the mere thought of it was completely liberating.

George found a low spot on the pier, down close to the water so he could stick his legs in and wash off the horse pee. He sat on the edge, putting his coat beside him on the damp wood. His feet dangled over the edge. He carefully stretched his feet down toward the water.

Just as they were at the water's surface, a swell surged up, soaking him up to both knees. Only then did he notice the floating brown chunks.

Human excrement! He pulled his legs out so fast that he almost fell in. As he regained his balance, he heard a woman's voice behind him. "Taking a dip?"

George twisted quickly from where he sat. There was Rebecca! She stood over him, radiating sexual, sensual beauty from every pore of her body.

She continued, "It's best to do that sort of thing on the far side of the island. The ocean has a more cleansing quality there."

George scrambled to his feet, nearly losing his footing, once again risking a fall into the brown soup.

Through shallow breaths of nervous excitement he squeezed out, "Are you ... Rebecca?"

"I've been waiting for you," she said.

Gazing up and down as if she were taking his measure, she continued, "We best get you some clean, dry, and proper clothes."

George picked up his coat from the dock, eager to go with her. As he did, Janie's lipstick fell from the pocket and rolled a few inches along the wood by his feet. Rebecca picked it up, looking at it quizzically.

"What's this?" she asked. "A tin whistle?"

Guilt flooded George's soul as if he'd been caught cheating on her.

"Lipstick—a friend's," he replied.

Rebecca turned with a sly smile and led him towards the town. He was all too happy to follow her like a puppy dog.

George marveled at the bustling business of Main Street as she led him up along the dusty cobblestones to a general supply store. Inside the store, George was quick to finger through the small stack of folded shirts. The storekeeper eyed him suspiciously. Rebecca stood next to the storekeeper, smiling broadly at George. He lifted a shirt up for the storekeeper to see.

"Are these permanent press?" George inquired.

Rebecca giggled. "I should hope not."

The storekeeper was confused by the question. "Them creases ain't permanent. They'll iron right out."

Rebecca said, "I've picked you a shirt and dry pants. Let's be on our way."

George picked up a fireplace bellows and started to pump it curiously. "I've only seen these on cartoons."

The storekeeper was even more confounded by this. "What kind of cart?"

Rebecca said, "Come, the day is wasting. You can change in the back."

Rebecca led George from the store dressed in his new clothes. The pants were black with a cinched waist and a black fabric tie instead of a belt. His shirt was eggshell white with billowing sleeves and pleated chest folds that puffed out in front of him. A V-shaped front closure flap hung open, exposing George's chest in true Errol Flynn fashion. In the store doorway, George stopped and picked up a long-poled bed warmer. "Hey! Let's get this popcorn maker."

Rebecca smirked as she removed the bed warmer from George's grip and placed it back where it belonged as if he were her young child gripping candy he wanted her to buy.

"Surely your sense of these things isn't as bad as you pretend," she scolded.

"It was a joke," George said. "Haven't jokes been invented yet?"

"Jokes we have. We've no tolerance for bad ones."

They continued walking. George slowed to a stop as he saw his reflection in a store window. The sunlight bounced off his new shirt and made it nearly glow in the glass. Rebecca stopped and watched him as he contemplated the billowing blouse.

"What is it?" she asked.

"There was a Seinfeld episode once ..." He stopped as he looked at her questioning face. "Never mind," he added.

They started walking again. Rebecca said, "I need you on your best behavior. You'll be meeting my father. He's in the oil business."

"Lots of money in that," George said.

"Money is not a ruler by which I measure."

George slowed to a stop again, turning serious. Fears invaded his newfound paradise. He gazed about slowly, taking in his 1840s' surroundings. He started hearing his father's voice again, started questioning his sanity. He fought back, grabbing at straws of denial.

He said to Rebecca, "I know this isn't a reenactment because I'm the only tourist. It's too elaborate for a practical joke. Who would play one on me anyway?"

Rebecca looked at him with pity. Their eyes connected.

"Is this like Dickens?" he softly asked. "Are you like the ghost of Christmas past?

A quiet terror spread across him, along with the loneliness of a little boy lost far from home. With a fluttering voice, he asked her, "What's happening to me?"

She offered only wide-eyed silence.

SIXTEEN

Sailing ship bowsprits jutted out in all directions. Rebecca led George beneath them on a maze of wooden planking that floated on the rolling swells of seawater between the ships' hulls. George felt like he was in a deep, dark canyon. He looked up in awe at the jumble of tall masts and long yardarms. Connecting it all was an impossibly intricate cat's-cradle-web of lines that fragmented the far off sky into tiny jagged pieces.

The wooden planks that they stepped on lifted and fell with the waves like a fun house conveyor belt. George had trouble timing his steps with the changing positions of the floating wood.

The ships' hulls creaked as they strained against their dock lines. The sound reminded George of those narrow stairs at the B&B. Elusive wisps of that same distant, disturbing memory danced just beyond his reach, defying definition. He had that same nagging thought that the creaking ships were calling to him, squealing in pain.

Rebecca steered George onto a gangplank that led up to the deck of a massive whaling ship. The day had grown old, and the sun slanted in from the west with the beginnings of its sunset-orange tinge.

Towering over them from the deck at the top of the plank was Captain Quentin Fulagar, Rebecca's father. Edged by that orange sidelight of sun, he looked all the more imposing. This was his whaling ship, The Eleanor May.

Fulagar looked down upon George with disdain. He was massive. His face was hardened and rutted by years of fighting the sea. If he got into a battle with a great white shark, he just might win it. He introduced himself briskly to George.

George tried desperately to make conversation. "Rebecca tells me you're in oil."

"Right she is, son," was Fulagar's terse response.

George looked around timidly and sniffed the rancid, fish-infused air.

"This seems like a fishing operation," George said hoarsely.

"Whaling!" Fulagar barked.

"Whaling?" George meekly returned.

"Where do you think oil comes from?" Fulagar had no patience for fools. "It don't exactly seep up from the flipping ground, you know."

Panic raced through George. "I guess I'm not in Kansas anymore."

"Kansas!" Fulagar bellowed. "You an Indian fighter?"

George hated himself for his stupidity. What did he think a Wizard of Oz reference was going to buy him?

Rebecca interceded, to George's great relief. "I'd like to show George the ship, if you don't mind," Rebecca requested.

Fulagar's eyes burned right through George's head. "Keep him topside."

"I will," Rebecca said.

For George, her words were like a reprieve from the Governor just as the noose was being placed around his neck. He gladly followed her along the deck, away from her father.

SEVENTEEN

George and Rebecca walked slowly through the disciplined chaos of a crew preparing their ship for nightfall. Lamps were being filled with oil, lines were being coiled, or Flemished. George was quiet, taking slow breaths, trying to calm himself enough to appreciate where he was. The old toxic self-talk that used to churn in his brain was long gone, replaced by obsessive thoughts of Rebecca and the toxic doubt of his own sanity.

This wasn't a whole lot better, but it was a little. *More than a little*, he told himself.

Rebecca returned his quietness. Somehow, she knew that it was what he needed. *It was as if she could read my mind*, George thought.

George tried his best to be in the moment. His eyes swelled to drink in his surroundings.

He was on a real sailing ship! The closest he'd ever gotten to this before was a Johnny Depp movie.

He smelled the mix of tar and wood and sea air that no movie could ever translate. All sounds reverberated through, and were amplified by the hollow space below that was sealed off by the hull. The gentle roll and dip of the ship and the soft creaking of her wood were as soothing as a baby's cradle.

As strange and new as this all was to George, it

was also hauntingly familiar.

As they reached the bow, they turned. The sun dipped close to the horizon, readying itself for the day's grand finale. George watched a crewman climb the rigging to hang a lit oil lamp on the end of a yardarm. Rebecca stood behind him. She gently ran her arm across his shoulder. Then she stepped up closer, putting her hands on each of his shoulders, squeezing them tightly.

George tensed as he wondered how things could have become so advanced, so quickly. Rebecca was very forward for a woman from this more restricted time period. George never had this much luck with women of his own time. It made him doubt the reality of it all the more. It MUST be a delusion, mixed with a fantasy. Still it felt so right, so real. It was so enticing. How could he resist it? He'd just go with the flow.

She rested her chin on his shoulder. He melted back in to her. All of his pent-up tension dilated into a free-flowing river of sensual calm. This gave him the courage to wonder instead of worry.

He spoke quietly to Rebecca. "Are we ... ghosts here? Am I?"

Rebecca silently ran her hands down the sides of his back and wrapped them around his waist. George gently continued his questions.

"Is this some kind of time warp?" he asked. He considered Ray's wormhole theories, but he didn't voice them.

Rebecca tightened her grip around his waist and nuzzled her chin deeper into that spot where his shoulder arched up to become neck. George was in heaven, but was it a heaven he dared give himself over to?

"How did you ever come to pick me?" he asked.

"Is it I who did the picking?" she asked.

He turned to her, taking her hands in his. It was

only then that he noticed scars on her forearms. She quickly twisted them away to obscure them. For the first time, George saw through Rebecca's veneer of mystery and control. He saw her anew as vulnerable, human. In that moment, his passion and compassion melted into one—his whole being throbbed for her.

"I'm sorry," George whispered.

Rebecca stepped to the rail and gazed out across the sun-painted harbor. "After mother died," Rebecca started, "I was eight ... Father couldn't very well bring me to sea. He's gone for years at a time."

As she relived the memory, her eyes turned glassy with tears that refused to fall. They reflected the harbor before her.

George waited quietly.

"I was put in a boarding school," she continued while rubbing her arms. "It was not the kind of place to tolerate eccentrics like myself."

Rebecca pulled a calico and lace potpourri satchel from somewhere within that dress. She lifted it gently to her nose, breathing in deeply with reverence. "Rose petals," she murmured. "My mother gave me this shortly before her death. It was my truest friend on all those lonely nights at that school."

George's heart melted as he watched her. In that moment, he fell completely in love with her. In her lonely childhood, he saw his own. He remembered those long, endless afternoons he'd spent as a boy, alone in his room, tracing the frost pattern on his window, wishing for a friend but instead focusing on the frozen, flat world before his finger. The little girl, Rebecca, huddling with her rose-scented satchel, was a kindred spirit, a soul mate.

He didn't understand how feelings that ran so much deeper than initial attraction could course through him with such all-consuming strength.

They'd just met, and it was like he'd always known her.

She brought the satchel gently to her nose again. She breathed in deeply, luxuriating in the scent. "It still retains its fragrance today," she whispered.

"After all these years?"

"Nantucket is indifferent to the march of time."

The moment of truth had arrived. If George lacked the courage to act now, he'd never forgive himself. He took her in his arms. The slipping sun edged them in its last orange rays. She delicately stroked his back. His lips went for her, but at the last moment, she turned away, offering only her cheek. He leaned his head against hers as they both breathed out, teetering on the edge of their passion.

She turned and leaned over the rail to watch the waves. George followed suit, standing close beside her, wrapping his arm around her waist. For the first time in his life, reality held all the wonder and beauty of his best fantasies—if reality it was.

His heart raced. His face flushed. Hot and cold waves rolled through him at the same time. He tried to steady his breathing and remain in control. He wanted no renegade body part to betray him in this moment.

They watched the last of the sun dip below the harbor. A fresh breeze came in like a broom to sweep out the remnants of the day.

As George looked out on the darkening Nantucket harbor, he noticed a beat-up schooner tied up one slip over from them. Something about that schooner sent terror up his spine. The pulse of romantic sensuality that commanded his heart now constricted with fear. Fear and rage took full control as George saw a wooden hatch cover tied to the main mast. Though his reactions were vivid, their cause was diffused. They came as sharp pinpricks of mental pain that dissolved on contact.

Rebecca watched him with concern.

"What troubles you?" she asked.

"What do you know about that ship over there?"

"First off, a schooner is a boat, not a ship, although that tub barely qualifies as even a boat. It used to fish the offshore banks. Now it's just a wrecker."

"Wrecker?"

"A scavenger. They plunder shipwrecks to sell their goods."

"Like pirates?" George asked

"Vultures really. They wait until their prey is dead before they pounce."

A strange fear nearly kept George from asking his next question.

"Do you know any of the crew?"

"Always different. It's a bad captain who can't keep a steady crew."

She walked to the opposite side rail, knowing George would follow. Once there, she turned to him and held up Janie's lipstick. "How does this work?"

George shook off his ugly thoughts concerning the schooner and refocused on Rebecca. He gently took the lipstick from her hand and removed the cover. "You just twist the bottom until the red sticks out. Then you slide it across your lips."

Rebecca laughed girlishly at the idea, revealing a mischievous quality beneath. "I would look like a harlot."

George smiled as he started to put the lipstick back in his pocket. Rebecca stopped him. "But it does appeal to my wicked side. Would you do the honors?"

George's insides dropped a foot. He was in the grip of a romance so deep, an attraction so strong that he could barely contain it. His hand quivered slightly as he twisted the red shaft out from the brass-colored base. They both watched with quiet excitement as the ruby protrusion extended further.

George's breath was short and shallow. His brain made him dizzy in its demand for more oxygen. Trying to still his shaking hand, George ever so gingerly brought the red tube to her waiting lips and moved it across them. He watched lustfully as the tube slowly pulled at her lower lip and then, just as slowly, released it to fall back along her beautiful gum line with a new sparkle of red.

Rebecca watched him. Her luscious eyes were filled with trust and love. George's shallow breathing deepened and turned hard. He could barely contain the sexual, romantic passion that boiled within him. The lipstick lowered, forgotten in his hand, as he leaned his head to hers, panting like a puppy. Their noses dovetailed. They remained locked that way for an endless moment before Rebecca broke away, resisting their mutual lust. She turned back to the rail.

George joined her. They looked across this new side of Nantucket harbor. The departed sun still shot its rays up over the horizon, painting red across the cloud-mottled sky, making a burgundy sea. The breeze stiffened, carrying a slight hint of cold that opened the senses. On a nearby whale ship, a fiddler was playing on deck. The orange glow of whale-oil lamps edged him warmly against the bluing, newborn night. A crowd had gathered around him, laughing, talking, some dancing a jig to the music. The sounds mingled together and lilted over to them, somehow amplified, displaced, and made haunting by the thick sea air.

George and Rebecca reveled silently in the magic of the moment. Slowly, the music faded to a stop. The crowd quieted. The fiddler began again with a sad, longing, rendition of Danny Boy. The group listened in silent reflection. The sound attained an even richer poignancy as it drifted across the water to George and Rebecca, deepening the moment.

"Boston Irish," Rebecca said quietly. "They'll sign on to any boat. They've already crossed one ocean in search of a dream."

"I'd have crossed oceans to be here with you."

Rebecca turned to him, looking into his eyes. "In a way you have."

As the music lilted across the waves, George kissed her, lightly, hesitantly, on her cheek. She put her hands flat upon his chest. Her fingers kneaded the fabric of his new, billowy white shirt. She tilted her head up to meet his. He kissed her cheek again, but more confidently. Then his lips slid across to hers for a truly passionate exchange. As they finished, she buried her face into George's chest, smearing her new lipstick on the end flap of his shirt's chest closure. She jokingly diffused the moment's intensity.

"Now I've gone and soiled your new clean shirt."

"I hope it stays there forever." His voice was hoarse and small.

"Forever is a wonderful thought. Tomorrow this ship will be gone, brought over the bar to load."

"The bar?"

"It would take too long to explain. Ships must be loaded down in the outer harbor, not here. Tomorrow, my father shall be gone a mile. After that, years."

There was a long silence. George watched her, not knowing what to add.

"Will you walk with me to the end of the wharf?" she asked.

EIGHTEEN

In the 1840s, Straight Wharf was just what the name implied. It was Nantucket's main pier. In fact, it continued straight down from Main Street. Much of the island's seagoing-related commerce continued right along with it. The pier was lined with shacks carrying bait for local fishermen and more shacks to sell the fish they caught.

That said, fish were of minor concern for Nantucket. This was reflected on Straight Wharf as well. Most of the shacks, some on stilts over the water, were dedicated to the biggest fish of all. Fish that weren't really fish. Fish who breathed air— whales. These shacks were outfitted for all the needs of whale ships on long journeys: sail makers, cooperages, rope braiders. The list could go on.

Silver-blue moonlight edged these dark, sleeping shacks. It caressed George and Rebecca's hair as they walked together to the end of Straight Wharf. A canopy of stars watched down from the heavens. A furious wind picked at their clothes and danced in their hair. Black, shiny-backed waves hurled themselves against the pilings, exploding on impact.

The drama of the night couldn't match the passion in George's heart. He watched the black ocean blast into a frenzy of moonlit white foam as it died against the pier. "A soul could get washed away," he shouted over the din of busy wind and roaring waves.

"The sea returns whatever it takes."

George thought on Rebecca's words for a moment as he breathed in deeply. He had so much to share, so much was happening inside him, but he didn't know where to start. "I've never felt so ... It's like all of my senses had been sleeping."

Rebecca listened patiently, gazing at the sky as they walked. There was a sudden wisdom to her, as if she knew everything that swirled within George but also knew that it was for him to discover on his own.

George looked up at the sky. A rogue flock of clouds raced across the moon, fluttering darkly across their faces. All of the words that occurred to him weren't merely inadequate; they were insults to what needed expressing. They were like stale pictures of a vacation that only served to kill the memory, not enhance it. Still, he thought, he must try.

"For the first time, I'm not regretting the past or fearing the future ... I'm right here, right now. I'm living in the moment. I want this moment to last forever."

A look of deep, knowing regret spread across Rebecca's face. She said, "That's the trouble with moments."

George tensed up.

What did that mean? he thought, finding no words or courage to ask.

They walked in silence for a while as George tried to gather his thoughts like spilt coins on the pavement. At the end of the pier, they stopped. George looked into the black waves. "The sea looks so hostile."

He turned to her. She responded in kind. He searched her glistening eyes for answers. Finally he said, "There's something else, isn't there?"

Rebecca was silent. Her lips pursed as if to speak, but no words came. George studied her face, waiting.

The pounding surf and howling wind were relentless. They mirrored the whirlwind within his head. It was all so real, but all so impossible. He never felt so marvelous and never felt so scared. Not a single thought would stay long enough for scrutiny. He needed to ask her—but ask her what? He needed to talk—but say what?

One thing he did know, he couldn't shout it over this wind. "Is there a place to find quiet?"

She led him behind the shelter of a fish shack, and they sat against a weathered plank wall, away from the wind, around the corner from the waves. It took him a while to start.

"I feel like I'm lost in a fog, on the very edge of clarity. I grab for answers that dissolve as soon as my mind reaches for them."

She lovingly stretched over and took his hands in hers. "Reach not with your mind, but with these." She gently shook his hands for emphasis. Then, she brought them to his chest. "And with your heart."

George closed his eyes to savor the moment. That same moment was shattered by the loud blast of a steamship horn.

George's eyes popped open. She was gone. The steamship horn blew again. He spun to see the fat modern ferry drift in towards its berth on Steamboat Wharf, a few slips over. The modern world surrounded him again. His heart shattered. He was dressed again in his regular clothes, his coat over his arm. This further confirmed for him that it must have been a delusion.

He plopped himself down on Straight Wharf's end and leaned against the back of a closed wooden store. There he spent the night.

NINETEEN

Morning brought no change. George was trapped, once again, in the present. Sleep had not rescued him from that fate. In a futile attempt to shake off his profound depression and wrangle in his wandering thoughts, he got up, straightened his clothes as best he could and wrapped his coat around him tightly against the morning chill. Then he got himself a cup of coffee and walked around the wharf.

His thoughts were no longer wandering. They were a stampede. Straight Wharf was still an extension of Main Street. It was still lined with businesses. Now they were of a different trade. It was one of the most tourist-oriented spots on Nantucket. The shops sold postcards and T-shirts, light baskets and saltwater taffy. Luckily, it was still refreshingly free of chain stores and franchises.

Most of the places were closed for the season, as were the restaurants and bars that also lined the wharf. It all disturbed George greatly as he shuffled by, bundled up against the cold, with his hands dug into his pockets.

There was something oddly disquieting about empty places that were built for crowds. Something about it amplified the emptiness and drew every last ounce of pathos it could from the absence of souls who had once inhabited it.

George remembered how he'd felt that same way as a child when his father brought him to Nantasket Beach Amusement park, just across the harbor from Boston. It was closed down. It had been closed for a while. The elements had long been feasting on the happy clown faces and bright paint that once adorned the fun rides. Those rides were now nothing more than spidery, twisted strands of rusting metal.

Nature seemed especially cruel to spots that tried to provide fun or hope. George thought about this as he worked his way toward the end of Straight Wharf. He passed workmen hanging a Christmas wreath from a light pole. He remembered how, as a boy, there would be a mini trauma after every Christmas when the tree that had brought them so much joy was unceremoniously stripped naked and dragged out to the curb.

George couldn't bear to look at it as he came home from school each early January day. It would lie there in the crusted snow with its bare arms opened wide, asking silently for a second chance, a reprieve from the chipper. Most times there would be a few stray strands of tinsel still clinging there in the cold wind as an even more ugly reminder of the good times it provided. Then, one day, he'd come home from school, and it would be gone. George would breathe out a sigh of relief.

Guilt had long been George's main set point. He'd often confused guilt with caring and compassion. His grand fantasies of performing heroic acts had always arrived stillborn in his reality, but at least he had the guilt. His heart could break for the bad things that befell people. At least he had that.

Rebecca was going to change it all. She'd already started to. With her, he could finally see a road to becoming the man of his dreams. The man he wished that he was and had always mourned that he wasn't. Now, with her disappearance, those hopes were gone. Worse than gone, they'd become added to the pile of evidence with which to indict his sanity, his worthiness to walk the streets, his right to be part of the human race.

George reached the end of Straight Wharf, the last place he'd seen Rebecca. It was barely recognizable. Where whale ships used to idle, there was now a maze of pleasure boats. Masts were steel or aluminum. Hulls were fiberglass. The late autumn sun blasted off polished chrome deck rails. There seemed to be only two kinds of boats here. There were the sleek, futuristic racers that flaunted their macho power and the luxury yachts that flaunted their decadence.

George sat on a tourist bench and looked out upon the sea of conspicuous consumption. He watched the bobbing sterns of all those million-dollar boats. Their names were spread proudly across their transoms. Joke names like Our Kid's Inheritance. Cutesy names like Suzy Q and Lovely Laura. He couldn't make himself read them all. Each one was a slap in the face.

Were these the captains of industry who came up with those names? Were these the people so much smarter, better, and more deserving of joy than him? Did he have to resort to insanity to obtain the same pleasure that they could achieve with a checkbook? Was there any fairness in the world at all? There had to be!

Rebecca was real, damn it! He'd known dreams. He'd known fantasies. This was different—different than anything he'd ever experienced before—different and better. Better than he'd ever dare to dream.

Adrift in the present, he'd felt closer to home when he was a hundred and sixty-some-odd years away. If he had a time machine like H. G. Wells had dreamt up, maybe he could sit in that very spot and dial back the years, watching them flip by like playing cards thumbed by a Vegas dealer. He wondered about that. After a blur of years, would she come up? Would she be with him on this spot, in their last conversation? Questions like that comforted him while they also taunted him.

A voice intruded into George's swirling thoughts. Perhaps it was a rescue? But George was far from seeing it that way. The voice said, "Just the man I want to see."

George turned. It was Bolgers.

Did Bolgers ever take a breath? Even one on one, he lectured or pontificated. "My dear boy—" he started.

Did anybody outside of old movies talk like that? George thought.

Bolgers continued, "You are the future of Nantucket ..."

I'm more the past, George thought, as he listened quietly.

"An island's problem is just that," Bolgers said. "It's an island. We need to keep connected to the mainland in order to keep pace with it. I have some ideas that I'll be presenting at the next town meeting. I'd like very much to present them to you first. If, after that, you'd like to be on my team, I could invite you up to speak at the meeting, and you could give your perspective on having Nantucket as a ready resource, an asset to you in ... Boston, wasn't it?"

"Yes, Boston."

"Fine then. For your time, lunch and drinks shall be on me."

"A little early for drinks, isn't it?"

"My dear boy, let's not be slaves to time."

TWENTY

Bob McKenzie stretched out his back from his spot behind the bar. It was nearly time for the lunch rush, and this would be his last chance to do it before two. He knew that "lunch rush" was a relative term. In Nantucket's off-season, the lunch rush wasn't exactly the dreaded onslaught it might be in July. But this *was* The Brotherhood of Thieves, so it could still be taxing, especially now when folks he hadn't seen since September were on the island to prepare for the Christmas Stroll.

In a few days, the place would be packed with tourists—not your standard summer folks, but an "in the know" crowd, a slight cut above. These were people who knew about the little-publicized week of Christmas Stroll in early December when Nantucket would be decked out for an old-time Victorian Christmas. Given the cobblestone streets and old buildings, it would all look like something created by Charles Dickens, especially if they were blessed with a dusting of snow.

Most of the stores would re-open with free cookies and eggnog, selling the perfect, distinctive gifts for the holiday. The bars and restaurants would re-open, too. It was Nantucket's last hurrah before those desolate cold months of January and February when the empty island would be given over to the whims of time and nature.

Bartending was fun for Bob, even though the long hours on his feet wreaked havoc on an old lower back injury from his high school football days. He got along with people, liked talking to them, liked being part of their good time or part of whatever time they could manage.

This, however, was one of Bob's least favorite moments. Mayor Bolgers was squeezing in through the door. This time he had some off-island nerd in tow.

Bob had no tolerance for pompous jerks and Bolgers held the first place title in that competition. It would always be the same thing when he came in. Bolgers would loudly order seltzer and lime, and Bob would have to make a big deal of squirting the seltzer gun into the glass.

Nothing stronger, Mister Mayor? was Bob's required response.

Of course not! Course not was Bolgers' standard reply.

With another obvious flourish, Bob would then have to put the lime in. Then, as clandestinely as was possible, he'd have to add a double shot of vodka—which, of course, Bolgers wouldn't pay or tip for since he hadn't ordered it, and it wasn't on the bill.

Bob kept a top shelf bottle of vodka in the well for just such occasions so he wouldn't have to turn around to the back bar for it and blow Bolgers' cover. Sometimes Bob thought about risking his job to expose the jerk, but then, who would really care? And he'd be out of work.

Bolgers strutted past the bar shouting, "We'll be taking a table, Bob."

Bolgers liked being seen as a man of the people, liked folks to see that he'd know the name of a lowly bartender.

"Scotch/rocks for my friend here," Bolgers announced before whispering to George, "Scotch okay with you?"

Bob did his pre-scripted duty. "And for you, sir?"

"Seltzer and lime, Bob. You should know that."

"Nothing stronger?"

"Course not! Course not!"

Bolgers and George took up a table near the back. Bolgers continued a conversation that he'd started with George way back on Straight Wharf, if you can call one person talking a conversation.

"People have the wrong idea of restaurant franchises and chain stores. They think of K-Mart and McDonald's. They're afraid that they'll wake up and find the whole island filled with Dunkin' Donuts and Burger King. We know different, don't we?"

George sipped his Scotch, wishing it were his only company. The fatherly, protective comfort he felt around Mayor Bolgers came with a price tag of self-consciousness, even intimidation. George was sure it was self-inflicted. It came from all of those years of abuse by people in that role. From his own father to teachers to Sheehan, he'd learned to fear those in a fatherly role. *Maybe Bolgers could heal that,* George thought, *if I'd just loosen up and let him.*

Bolgers continued, "Those of us in the outside world know that there's been a revolution in the franchise market. Oh, sure, we can all point to Starbucks. By the way, did you know that's a Nantucket name? Without Nantucket, there'd be no Starbucks, but that's a story for another day."

The pressure to listen was too great for George to be able to listen. Besides, he had other things to dwell on. Rebecca commanded his thoughts. George continued to feign listening. He was terrified that Bolgers would ask for a response or an opinion. It would be like being called on in school when he was daydreaming, which had been always.

Bolgers went on, "People here get mighty tired of quahog chowder and cod fish. More tired than they even know. What would they think if they could go to ... say ... a California Pizza Kitchen? Bubba Gump Shrimp? Chef Chang's?

"These are only 'off the top of my head' ideas. The possibilities are endless. These places aren't your standard chains. We're not talking Denny's or IHOP. These are classy places, places that would respect Nantucket's nautical theme but open up this place to a whole new market.

"I'm thinking we could start a high-speed ferry right from Boston Harbor—one of those Catboats. It could leave from right down at the end of Quincy Market in Boston, and screw Steamboat Wharf, we'd have it come right in to Straight Wharf. It would be like Main Street, Nantucket, was an exotic extension of Quincy Market! Think of the business we'd do!"

George swilled down the rest of his Scotch. He was glad for the warm honesty it wrapped around his insides. Bolgers called for the bartender to give George another drink. He was thankful for the refill. He heard oblivion calling.

"Why are you telling all this to me?" George asked. "I'm not exactly a mover and shaker. It's not like I'd be much help."

Bolgers looked at him for a long, silent moment, sizing him up. *Why AM I telling him this stuff? If this coof was a spy, I should be tight-lipped.*

"I don't know what it is," Bolgers said. "Something about you just clicks with me. That son I never had, I suppose." Even Bolgers didn't know if that was truth or bullshit. It had been so long since he'd known the difference.

Still Bolgers droned on, "I'm getting some resistance from the year-round townsfolk, but once they get a taste of it, they'll come around. I'm already courting these franchises for my building site out there on Surfside. It won't be long before we get those things in town. What do you say? Will you join me?"

"I'm not sure I'll be here."

The Scotch came. George ignored the ice and drank it like a shot.

TWENTY-ONE

George climbed the steps to his room at the Quahog B&B with leaden feet. What was the point of anything? The best moments of his life had been a delusion. He'd be going home feeling worse than before he left. At only thirty-five, what would all those years ahead of him have in store?

He remembered the last subway ride he'd taken, home from work on Thanksgiving Eve. He thought about the old man with the McDonald's meal. Would that be him one day?

The buzz of lunchtime Scotch was now solidifying into dull fatigue, further reminding him of that lonely Thanksgiving Eve night. Maybe Bolgers was right? They could join together. George could stay on Nantucket and even make some good money.

Something scared him about it. Just pondering it brought on another panic attack. He remembered the evening with Rebecca and seeing that old, beat-up schooner of Bolgers the First. Was any of it real? Did it have some bearing on things today? It was all too confusing.

He fumbled for his key and opened the door to his room. He dragged himself to the bathroom and turned on the tub water, bending to his knees and twisting the rubber plug into the drain hole. Putting his hand under the water flow to test the temperature, he stared at the mesmerizing fall of water over his hand, the black hole of his life threatening to draw him into the pit of no return. Tears of desperation rippled through his eyes.

With a deep breath, he forced them to stay in. He knew that if he let them out they'd never stop. He'd be forever lost. He broke away from the tub and walked into the main room to undress.

As he went to take off his coat, something on the bed caught his eye. He stepped over for a closer inspection.

There, on the comforter, all laid out for him, were the black pants and that white puffy shirt that Rebecca had bought for him. His eyes shot to the chest-closure corner. There it was—the lipstick smear that Rebecca had left there.

He gathered the shirt into his arms. He pressed it tenderly to his face with quivering hands and slowly breathed in its scent, letting it intoxicate him with memories of bliss.

The present-day streets of Nantucket were cold—too cold for a person in a light cotton puffy shirt. After all, these were the waning days of November. The weak afternoon sun was nearly gone, and transitional winds swept through the town, stealing what little remained of the sun's warmth.

None of that mattered to George. He stepped out from the B&B in that shirt and those pants. Faith told him he'd need little more, and faith was what he'd follow. He headed for Straight Wharf.

As he got to Main Street, he was met by a small crowd of people who'd recently gotten off the ferry. After Thanksgiving weekend, Nantucket's meager, off-season crowd swells in anticipation of the Christmas Stroll. The newcomers who noticed George reacted with concern or puzzlement. A few of them wondered if he was part of some historical re-enactment show.

A young boy tugged on his mother's coat as he gawked and pointed at George. "Look, Mommy, a pirate!"

George ignored all of it. He let nothing deter him from his mission. The cold was starting to numb his face, arms, and chest. He could feel his breath shorten. No matter what, he would continue on to Straight Wharf.

TWENTY-TWO

In New England, November skies are famous for their gray and purple bluster of clouds. They warn of the dangers posed by the coming winter. November dusks and sunsets speak in an even louder voice. The ominous moods they bring are felt deep in our bones and psyches. They are the reasons for a multitude of traditions and rituals that, in mythic times, were meant to ward off the evil spirits.

In modern times, they've been distilled and homogenized into tamer things like Halloween, but peel back today's comforting accoutrements, and the visceral fear still remains.

Nantucket, off-season, magnified these things. For the few hardy souls who stayed here at this time of year, it was a time for the comfort of friendship around warm fires, sipping mulled cider with cinnamon, counting their blessings as cold November blasts rattled the windows looking for a way in.

George didn't care about any of that, not anymore. He was running on faith.

Having long ago rejected religion, faith was not a regular part of George's life. Now he was coming to understand the value of faith, not connected to God, at least not necessarily, but just faith alone.

He wasn't sure what his faith was in—perhaps some kind of cosmic justice? He just knew that he had it somewhere inside of him. Faith made George strong even in his weakness. It made him brave through his fear. It allowed him the courage to don that shirt.

He stood at the end of the pier, letting the cold wind blast upon his lightweight shirt, lifting it up like a balloon around him and stabbing directly at his bare chest beneath. The longer he stood there, the more his faith began to fray.

A little voice started to make itself heard.

What are you doing, you nut? It was small at first, but it started to grow larger.

He started to become aware of the people around him, aware of their staring. He started to feel stupid and self-conscious. He tried to fight his way back to his newfound faith, but it was an uphill battle. He closed his eyes to better concentrate.

Nothing!

As he opened his eyes again, he was shocked by the flash of a brass cylinder before his face. It was Rebecca, holding Janie's lipstick up to him. "I do believe this is yours, sir."

A flood of bliss swept over him. He couldn't shed the negative ones fast enough for the good ones to flow in. They collided with one another in passing.

Rebecca studied his face curiously as all of the changes and realizations came upon him. The air was now warm and crisp, like a late spring day. Whale ships once again bobbed at their berths.

"You look troubled."

"Overjoyed!" he said.

"But still something nags at you."

"I think I left my tub running."

She laughed at that, looking at him with confusion. "How does a tub run?"

George started to explain but then realized that there wasn't much point.

"Step lively now," she said. "A rantum scootin'

day it is."

"A rantuh—what?"

"Rantum scootin'. A day for romping."

"Romping sounds good."

She led him up Main Street through the hustle and bustle of morning business. Horses clopped over the cobblestones, pulling open-backed wagons. Storeowners stood out front of their shops to catch the fresh sun. Townsfolk weaved past each other.

George noticed that most of those townsfolk were women. "Must be easy for a guy to get a date in this town."

Rebecca didn't slow her pace. She just looked at him with more confusion. "Date? Date on a calendar? Appointment?"

"You know, going out together."

"Out? Out to sea?"

George smiled inwardly at this confirmation that he was in a different world.

She tugged him onto Orange Street, and they headed out of town as he tried to explain. "A date is a way of saying ... courting."

"Oh, I see. You come from a place of strange phrases."

Again, George had an inner glow as he pondered this. "I sure do."

"Now that I understand your question, Nantucket continues to be a man's world, though they be half a world away on a whale hunt, gone for several years at a time. The hardships of life here are left to the women, but not the control. A few of us aim to change that."

George started to respond, but he was cut off as Rebecca ran ahead to a wooden washbasin that had been left to catch drips off of a leaky gutter. She lifted it on its side and rolled it with glee. "Look! The tub is running!" she laughed.

As she chased it, George chased her, catching

up with a lusty grab around her waist. He turned her around, and they spun in a steadily tightening embrace. Nose to nose, with the world swirling around them, their eyes traded passion. Slowly their lips neared, opening and reaching out to each other, rejoicing in contact as their spin slowed to a stop.

They continued walking with their arms locked. As they got further from town, the houses changed from imposing, squared-off, Captains' houses that sported widows' walks on their roofs, to small cottages with tiny little front yards. They came upon just such a cottage with a white picket fence wrapped in wild roses.

George picked the prettiest one he could find and gave it to Rebecca. She blushed with the gesture and took it, bringing it gently to her nose, breathing in softly. "Roses are my special joy."

George went weak at the knees as he watched her stunning beauty. It was far from the beauty that was sold in the world he had grown up in. Rebecca's beauty had depth and subtlety. It was hardwon, not by a beauty regimen, but by the graces of life's hardships.

She brought him to the bluffs at Seaside. What had been an arduous moped trip for George in the modern world was a short effortless stroll in the trance of his love. They stood for a moment surveying the windswept beach below them. Bolgers' present-day construction site was conspicuously absent to George.

Rebecca turned to him with girlish, giddy excitement. "Let's go down, perhaps get our feet wet?"

George would follow her anywhere.

Minutes later, they were playing tag with the final push of each wave across the flat, wet sand. They laughed and played like children, without a care in the world, living exactly in the moment.

Later, as they walked away from the sea edge to the dry, thick sand, out of breath from the frolicking, George turned and fell back on the sand, staring straight up at the sky. She fell beside him with loving giggles. He sucked in a deep breath and blew it out. "For the first time I feel like the world is on my side."

Her girlishness gave way to wisdom. "Perhaps the world is but an innocent bystander?"

George felt more satisfied, comfortable, and safe than ever before as he lay there on his back and watched billowing white clouds drift by against a bright blue summer sky.

Rebecca stretched out beside him to share the view, absorbing George's emotions. She slowly propped herself up on one elbow, watching him watch the sky and drink in the sun's heat. She lifted up the fresh rose that George had picked for her and gently brushed it across his face, sending him to heaven. He closed his eyes, getting lost in the rapture.

"In your world, it is winter now, nearly Christmas," she said

George opened his eyes and looked up at her in continued bliss.

"*Was* my world," he said. "This is my world now."

"Winter comes in all worlds. Here you are but a visitor."

Fear rippled across George's face.

She said, "Stay calm, my darling. Close your eyes once again."

He complied with her request as she pulled a rose petal and brushed it lightly across his face.

There was comfort and safety in the darkness. It was something he'd felt since early childhood, something that he'd often retreated to when the world's reality became too much. In the hostile territory of his thoughts, darkness was a kind friend. It allowed him to listen to his heart or his soul instead of his self-hating head.

Though her words alarmed him, the maternal comfort of her soft tone soothed him and set him adrift through the darkness to the fringes of sleep where language morphed into images.

"I've come thrice to you. It is you who next must come to me," she said.

His face tightened. He started to open his eyes. She brushed the rose petal across his eyelids as he trustingly closed them once more, drifting back into her spell.

"You must come by Christmas," she whispered. "You must write it."

Suddenly the delicate rose petal turned scratchy on his face. He fell like a stone through the weightless dark, landing back in own body with a thump.

His eyes popped open. Instead of a rose petal, on his face was a dead, dry, brown oak leaf. As soon as his brain registered the leaf, cold November wind blew it away. He was back in the present. His coat was wrapped around him. He screamed a tortured howl of frustration to the sky. He realized that he was again wearing his normal, modern, weather-appropriate clothes. Was ALL of it just some fantasy or delusion? Even that shirt? Was he completely insane?

Driven by passion and fear, he waded through the thick sand to the bluff, figuring he'd retrace their steps. He noticed that the Bolgers construction site once more scarred the scene. He grabbed desperately at the thorny underbrush, clawing his way up the steep bluff side, not caring about or even feeling the pain.

Rejection was a familiar friend to George, but never had he suffered one so deep and complete. This was the kind that could not be recovered from.

He'd long stopped worrying about what was real or imagined. He no longer cared what sanity meant or whether he fit the parameters.

Like a heroin addict, all he cared about was getting his next fix, his next fix of Rebecca.

He knew in his heart and soul that it would no longer be a question of awaiting her returns. He knew it was different now. He was cut off from her. He had to do something to reach her, but what?

He came upon the house where, just hours or centuries ago, he'd picked Rebecca a rose. The house didn't look much different, though it was boarded up for the winter, and a Brinks Security sticker stood watch on the front door. The picket fence had been updated but kept in the same basic style. The thick, gnarled branches of a rose bush still wound itself around the pickets.

He remembered Rebecca's words about her rose satchel. *"Nantucket is indifferent to the march of time."* He clung to the faint hope that those words provided, but now they also had a haunting quality to them. They gave George a chill of ominous expectations. He knew deep inside that, if he succeeded in what had to become a quest for her, it would not be an end, just a beginning. It would be like jumping off a cliff into the dark unknown.

Fears carved through his brain like a chainsaw.

How could I possibly see this through? Just a few days ago, it took every ounce of my courage just to get on the damned ferry, just to go to Hyannis, for Christ's sake. Could I love or need somebody so much that I'll brave these challenges? Will I falter and fail along the way? Will I give up?

These scenarios tortured him as he made his way back toward Nantucket's town center, but as he asked them, his heart knew the answers. For the first time in his life, he'd see something through. His desire would overpower his fears.

By the time he got to the town's edge at the far end of Orange Street, he was chilled to the bone and drained of his strength. He felt like only his passion was driving him on.

He came upon the spot where the wooden tub had caught the drips from the leaky gutter. A plastic garbage can had now replaced it to do the same job. A dozen decades had not stopped that drip. Like grass pushing its way back through a cement sidewalk, some things just persist in being.

"Nantucket is indifferent to the march of time." It made George's brain feel itchy, with no way to scratch it.

When he finally made it back to the Quahog B&B, he was a shell of himself. He thought only of falling across the soft bed in his room and drifting off to the safety of sleep. He didn't even plan on undressing.

Perhaps, in the morning, things would look different? Maybe this was all a dream within a dream, and he'd wake up refreshed, ready for the ferry ride back to Hyannis and the bus trip back to Boston. He'd slip on the life he'd left as if it were an old shoe. Its familiarity would outweigh any discomfort. He'd regale Jim and Ray with stories of the trip and of the dream that made him think he was going crazy. He'd tell them about Bolgers nearly giving him the key to the town.

As he shrugged off his coat, the first thing he heard when he stepped into his room was running water. More than running—spilling, too. It confused him for an instant. Then he remembered.

That goddamned tub! I knew I left it running. He stomped past the bed to the bathroom. As he rushed in to turn off the water, his heart nearly stopped, nearly exploded on the spot.

There, on the bottom of the full and overflowing tub, was Rebecca, dead as yesterday's catch. Her eyes were wide-open buttons. Her Victorian dress floated around her in the swirl of bathwater.

Tears raced down his frenzied face. With a grief-stricken shriek, he dove into the tub, as if, somehow, to save her. When his body hit the water surface, the disturbance broke up Rebecca as if she were old, waterlogged tissue paper. Rebecca's dissolving body turned the water a sickening blend of colors as George thrashed around, grabbing for her.

As he continued to roll frantically in the mess, screaming and crying and reaching, the water gradually lightened. Rebecca continued to break up and dissolve until the water was clear and she was completely gone.

Finally, George stopped his tirade and lay back against the tub wall, physically and emotionally spent. His world had changed once again—once again and forever. There would be no ferry home, no regaling Jim and Ray. He had a mission. He had no clue what that mission was. He did know one thing; if he failed, he'd be as good as dead himself, better off dead.

Part
Two

TWENTY-THREE

Sheehan's desk could've been an aircraft carrier. It spread out before him in all directions. Even so, he wasn't diminished by its size. He was an imposing figure as he sat behind it. He was in command of it, in command of all he surveyed. Everything about the office said power: the commanding view, the rich wood paneling. That's the way Sheehan demanded things. Sheehan didn't 'want' things. Want was a weak man's word. Sheehan demanded.

At more than sixty, he could still take on all comers. He'd fought his way to where he was with a magically rare combination of brains, cunning, courage, and strength. At least that's the way he saw it. As a young guy, he'd been one of the prime movers in Boston's re-emergence onto the world stage. The city's redevelopment in the mid-'60s was only the spark that set the fuse. In the 1970s, he rode the wave of new wealth like an expert surfer. That was not an image he'd warmed up to.

Surfers were too laid back, too "California soft." Sheehan would rather see himself as having ridden a bucking bronco, as taking a tiger by the tail, something a "man" would do.

He looked like old Boston power, like Tip O'Neill. He had a hard scramble of white, Irish hair that no comb or brush would dare tangle with. His face was red with tiny, purple veins at the tip of his bulbous nose. He tossed his two-hundred-dollar pen on the desk before him and pushed an intercom button.

"Get the hell in here."

Almost instantly, Jim timidly crept into the room and up to Sheehan's desk. Gone was all the bravado that Jim had displayed to George and Ray in the bar.

"Where the hell's your little friend?" Sheehan demanded.

"George?"

"No. The f'in Pope! Who'd you think I mean?"

"Well, you did fire him," Jim offered.

"Bullshit! He's still got to finish out the week."

Sheehan studied Jim's nervous and guilty face.

Jim felt the weight of the scrutiny.

"You didn't even have the balls to tell the little shit, did you?"

Jim gathered all his courage to answer, "I thought I'd let him enjoy the holiday, at least."

"You thought! I don't pay you to think. If I needed thinkers, I'd hire them." Suddenly the situation caught Sheehan as funny. "That little bastard is a no-show for a job he thinks he still has."

As Sheehan chuckled to himself about this, taking great satisfaction in it, he waved his arm dismissively at Jim. With great relief, Jim turned and slunk from the room.

As Jim drifted by the sea of cubicles, Ray popped his head up over one of the partitions. A *Homestar Runner* STRONG BAD coffee mug dangled from his finger. Jim noticed the cup.

"Where's *Doctor Who*?"

"He's soaking."

"Those British."

"Where's George?"

"Who knows? I left lots of messages at his place. I tried his cell, too, but it's like he turned it off."

112

Ray said, "Maybe he spent the weekend with that girlfriend?"

"Bullshit. If he did that, we'd be talking him down from the window ledge right now."

Ray got excited. "I know! In *Twilight Zone* once–"

Jim cut him off. "Get a life, Raymond."

TWENTY-FOUR

November 30th

Christmas trees lined Nantucket's Main Street. Though Christmas Stroll had not yet started, the town was beginning to bask in the Victorian splendor of the old time holiday. Carolers drifted over the sidewalk, singing *O Christmas Tree.* The day was cold, raw, and gray. Swags of fresh pine, laced with red ribbons, hung low over the cobblestone street. The sea air was mixed with the scents of all that fresh-cut pine, chestnuts roasting, and wood fires from the stately homes and B&B's.

George staggered along the street in a tortured frenzy. His eyes were that of a zombie. His clothes, still wet from the tub, were starting to stiffen and freeze on his back. He barely noticed. His brain was a raging inferno. His soul mate, the person who would make all life worth living, he had found dead right in front of him. The height of his bliss had become his deepest tragedy.

An old man sitting on a Main Street bench watched George apprehensively. To him, this soaked, barely clothed man was consumed by madness—the wild eyes, the disoriented steps of confusion, it all added up to crazy, perhaps dangerous.

The man shouted out to George, "Hey buddy,

you'll catch your death of cold."

The explosion came. George's shaky eyes bore through the man.

"Catch MY death? Catch my DEATH!"

Fear shot through the old man. "Take it easy," he said. "Take it easy."

At that moment, George noticed one of the Christmas trees tied to a lamppost. It was a particularly sparse one. Its branches reached out longingly. Ornaments hung from the ends. Something about that tree set off sheer horror in George. In a lightning quick flash, something burst in his brain. It was the split-second vision of something he couldn't recognize, something horrible, something like that tree but bigger, even more sparse. Things dangled from the ends.

Then the vision was gone. It had crystal clarity, but it was too brief for his mind to fully capture or understand. He grabbed at his head as if a rail spike had gone through it. He spun, falling to one knee. The old man sprang from the bench and edged himself away to safety.

George was in a whirlwind hell of fear and fury. He was racked with grief, guilt, and regret. As high as the pinnacle of his happiness had been, so now was his devastation as deep. He stumbled wildly along the sidewalk like a landlubber on a pitching ship's deck, clutching his head as he went.

A man called out from across the street, "Pretty early in the morning, isn't it?"

If George heard him at all, he ignored him.

A short time later, George found himself at the ferry dock. He didn't even remember how he'd gotten there.

The confused sea leapt and spat as the ferry's powerful screws churned against it. George's mind raced as he watched a crewman casting off the lines. Though George didn't even have his duffle with him, he thought about what comfort escape to the mainland might bring. He could just hop aboard and be on Cape Cod in a couple of hours.

He didn't seriously consider it. He knew that running now would introduce him to a level of self-hatred that even he had not yet plunged to.

As he undid his last stern line, the crewman called over to him. "Hey! You going to Hyannis?"

George was too self-absorbed to even hear him. This pissed the guy off.

"Fuck'ya, then," the crewman yelled as he jumped aboard the fat boat.

George watched the ferry until it cleared Brant Point, trying to get enough of a handle on his grief-stricken fear to come up with a game plan.

Rebecca needed saving. He didn't know from what or where or in what time, but he knew she needed it, and it was up to him.

He shuffled ideas like cards in his brain. None of them made any sense. None of them connected to one another. He might as well have tried to nail a board to a cloud. Where could he possibly start? Why did she come to him of all people? Would somebody, anybody else have been a better candidate?

The very marrow of his bones told George it had to be him. By the cosmos or God or Rebecca herself, he'd been chosen, and no matter how much it scared him, he'd see it through. Failure was not an option.

That last thought gave him a chill of self-doubt.

Failure may not be an option, but it sure is a probability, he thought.

Back at the B&B, he needed to book extra days. The room was vacant for the next few nights, but after that, because of the Christmas Stroll, every room would be full. George's funds weren't in the best shape, either. The one credit card he'd allowed himself was close to maxed out. He wasn't sure of how much room was left on it because, as it got close to the limit, he was always afraid to look.

He'd always let money terrorize him. He even preferred ATMs to bank tellers, feeling guilt for requesting his own damned money. As if the teller would say, "Didn't I just give you money last week? What'd you do with it?"

George thought about this while waiting for the B&B desk clerk. He used it to beat himself up even more.

Some hero she picked!

The desk clerk cleared him through Friday.

Cleared to do what? His brain taunted, *You have NO CLUE!*

TWENTY-FIVE

The moped ride out to Surfside felt longer this time, longer and colder. Purple clouds darkened the sky. A headwind battled him the whole way, pushing him back so hard that it like he was riding on a treadmill.

After a night of staring at the ceiling of his room, he'd decided that any action was better than none. Even if he didn't know what to do, he'd do something. As King Lear once said, *"Nothing comes from nothing."*

George decided that somehow he would stir the pot. But could he even find the pot? He doubted it, but in a new surge of courageous commitment, he vowed to try.

He figured that the best place to start might be the last place he saw her alive, the place she'd brought him. It must mean something. Maybe the place would tell him?

He stood on the high bluff, looking out over the sand and the sea, listening to the wind for answers. If any were forthcoming, they were lost in the wind's howl. There was an ominous, lonely quality to the sound, but no new wisdom was held there.

George noticed the Bolgers construction site far off to his left. To him, it looked like a scar on the land, like blight. This time it bothered him tenfold more than it had the first time, as if it were a personal slap in his face. He knew in that moment that he disliked Bolgers. Any pretense of his being the benevolent father figure was just that—pretense.

As he continued watching the sea, he visualized his romp with Rebecca on the sand. It seemed like a long-ago memory or dream, but at the same time it felt as fresh and recent as the last few seconds, as if he could close his eyes and be back there with her. George filled with tears. He tried to force his whole body not to cry for her, not to turn weak and become a blubbering puddle. He had a job to do, a mission, and he had to hold it together.

Then he came upon a new realization. *What if my only road to her is emotional?* he thought. *How can I get there if I close off my emotions?*

In that second, he knew that the pain he wanted to cry out was the thing it took the most courage to face. Perhaps what he thought was weakness was really strength? With that, all of his pain, rage, and fear flowed out. His crying became convulsions. He screamed from the depths of his soul. He cried every last little bit of pent-up grief, fear, and guilt that he could find. He wrung it out of his brain as if it were a sponge. He cried until he could produce no more tears. He screamed until his vocal chords whispered hoarse pleas for mercy. When he was done, he lay there spent. It was a moment of catharsis, like that brief time after sex, when fatigue brings a friendly clarity.

Just then, something tugged at his memory.

He'd met Rebecca's father. His mind scratched for the name: Quentin Fulagar. He was a ship's captain! There must be registries on file: records, ships' logs ... Finally, George had a place to start his search, a place to prove to himself that Rebecca was real. He couldn't know where it would lead, but at least it was a beginning.

TWENTY-SIX

The Nantucket Atheneum was a stately building in the center of town. Tall columns towered across the front of it. George had been looking for the local library, but everyone he asked kept steering him to this place. George didn't know what the hell it was. He couldn't even pronounce it.

Turned out it was better than a library; library was one of its functions, but it was so much more. Atheneums were more common a couple of hundred years ago. They were started as centers of knowledge where people could congregate to share and acquire new wisdom and information. Famous writers and thinkers of the time would make speeches, research could be done, books could be read or borrowed. The name came from Athena, the Greek goddess of knowledge.

George strained his neck looking up at the imposing columns. This was going to be worse than facing tellers at the bank. The very size of the place told him he was already in trouble for even thinking he could go in. He had visions of the lion standing in front of the giant, flaming, orb-headed Wizard of Oz.

"Maybe I've seen that film too much?" George said to himself as he realized how much he referenced it. He put his foot on the first step. Now he was committed. He remembered that day, as a freshman, taking his first step up the front stairs to his high school, wondering what hidden terrors lay in store for him. It felt good as he ascended the stairs, overcoming the silly fears that had dogged him since childhood. Even small victories were victories still the same.

Inside, the Atheneum had a cool, dark quiet that was as comforting as it was imposing. In a place like this, even if you tried to speak up, it would come out as a whisper due to the automatic reverence the room demanded.

George looked up in awe. Sunlight streamed in through high windows and sliced through tiny dust motes, like heavenly rays glowing against the darkness.

Books have a distinct smell to them—not an individual book so much as a collection of books. Anybody who has gone into a Barnes and Noble knows that smell. George had always liked it. He loved hanging out in bookstores. New book smell, like new car smell, probably came from chemicals that gave you cancer as you whiffed.

For old books, the risk was much lower and the experience that much better. Library books had an enticing smell, too. It was partly that new book smell, mellowed like a fine wine, with organic complexities and subtle tones that no new book could rival. But there was something else that only age supplied. It was a smell of safety and wisdom. It could cradle you, comfort you like an old covered porch in an April rain.

For George, there was the added thrill of a million adventures between the dusty pages. There were millions of heroines to be saved and millions of heroes to save them.

Betty Bolgers gently interrupted George's thoughts with the well-known icebreaker "May I help you?"

George focused in on her aged, careworn face. There was a friendly, open quality to her, a gentleness in her eyes, an energy that told George she might be younger than he'd first thought, but he couldn't tell for sure. Her nametag just said Betty so he made no connection as to whom her husband might be.

"I'm looking into Nantucket history."

"This is the place to start."

George admired a certain sparkle she had about her.

"Is there a particular part of our history you're looking for?"

George tried to focus his thoughts. "Whaling, I guess. Mid-1800s."

She led him down a long dark hallway. "You might find it better to focus on the early part of the century. By 1850, whaling had run its course on Nantucket."

"Why is that?"

"Our harbor had a rather big sandbar. It kept growing until the ships couldn't get over it. Lots of things were tried, but eventually New Bedford eclipsed us in the trade. We just couldn't compete."

"I thought Nantucket was the world king of whaling."

"It was. We were blessed with wealth and world renown. Everything falls victim to time, I suppose."

"You sound like you lived it," he said.

"I'm not quite *that* old," she said. "I absorbed it, more likely."

George thought about her sandbar story. Rebecca had mentioned her father getting his ship over the bar. He hadn't known what it meant at the time and so he'd let it pass. If she had been a product of his crazy mind, she wouldn't have talked about the bar because he didn't know about it. It didn't come from him. This realization sparkled inside him.

She must be real! The thought came like a B-12 shot.

"Do you have ships' logs?"

"That's a lot to sift through."

They came to a door. She opened it with a key and motioned him inside.

George was awestruck by the sheer volume of old wooden file cabinets. The room was thick with the dust of age.

Betty saw the intimidated look on his face.

"Some of this has been entered on computer. Perhaps you'd rather search there first?"

George looked around, breathing in the thick, history-laden air. "No. Thanks. I need to be here. I can feel it."

Betty took this as a bit odd but kept it to herself. "Very well."

She pulled out a pair of white, light cloth gloves. "The logs are original documents, very fragile. I'll have to ask you wear these."

George agreed and took them from her with reverence for the fragile value of what they meant he was about to handle. He struggled to get them on his hands. He watched Betty leave and then turned back to the mountain of files. They were daunting.

Left alone, his hibernating fears began to stir. The little lost-boy parts of him wanted to call Betty back and savor the comfort of her maternal presence. He resisted the urge. He looked up at the stacks, taking a breath full of courage, like David preparing to face Goliath.

Since Rebecca had mentioned 'the bar,' he decided to start at 1850 and work backwards. Even by that definition, the volume of material he had to sift through was immense.

He pulled out the first leather-bound, ledger-sized book. As soon as he opened it, he knew this was the right decision. These were handwritten originals, done with a quill pen. The heart of each writer was there on the page. A computer screen could never hope to match what he could absorb from these.

The actual logs were formal, constrained by the language of the times. They read like Melville without the artistry. Even so, raw emotion would oftentimes shine through. He read between the lines about hints of hardship, of desperate crews and uncertain futures.

The real gold, though, was in the letters. They were interspersed with the official logs. Here men had written home to loved ones, sticking their letters in a Valparaiso tree hole—used as a makeshift mailbox—hoping against hope that another Nantucket whale ship would find them and carry them home to their intended reader. Valparaiso, Chile, had become a favorite port for Nantucket whalers, either resting up from their trip around The Horn or re-supplying for their trip back around The Horn for home.

These letters, written in the same quill pen and the same *Moby Dick*-style language, talked freely of negligent captains, abusive first mates, hardships, and fears. They inquired about children and lamented about lost ones. The emotions that rolled from the pages swept George up and told him about life in terms he'd never dreamed possible.

Some of these letters brought tears to his eyes. One indentured seaman wrote to his young wife, describing his condition as one-half-step above slavery. He talked of the floggings, the weevil-infested, rotting food, the endless hours of dangerous, backbreaking work, and the hole in his heart that came from being yanked from her soft comforts.

Another told of life lived in terror of an evil, sadistic first mate. This was not uncommon, George learned as he sifted through more letters.

As he continued to read about shipboard life, he felt it in his very bones, as if he'd lived it himself. He mocked himself for being so suggestible. He figured it was the same thing that made him cry at movies. He even caught himself crying at TV commercials.

He shook off his inner critic and continued reading.

Some letters were from wives and mothers, given to outgoing whale ships in the hopes of being picked up by the right person in that same Valparaiso tree hole and reaching the intended husband or son. These letters spoke in equally dire terms about babies or mothers dying at birth, illness, and loss of all kinds.

One thing most letters had in common was that they weren't complaining or self-pitying. The worst hands life could deal a soul were taken as a matter of fact, to be expected.

George wondered how he'd have fared in that world and didn't like the answer. In their stoic nobility, he saw the true stuff of heroes. Nothing big, like a movie hero, just day to day, doing what's needed for children and family, all done with quiet dignity and courage.

The emotions of those pages flowed over him and filled him with tears. In his bones, he knew that he was meant to come here, meant to find this. He knew in his soul that the trauma of these lives was strong enough to leave permanent scars in the very spots they occurred in, wrinkles in the thick sea air, folds in time and space.

He could feel these tragic souls all around him in the dank chill of the room. In that moment, George believed in ghosts, a concept he'd never given much thought to before stepping on this island. These were things he felt in his heart and soul, but his brain remained skeptical, ready to ridicule it all and remind him of his family predisposition for insanity. For now, those doubts remained a sleeping giant as George gave himself over to his less-discerning side.

Hours more of reading left George bleary-eyed with still no discovery of a Quentin Fulagar, no letters to or from a Rebecca. He kept telling himself that he'd only made the tiniest of dents in a mountain of material. This reassured him that not finding her wasn't proof that she wasn't there. It also discouraged him to the limit. Finding records or further clues in this mess would be as likely as winning the lottery. The logs weren't filed alphabetically by captain, but by ship.

George strained to remember if he'd been told the ship's name or had seen it, but he drew a blank. The letters weren't filed alphabetically, either. They were filed by month and year.

George knew that if he continued on this path, the Christmas deadline that Rebecca had given him would come and go before he'd even scratched the surface. There had to be a better way. Thinking about it made him even more tired. His eyes were like heavy window shades. Dreams knocked on the door of his consciousness.

Stars burn through the darkness of a moonless night. Before them, masts of a giant ship tower against the sky. Creaking and grinding are loud. A man's disembodied voice screams over the wind, "Get a line around! Get a bloody line around!!"

George woke up with a jolt. He barely remembered the specifics of the dream. What he could recall was quickly dissolving before his eyes, dissolving like Rebecca had in his bathtub.

The records room quickly lost its appeal to him. It felt dark and ominous.

Time to leave.

As George shuffled near zombie-like past the front desk, Betty called out to him, "I was just about to come and get you. We're closing in ten minutes."

He nodded to her vacantly and asked, "What time do you open in the morning?"

"No luck, huh?"

"I think the computer room might be a better bet," he told her.

"Fine. We'll be here at nine o'clock."

"I'd hoped I'd have a more productive day."

"Oh, well, there's always tomorrow."

That struck him oddly.

I hope so, he thought.

TWENTY-SEVEN

Tristram Bolgers waited impatiently at his dining room table. Mashed potatoes steamed from one bowl, multicolored vegetables steamed from another. But where was the meat? *Where was the GODDAMNED MEAT?*

He could hear Betty bustling about in the kitchen, busy as a bee. Instead of reassuring him, it infuriated him.

Why do I have to put up with THIS bullshit? It made him feel better just to think the word. It was therapeutic. *Bullshit at work all day. Bullshit at home. Bullshit. Bullshit. Bullshit.*

Betty hurried into the room with a hot platter of prime rib and laid it in front of Bolgers' plate. He quickly piled some on.

"About time."

She bristled slightly, but mostly hid it, preferring to endure her pain stoically. She sat down across from him in stiff silence. They ate half of their meal in awkward wordlessness. Finally, the guilt became too much for him.

"A very lovely meal. Thank you."

She dabbed a single spot on the corner of her mouth with her napkin. "You're welcome."

More stony silence.

He tried again. "Anything new happen at the library?"

"You of all people know it's not a library."

He smiled wickedly. He liked to kid her about the things that were important to her. He saw it as a lover's game. She saw it as abuse. At least she did way down deep in the still-smoldering embers of her self-worth.

"Alright, alright," he said. "It's a real hot spot, okay, a real 'happening place' as they say. So what exciting things unfolded? Was Paris Hilton there?"

Her anger simmered. "That's your wet dream, not mine."

Her answer sent real shock waves through Bolgers' sense of security. "Who's been teaching you THAT language?"

"Brad Pitt! Every day at the LI-B-RARY!"

She slammed her fork on the table and shot to her feet. Bolgers meekly watched her march into the kitchen. He heard her quietly sobbing from someplace over near the stove.

The warm flow of regret rolled across his face with icy pins of shame. He knew he always went too far. He feared someday there might be no return. In front of him would be a lonely life of regret. Who would take care of him, be his harbor of comfort, his rock of strength?

Suddenly he was staring into the dark pit of his fears. It was a darkness he had run from since early childhood. Everything he'd done in life had been an attempt to avoid it. Money and power could scare it off or buy it off, keep it at bay, or so he thought.

It never worked. No matter what, there it was, like a boogieman in his closet waiting for his chance to strike. The monster lurked just behind the face of any failure. Any misstep could cause it to spring. He'd always tried to outrun it, striving for more and more power and wealth but nothing was enough.

He couldn't admit it except in times like these, but Betty was his best weapon to keep that boogie-man away. Her mothering charms soothed the boy inside him. If he lost her, he'd be done. The monsters of darkness would flock in to feast on his soul. He never saw darkness darker or scarier than when pondering the prospect of losing her.

He gauged the severity of their fights by length of time. Through dinner was bad—through dessert, worse. If it interfered with TV time later, it would get critical. He knew from the anger in her eyes and from the fact that he didn't go to her in the kitchen, that this one was bad.

This one might go past those levels. This one might go all the way to the bedroom. That was DEFCON ONE, condition red, the worst—time to panic.

Later, they sat silently together watching *Risk Factor*. The blue, changing light of the TV flickered on their faces and reflected in their eyes.

Bolgers' guilt drove his thoughts. *She always complains about me hogging the remote. Maybe if I let her watch some chick channel it'll patch things over. I'll even watch the stupid thing with her. That'll show I care. Look at her over there, stewing in her own juices. I'll say something to break the ice ... as soon as the next commercial comes.*

The picture changed to a male enhancement commercial. He turned to her, sheepishly offering out the remote. "You could flick around, if you'd like."

"So generous."

This wasn't going to work. He knew, as distasteful as it might be, that he'd have to revisit the source of the pain if he really wanted to mend things. "How was your day?"

She crossed her arms as if she were hugging

herself. Her silence told him that he was just making her angrier. It looked like a bedroom of sorrows lurked in his future.

It was time to push forward with the nuclear option: a performance of complete contrition. What woman could resist a man who laid his weaknesses and faults bare at her feet. It was like handing her a knife and saying, *"Now please don't stab me."*

Honesty—it worked every time if you were a good enough actor to pull it off. He muted the TV just to prove his sincerity.

"Sometimes, when I've had a bad day, I take it out on you without even realizing it. I'm sorry if I hurt you. I really do care about your life."

More silence.

Oh no! Now what? he thought as he sat there drowning in the heavy quiet.

Finally her words came, small and tentatively.

"We had an off-islander come in to do research today."

"A coof? In the Atheneum?"

She angered again. "I am a coof, too, you remember."

"You've been here decades. Your coofiness has worn off."

"So accepting of you."

Bolgers had no time for her anger now. He was off on another tangent, a paranoid one. "What did he look like?"

Her description of the man told him positively that it was George.

"So, he IS a spy!"

"Who's a spy?"

"The coof, the coof! Can't you even follow your own story?"

Her anger was back. She stood up. "I'm going to bed."

Bolgers didn't care so much anymore. He was

too focused on his imagined enemy, George. He called out after Betty. "If he comes again, keep an eye on him."

She spun back to him. "I won't indulge your paranoid delusions."

Bolgers was ready to blow, but he reigned it in. "It just happens that I have information on good authority that a Boston redevelopment firm wants to horn in on my plans. They'd send spies first, then corporate hit men!"

"My, my, such intrigue," she said as she turned back and headed for the bedroom, leaving Bolgers to stew in silence.

Things didn't change much by breakfast. Bolgers was still consumed by thoughts of George. At the table, he interrogated Betty about when George came, how long he stayed, what he wanted, what he said to her. She endured his third degree with the same grace that had seen her through most of her marriage.

Oh sure, she had the occasional blowups, like last night, when the pressure and the anger had built up over the weeks and months to the breaking point. Many of the times when she had blown, it was over petty issues that only served to make her look small and unreasonable. There was no way to communicate that they were the result of long-repressed, larger issues. She lost either way, so mostly she suffered in stoic silence.

As she buzzed about the kitchen waiting on her husband, he silently schemed for his enemy's destruction.

TWENTY-EIGHT

George was at the Atheneum ten minutes before it opened. He quickly drank his coffee so he could discard it empty when the doors finally opened. He didn't notice Bolgers watching him from across the street, near the Post Office. He didn't think to look.

Needless to say, George was first in through the door as Betty Bolgers opened it. She hid her shock, suspicion, and fear as she directed him to the computer room. She was used to hiding a multitude of emotions at one time.

Amazingly, this never stopped her from prizing honesty as a virtue and successfully striving for it most of the time. She was now torn about what to do.

Should she spy on him like she'd promised her husband? If she didn't, she'd be lying to him. If she did, she'd be dishonest to the off–islander, and worse than that, she'd be betraying her own sense of personal integrity. At times, she felt like that integrity was the only thing of value she had left.

George took a seat at one of the computers and booted it up. Static electricity buzzed on the screen as it came to life. A sick feeling instantly overcame him. For a flash, he was back in his gray cubicle in Boston, pecking away like a bird at his company computer and living in dread of Sheehan's booming voice.

He shook those feelings off and focused on the subject at hand: finding Rebecca. There wasn't a mountain of info. There were a lot of links to other libraries, historical societies, and Nantucket books but nothing screamed out at him. Nothing yelled *HERE—SHE IS OVER HERE!*

He started to regret the attention he had failed to pay in classes about using the library and researching papers. He kept searching, but there were few, if any, leads. He tried name searches for Quentin Fulagar, Rebecca Fulagar—zip. Was he spelling it right? Were records this old so incomplete?

Just as he was about to take a break, Betty Bolgers slipped in. "I don't want to disturb you, but you've been in here so long that I began to worry."

"I was just about to break for lunch. What do you recommend around here?"

"The Atlantic Café is always good, and it's one of the few open year-round. It's just down on the corner of Water Street. When you go out, turn left toward the water."

"Thanks." He saw something in her eyes that told him she was curious, but about what? He waited for an instant in case she had more to say.

"Are you coming back after lunch?" she asked.

"I think so."

"Is there anything I can help you find?"

She seemed to be pleasant and helpful, but George couldn't shake the feeling that there was more behind it.

"I'm researching the 1840s. I'm looking for whaling ships—"

"Yes, I remember that," she interrupted. "Anything more specific so that I may direct you better?"

"Have you heard the name Quentin Fulagar, a

sea captain, or ... Rebecca ... Rebecca Fulagar?"

"I'm sorry, no."

She didn't want to do this, her husband's bidding. In fact, she wanted to tell this off-islander to run, hide, take the next ferry home. She couldn't betray her husband any more than she could carry his water. She'd have to settle for some middle ground.

"Perhaps you'll find what you're after at The Whaling Museum. They are right down by The Atlantic Café. Their logs and historical accounts may be better organized and more thorough for that time period."

George watched her anguished face as she talked. It gave him an uneasy feeling. He couldn't put his finger on it. Something was wrong. She reminded him of a hostage on TV, trying to find a way of communicating the truth while speaking the words their captors forced them to speak.

He knew it was silly. Nobody was holding a gun to her head. His decided that his overactive imagination was conjuring up some stupid, paranoid stuff.

TWENTY-NINE

George thought to himself, *That lady steered me right,* as he huddled over a steaming bowl of one of the best chowders he'd ever eaten. The chowder would be his one nod to being on this sea-swept island.

He needed reminders of home right about now. He lusted after the plates of burgers and fries he saw come out of the kitchen. That's what he'd have, along with a beer.

He'd finished the chowder, and was just about to get that burger plate, when Tristram Bolgers sat down across from him.

"Well, well, well, my Boston friend. I thought you'd be long gone by now. Thanksgiving weekend, wasn't that your itinerary?"

"You made the place so friendly I decided to stay a bit longer."

George's burger came. Now he was too self-conscious to eat it. He always felt awkward eating in front of people. This was especially true of people he cast as authority figures, which was almost everyone.

Bolgers was a special case. George still wanted to impress him, to be cool around him, even though he'd also begun to hate him. Unfortunately, those dueling thoughts only served to make George act less cool.

Bolgers continued the inquest. "Have you no job to go back to?"

George didn't want to answer. He knew the question was an invasion of privacy, but his people-pleaser part got the best of him. He spilled his guts. He told Bolgers all about the office and Sheehan, his crummy apartment in the Somerville triple-decker. You'd never have to waterboard George. He'd tell all before you even filled the bucket.

Bolgers absorbed it all like a sponge. To him, information was power. All of it could be used in some way to vanquish an opponent. He had become an expert at extracting the truly damaging things to be learned about people and then spinning the rest as needed. He was proud of those traits. He considered them necessities for anyone holding public office. He saw his skill level at this as being downright presidential.

Now it was time for him to grease the skids so he could pry a little more.

"I wish you'd have let me know you were staying. I could've taken you to dinner."

George's burger was cold now. He tried to wolf it down while he could. He was intensely aware of some kind of juice or glop that dripped from the bun onto his shirt. He took no joy in this eating experience.

Bolgers took out a twenty and slapped it on the table. "At least let me buy you lunch. This should cover it, unless you've got martinis coming that I don't know about." Bolgers laughed hard at his own joke. "What really made you stay on, if I may ask?"

"I'm researching some things."

"Such as?"

He truly didn't know what to tell him. If he told Bolgers the truth, he'd think George was nuts. He couldn't risk that. "Just ... things ... whaling history, stuff like that."

"Why does a coof need to know about Nantucket whaling history?"

The word caught George unexpectedly and hurt him. "I thought you didn't like to use that word."

"I apologize. Because of the way we met, I'm using it ... affectionately."

Bolgers stood up, pushing back his chair. "Perhaps I've been too nosey. I just want to be the best help I can. My door is always open. I'll leave you to enjoy your lunch."

Before he got to the door, Bolgers turned back to George. "One more thing. Now that you've decided to stay, perhaps you'd give some thought to attending my town meeting presentation?"

George hesitated. *What presentation?* he thought in a panic.

"You remember. The one we discussed at The Brotherhood of Thieves."

George nodded. "Perhaps."

When Bolgers left, George looked down at his plate. He had five cold French fries left. He was determined to enjoy them.

THIRTY

George looked up in awe as he wandered under the fifty-foot-long sperm whale skeleton that hung from the Whaling Museum's ceiling. Nearby, a crusty old man led a small tour group through the exhibits. An unlit corncob pipe dangled from his hardened lips. George decided to tag along at the end of the group and get some good background info.

He learned all about the whaleboat that sat under the hanging skeleton. The details that the old man pointed out were all on the whaleboat that George had seen the man working on during his first excursion to the past. That leg brace thing was called a clumsy cleat. Harpooners used it to brace themselves when hurling their spears at the back of a whale. The box in the middle was for coiled rope to be paid out quickly once a whale was harpooned. The post at the stern was called a loggerhead. The rope would be fed around that and run the length of the boat to where it was attached to the end of the harpoon.

George was elated. If his trips to the past had all been in his head, they wouldn't have contained all that detail of what existed on a whaleboat. They weren't things he'd ever known about. He felt his heart race. Rebecca had to real, too.

He needed more confirmation to seal the deal. He raised his hand. The old guy called on him. "Was there ever a cannibal on Nantucket?"

The rest of the group looked at him like he was crazy, but the old man seemed to light up.

He said, "You must be thinking about The Essex. Terrible story. The ship was sunk by a sperm whale in the Pacific. The men went four thousand miles in tiny whaleboats like this one before reaching safety. The ones who survived did it by eating the dead. In the Captain's boat, they even drew lots to see who'd be killed for food. Short straw was pulled by the Captain's own cousin, a kid that Captain had promised to protect. Ended up eating him instead."

The old man delighted in the shocked reaction from the group. George took a deep breath and forged ahead. "Did the Captain survive?"

"Yep, came right back here to Nantucket, lived out his life in shame, right up close to where The Jared Coffin House is, corner of Centre and Quince, it was."

George wanted to do the happy dance but kept it to himself. Then he had a scary thought. Since seeing that house on Centre and Quince was the event that kicked off his first trip to the past, maybe it was a major part of Rebecca's story? He asked his next question tentatively. "Was the Captain named ... Fulagar?"

"No, no, no ... This happened around 1820 or 21. Fulagar was at least fifteen or twenty years later."

George was ecstatic!

"Quentin Fulagar?"

"I see you've done your homework," the man said. "Fulagar came along near the end of whaling in Nantucket. A bad time, really, not a lot of history kept about that period. Too depressing, I suppose.

I'll show you a picture though."

The man led them into a room filled with oil-painted portraits. The deep green walls and plush carpet called for quiet reverence. All but the most oblivious would automatically keep voices at a whisper.

The paintings weren't Rembrandts, but they were competently done. As well as being a good likeness, they captured the pride of being a whaling ship captain and sometimes even the hardship. Each man had sat stoically for his painting, trying not to let any emotion show through. Emotions could betray manhood in their world. They were things best left to the women. Still, many of these portraits did as the name implied, they portrayed. They caught a certain truth behind the eyes. This gave them the depth that, all these years later, commanded the reverence in this room. It wasn't the walls or the carpet. It was the eyes, their eyes.

It didn't take long for George to see him. There he was, immortalized on the wall, Quentin Fulagar. He went straight to the painting as if drawn by a tractor beam. His mouth opened to speak but then closed again. He was too overcome.

The old tour guide stepped over beside him. The group gathered in a wide circle, allowing enough room for the drama that they saw unfolding. George looked into the old man's eyes. "Fulagar?"

"That's right, Quentin Fulagar."

George tried to reign in his raging emotions, but his body shook and his lips quivered. "Did he ... have a daughter?"

The old man removed his pipe, and with the back of his hand, wiped the spittle from the white whisker stubble of his chin. "Don't know about that. We're not so much on the personal side here. You might want to check out Mitchell's Book Corner. They got a whole Nantucket section. Might find something." He reinserted his pipe.

George left the museum at early dusk. He stopped to look at a black cast iron cannon situated out front. He slowly reached out his fingers to touch its barrel. That's when it happened again.

Dark night, on an old sailboat of some kind. A cannon fires out a padded ball with a plume of orange that lights the world for a millisecond. The ball arcs into the rigging of a huge sailing ship. Thunder ruptures the air ...

Then it was done. Terror rippled through him. His face broke out in a warm sweat that quickly chilled in the late day air.

THIRTY-ONE

On the outside, The Even Keel Café was pure Nantucket. The white-trimmed, brick exterior looked like it had grown right out of the sidewalk bricks. Inside, there was a long counter on one side and tables on the other. It wasn't an old-time drug store or cafeteria-style counter. This was upscale New York. The cream-colored walls featured sophisticated artwork, not so much "pure Nantucket."

Harry Beal had a table near the window. It wasn't the place he felt most comfortable in, but their dark roast coffee was great. He strained his neck to look back towards the kitchen. He knew his eggs would be on their way. Another thing he liked here, he could order sunny-side eggs, and they'd always come with warm, liquid yokes, and he wouldn't have to worry about any of the white still being clear. That clear liquid part made him want to hurl. He knew cooking those eggs was a delicate operation. Wait too long for the clear to whiten and the yolk becomes cement. These guys could walk that tightrope just right. And their toast was always the perfect sponge for the yellow goo.

Such were life's small pleasures for Nantucket's chief of police. But this day, just as the eggs were coming out, Bolgers sat down across from him. This guy could ruin more meals ...

"We got trouble."

"Right here in River City!" was Beal's mocking response.

Bolgers didn't even get it. He continued on with a look of minor annoyance. "There's a coof here who's up to no good. I'm sure of it. He'll do harm to Nantucket."

"Nantucket, or you?"

Bolgers was incensed. "I am Nantucket!"

"You take a poll on that?"

"Everything's a joke with you, isn't it?"

"Not everything ... or everyone."

"What was that last part?"

Beal remained silent. Bolgers took that as a triumphant reassurance of his power. "I thought so!"

Bolgers launched into his rant. "We can't allow troublemakers to come here just to meddle, just to screw things up. I want it stopped."

"Should I load my gun?"

Bolgers ignored the comment. "His name is George Cooper. I have a complete dossier."

"If I read it, will it self-destruct in ten seconds?"

"Do I have to remind you of what you owe me? Everything I've done can be undone."

The humor drained from Beal's body. Something in Bolgers' words scared him, scared him a lot. Bolgers continued in his take-no-prisoners style. "You were in a pretty tight spot as I recall."

"Okay. Okay," Beal snapped. "You got what you paid for. You own a cop."

"I don't like having to remind you."

Bolgers paused to make sure he'd made the impression he wanted to. Then he continued, "We need to set the trap. I want to catch him like a little bird. We'll build a case, make it good and legal."

Harry Beal looked down regretfully at his cold eggs. It no longer mattered how perfect the yokes were.

THIRTY-TWO

George had slept the morning away. His night was fitful, tortured by demons of doubt and fears of what lay ahead. He needed an infusion of passion in order to continue. The Atheneum and the Whaling Museum had fed his brain, but that was only half of the journey he needed to take. What would feed his soul? Instead of going straight back to his research, he needed to clear his head, listen to his heart. He thought about going back to the end of Straight Wharf, but he opted instead for a long walk.

It was three miles out to Surfside, three miles to think, to clear his head. He traced the same route along which Rebecca had led him at the height of his bliss. Maybe somehow this would bring him closer to her?

The bare tree branches clicked their fingers together. The wind cackled through them. The ground was hard and frozen. Even the sky seemed to warn him back with its threatening gray. George was intensely aware that every step he took towards his goal was another step further from the safety of town. He almost talked himself into turning back several times, but then at the last moment, decided to push forward.

He finally came upon the cliff and started down

the steep path to the sand. The sea roared, sending its frenzied surf to explode on the beach. The wind was now a full blast that he could barely stand against. Self-doubt tugged at the edges of his frayed brain, but still he pressed on across the blowing sand, squinting to keep the airborne grains from stinging his eyes. The world seemed to be saying, *"GO HOME!"* This time, life's challenges weren't making him run. This time, they inspired him to continue on.

He walked until the edge of the ocean was licking at his toes. He looked out across the tormented waves. He thought about how this very spot, the world within his view, was immune to time. It looked the way it always looked, always would. It didn't care whether Lincoln was being shot or Kennedy, didn't care if people drove cars or rode horses. Time did not exist, did not apply from the sea's perspective.

Something about that concept touched him. It called to his soul. Maybe what he was searching for wouldn't be found in books or museums?

In that instant, George knew that he would get what he came here for. He knew he couldn't find Rebecca by following a single trail. The task demanded a multifaceted approach. Part of it would have to be relearning to feel things in his gut, to trust his instincts, to listen to his heart.

He looked out across the white-capped swells and quietly spoke her name. He heard no reply but the wind. Then he made his promise. "Rebecca ... I'm coming for you."

THIRTY-THREE

Sasha's Seance wasn't the kind of place that was acceptable for Nantucket's Main Street, or for anywhere in town proper. After finding it in the Yellow Pages, George had to trek out past the traffic rotary and into the boonies to find the little shack, next door to a tiny, wood-shingled gas station.

Even after that walk, he still hesitated to go in. He reminded himself of his decision out there at Surfside. He had to explore all angles, all possibilities, if he was going to find Rebecca in time. He still didn't understand the time limit that she had set, but he believed it.

The door to the place had obviously been painted sometime within George's lifetime, but it hadn't been kept up. When the weather had finished devouring most of the paint, it had started on the unprotected wood beneath.

George looked around for a doorbell but instead found a rusted iron pull chain connected to a gargoyle-shaped bell. The bell, at one time, might have been brass, but the sea air had crusted it in a whitish-green coating. George pulled the chain, awakening the bell from what might have been like decades of sleep.

Sasha came to the door. A plump sixty and dressed like a Gypsy from central casting, she did little to instill confidence in him. She led him into a tiny room with a small round table in the center. A crystal ball sat in the center of that. Loose hanging Indian print silks hid the ceiling.

The clichés of this room weren't doing much for George's faith in what he was about to go through. Tiny nose-cone-shaped incense pellets burned from saucers on cluttered shelves. Long sticks of incense smoked from an array of ornate, upright holders. George wondered if secondhand smoke risks applied to incense.

Sasha swept into a seat at the table with dramatic flair. She motioned him to join her. "Join hands with me and stare into the crystal," she said.

George obliged her, but the longer he stared the more nothing he saw—no smoke, no lights, no Aunty Em calling to him.

"Are you sure it's plugged in?" he asked.

"The crystal needs no plug to see your future."

"I don't care about the future. I'm here about the past, the way past, lifetimes ago."

"Oh, why didn't you say so?"

"I just did."

She bent down to reach under the table as she spoke. "Like any profession, the right equipment is needed for the right job."

From under the table, she brought out a Ouija board and laid it between them. Then she started in on her spiel. "Place your hands over mine. Cleanse your mind of all daily debris. This debris clutters your thoughts and keeps you from actualizing your true essence."

George's skepticism was growing by leaps and bounds. As she spoke, he stole glances at the dense collection of strange trinkets that filled the room. Sasha was obviously a packrat. She had stuff that probably had its own stuff. He saw everything from Jesus to Buddha to voodoo dolls. Something hanging from a rafter might have been a shrunken head.

She continued, "Keep your eyes focused on mine and breathe in deeply. This shall cleanse your soul."

George thought, *Did anyone ever cleanse this room?*

By now, he was looking for a way out. "How much is this going to cost me?"

"What's money compared to finding a lost love?"

George knew that probably meant it would cost a lot. "Do you take checks?"

The question frustrated her. "This is a place of truth and passion, not the local K-Mart. I can't do checks."

"How much?" George persisted.

"Two hundred and fifty dollars."

George immediately stood up.

Sasha switched gears, trying to keep his business. "I do take Visa and MasterCard, debit cards ..."

She pulled a charge card/ATM scanner from under the table.

"I see you have something plugged in," George said. He leaned over the table. "You mentioned K-Mart? That's where they sell those Ouija boards."

"It's not the tool, but the user," she said.

In a show of personal strength, George turned and left. In the days before this trip, he would've let someone like Sasha sucker him in. George thought about this as he stood outside her little shack. Then the old George started to return. He pulled out his wallet and looked at his ATM card.

"What am I doing?" he said. "I must be crazy."

He fought back his weaker self and stuffed the wallet in his pants. As he walked slowly back toward town, he thought about the promise he'd made to Rebecca when last he stood on the sand at Surfside. He knew that the research route alone was too slow. He had to "think outside the box" as they say. But this might even be a worse route.

He had one more stop to make. This place was closer to town. Maybe that meant it would be more respectable?

The name on the door didn't do much to encourage him. It read DR. FLIM. Under the name, it said LICENSED HYPNOTIST: SMOKE ENDING; PAST LIFE REGRESSION; WEIGHT CONTROL.

George discounted his doubts, saying to himself, "A guy can't help the name he was born with."

Still it bothered him. Flim sounded more like the name of a Dickens character than a real person. He put his skepticism aside and walked in.

Inside, Dr. Flim sat at an Indian print table, wearing an Egyptian headdress. He was a chubby fifty, with a gray goatee. With no introduction, Flim started right in.

"I was an Egyptian Pharaoh."

"I was a Cub Scout," George replied.

"You need help," Flim said. "I can feel it. An adjustment will center you in your quest for financial success."

"Your sign says hypnotist."

Flim sprung up and fluttered around George with two Japanese fans. "I'm a chiropractor for your head. By redistributing the electrical energy, I can change your future."

George backed himself out of the door. "You've changed it. I'm out of here."

Before he knew it, George was once again out on the cold, gray, winter street. *Now what?*

Was this what "outside the box" would yield? What should he do?

On his way back to town, he made a slight detour, ending up at the end of Straight Wharf, the other place he felt connected to Rebecca. The short winter day was already waning. The gray of the sky was deepening to a chalky charcoal with only the slightest suggestions of sunset pink struggling through the western horizon. The damp cold of the air worked its way through George's clothes and started to gnaw on his bones.

George stood on the edge, staring into the lifting and falling swells, letting himself become mesmerized by the rhythm. A few rogue flakes of snow swirled to their deaths upon the water's surface. George's emotional turmoil throbbed harder than the waves. No longer did he alternate between the warmth of Rebecca's love, his grief over losing her, and his self-loathing fear that it was all a crazy delusion. Now all of those things existed simultaneously. Instead of sharing space, they fought over it.

His head was trying to explode, but he forced it together. The rhythm of the waves helped him focus and reprioritize his thoughts. Priority number one was Rebecca and always would be as long as he was in charge. At least, that's what he told himself.

He attuned himself further to the pulse of the sea. It made him feel like Rebecca was close, but in that very closeness was an immense, indescribable distance. Was he a century and a half away from her or were they separated by the thinnest of membranes between dimensions? Was traveling there a linear thing or something else? If there was another way, what?

He thought back on his attempts to find her so far. To him, they seemed like one big waste of time, and time was something he couldn't afford to squander. That struck him oddly since he was no longer sure what time was or what it meant.

He made his way back toward The Quahog B&B feeling no further along than when he started.

A *huge sailing ship rolls on her side in pounding surf. She towers in the moonlight like a black monster from hell. The sound of splitting wood ruptures the darkness ...*

George sprung up with a yelp from the bed. The nightmare paralyzed him with fear. Sweat beaded on his forehead. He looked around in a panic. The familiar forms of his B&B room were there, half-hidden in the darkness. They offered him little comfort. He got himself out of bed and stepped over to the bathroom. He looked in at the empty tub, pining mournfully for Rebecca.

THIRTY-FOUR

Amber Baskin sat at a card table that had quickly been set up just inside the window of Mitchell's Book Corner. In front of her was a long line of fans waiting for her to sign her latest book. Like most of her books, this one dealt with Nantucket. Like her last two, the book documented ghosts on the island. This info was all displayed artfully on a promotional poster that sat on an easel beside her.

Amber's salt-and-pepper hair put her in her mid-forties but attractively there. If she wore makeup, it was light. Her natural, honest quality spoke of a life lived close to the earth. She was reminiscent of the "back to nature" strain in the hippie culture's waning days, circa 1972.

As she looked up to greet the next fan, she was pleasantly surprised to see Dr. Pantone standing before her. He was the professorial, leather-patches-on-the-elbows type, with distinguished gray at the temples. She broke into an easy smile.

"And I thought you psychologists looked down on all this occult hocus pocus," she said.

"Never hurts to know thine enemy."

He handed her a copy of her book for signing. She scrolled in big letters *Science keeps an open mind!* and then she signed it.

He looked at it and smiled as he said, "When you're done we could go for coffee."

She craned her neck around him to see the long line of waiting fans.

"Make it Scotches instead."

George dug his hands deep into his pockets as he walked up Main Street. All trees except for the decorative Christmas variety were bare. The sky was just a few shades shy of white. It spat infrequent, lonely flakes of snow.

As George got to the multi-paned window of Mitchell's Book Corner, he stopped and looked inside. He saw the crowd that had gathered for Amber Baskin's book signing and thought it might be wise to wait until the crowd thinned out. He crossed the thick cobblestones, got himself a cup of nice warm coffee to go, and sat on a wooden bench that was situated almost directly across the street from Mitchell's. He sat there sipping and berating himself for letting something so mundane as crowds intimidate him.

Police Chief Harry Beal sipped at his own coffee-to-go as he turned onto Main Street from Centre. He spotted George there on the bench.

As George continued watching the bookstore, he gradually realized that somebody was standing next to him—not just standing, but also watching. Fear and guilt danced together on George's shoulders. It was the guilt from years of feeling like he was doing something wrong even if he didn't know what. The watchful eye of a teacher or employer always triggered it. George slowly turned his head to acknowledge Harry Beal standing there. Harry started up the conversation.

"Hope you're not waiting for a bus."

"No, not waiting for the bus."

Beal took a seat beside him without waiting for an invitation. "That's good. Know why that's good?"

"Why?"

"Because there is no bus."

George was keenly aware that Beal was studying him.

"Soaking up the sun, then?"

"What?"

Beal repeated, "Soaking up the sun?"

George squinted his eyes into the white, sunless sky. "No."

"That's good," Beal said. "Know why that's good?"

"No sun?"

"Went the way of the busses."

George was too nervous to even crack a smile, but he liked something about Harry Beal.

"Here for the Stroll?" Beal asked.

The question made no sense to George. Beal saw his look of confusion.

"Can't be here for the Stroll 'cause you'd know what 'Stroll' was when I asked you."

George finally made the connection. "Oh, the Christmas thing."

"Yeah, that thing."

"I came for Thanksgiving weekend and just ... Well, I just decided to stick around."

This guy is a bundle of nerves, Beal thought. *A rookie could see it.*

Beal would do anything to avoid proving Bolgers right, so for now, he was liking George. He'd give him the benefit of the doubt.

"Going to spend all day on this bench?"

"No," George said without stammer, "I'm going in to the bookstore as soon as I finish my coffee."

Beal gave him silence. George tried desperately to fill it.

"I mean ... I'm sure they wouldn't want me to bring it in there."

More silence.

"I mean ... I don't just go around breaking rules about where people want coffee."

Harry Beal stood up. George went into full panic mode but repressed it so Beal wouldn't see. Beal slapped him on the shoulder. "You get a real 'A' for citizenship."

He started off down the street calling back to George, "Have a good one."

George gave Beal a fainthearted wave as he watched him walk off down Main Street. He took in a deep breath and let it out in a plume of steam as he tried to steady his nerves.

George watched Beal disappear around the corner by The Pacific Club. He gathered what strength remained and ventured across the street toward Mitchell's Book Corner.

He pushed the bookstore's door open, causing a cluster of three small brass bells over the doorjamb to ring. He was intensely aware of the people who looked over to acknowledge his entrance.

Once in the door, he quickly spotted a little cubbyhole of a room. A sign over its archway labeled it *The Nantucket Room*. The cozy nook seemed to beckon him with the promise of comfort. He walked straight to it.

Walter, the Book Corner's proprietor, was manning the cash register. He watched George walk through. Since he'd never seen George before, he thought about calling to him and offering help.

Something in George's determined focus on the

Nantucket Room told him that there was no need.

This guy knows what he is looking for, Walter thought.

A tiny alarm rang in the back of Walter's mind. George's eyes were so intense that they hinted at darker possibilities. Was that determined look in his eyes an avoidance of eye contact?

Walter thought of the shooter in that Virginia Tech massacre a few years back. He quickly brushed the thought from his mind. After all, this was Nantucket.

Still, a tiny nugget of fear remained. He told himself he'd go in and check on the guy after a while.

In The Nantucket Room, George was accosted by everything related to the island. He didn't know where to start. He pulled out a coffee-table-sized book with a soft cover, titled *Nantucket Then & Now.* It contained new photos of island spots placed next to old photos of the same places. He thumbed through it. He knew it would at least be good for inspiration.

There were a multitude of titles on whaling. George pulled them out in a frenzy, quickly checking tables of contents and indexes for the most relevant subjects. Instead of taking the time to put the books back, he discarded them at his feet in case he needed to go back to them.

He found a small section of books on Nantucket ghosts. They were all by the same author, Amber Baskin. The floor became slippery with discarded books. Finally, Walter came to the doorway. He looked upon the scene with both anger and fear. "Sir, are you planning to buy any of these books?"

When George turned to address him, he slipped on a discarded book and nearly fell. "Yes. Sorry. I'll put them back—I mean the ones I don't buy. I'm buying a bunch."

Walter wasn't sure what kind of nut he might have in his Nantucket room or what kind of danger he might pose. He started to ease himself out of the room. "Very well. Just make sure nothing's harmed. I'll be right out here."

When George finally came out with an armful of books, Walter eyed him with covert suspicion. George handed over his ATM card, afraid that the purchase might break the bank. In these moments of purchase, he always held his breath, hoping for approval, but ready for the worst.

Walter checked him out carefully as he ran George's card. He could see the shifty fear in his eyes, as if he was ready to be caught for something, or at something.

APPROVED!

Both men breathed a sigh of relief that no confrontation would be coming.

In that moment, George saw the poster for Amber Baskin's book signing. "Is that the ghost book author?"

Walter was wary about giving out any information.

"Yes."

"Will she be back?"

"No."

"Does she live here on the Island? Could I visit her?"

"We don't give out personal information."

Walter bagged the last of George's books with of a grimace. George took the bags and headed for the door, stopping for a moment at the poster, inspecting it for contact info but finding none.

The cold hit George's face as he opened the door from Mitchell's. The day had darkened to deep dusk-blue, warmed in spots by the orange lights of store windows and old-style street lamps. The pin-light colors of Christmas tree lights also glowed from the decorated trees along both sidewalks. The sidewalks were empty. The whole thing looked like a Christmas card, or one of those Thomas Kinkade paintings that they sold in shopping malls.

As the cold settled in on George's face, he smelled the smoke of a wood fire wafting over him from somewhere. He heard the sound of Christmas carols playing softly from hidden speakers that also lined the street.

For all the cheerful warmth of the scene, it made George feel all the more lonely. He envisioned families sitting around that warm fire he smelled, sharing their love for each other. He thought of families all over town having similar moments, but none of them involved him. None of it ever would involve him. He was alone in the cold, blue, and darkening night. The sound of Christmas carols and the nostalgia for past Christmases it stirred was always a comfort cloaked in sadness.

That was what he had felt watching the Salvation Army Band playing at Quincy Market, before joining Jim and Ray in the bar. Solemn endurance mixed with a strange, resolute innocence.

George made his way across Main Street and along Centre Street to his B&B as night fully settled in. Once in his room, he began to pour over the books. While he read, bare tree branches clicked and scraped against his window as the wind knocked them back and forth. George felt like the very night itself was haunting him. He picked up one of Amber Baskin's books. The cover said that it contained twenty-two true-life accounts of Nantucket ghost encounters.

"*True life.*" George repeated it silently. Was this where he'd find Rebecca? As he read on, the book was an almost routine account of smoky figures and bumps in the night that offered him little insight. The subjects of the book seemed so matter-of-fact about their ghosts. It was as if they were talking about picking up their dry cleaning.

George became both frustrated and intrigued. He knew there was more to it. His encounter was nothing like these. He had to talk to this author, but how? He could barely muster the confidence to talk with normal people. The writer of a book had automatic celebrity, and celebrities cornered the market on automatic authority. George recoiled just hearing the word authority, let alone having to encounter it.

He thought to himself, *Maybe this is a test that Rebecca has set out? "How brave will you be? What will you risk to find me?"*

He felt courage throb into his veins. He checked the book cover for any contact info. No web sites, no e-mail addresses, no phone numbers—nothing. Strike one.

He sat on his bed thinking. Suddenly he realized that his room probably had a phonebook along with its Bible. On a small island like this, maybe she was actually listed?

He found the book in an end table by the bed. Eureka! There she was in the "B's." George whipped out his cell phone and stopped short. He took a deep breath to strengthen himself before calling. He even tried to talk himself out of it, but the new seeds of personal power had grown too strong. He flipped open the phone to call.

Nothing—the phone was dead. While quickly, angrily packing for this three-day trip, he had never thrown in his phone charger. The thing had probably been dead for days.

A new sense of aloneness flowed over him. He was out of contact with the world. He had been since he'd gotten here.

What if there was an emergency at home, and somebody was trying to get in touch with him? Immediately following was the question *Who?*

There was nobody to call, nobody to worry.

For the first time, he thought about his cat and bird. They couldn't use the phone.

What if they were in trouble?

He knew he had left a week's worth of food for both. He always overdid things like that. It was part of his worst-case-scenario thought process.

He decided not to worry about Garfield and Petie. They would be fine. He'd even moved Petie's cage out of the cat's reach before he had left.

He refocused on Amber Baskin.

Maybe the dead phone was a sign not to contact her?

Bullshit!

He wouldn't let that sidetrack him. "Fuck it," he said. *Fuck it* felt good again. It would still be his beacon.

Maybe it's too late to call?

"Fuck it!"

Maybe she's not home?

"Fuck it!"

Without worrying about hidden charges, he used the room phone. Amber picked up on the third ring.

George explained himself as best he could.

She said she'd see me! Was this for real?

He didn't know what to say. An appointment was made for ten o'clock the next morning at her house—*HER HOUSE, YET!*

THIRTY-FIVE

Morning sun streaked in through diamond-shaped windowpanes and dappled on the lush, hanging greenery in Amber Baskin's kitchen. Amber stood at her ceramic-tiled kitchen counter steeping coffee in a steel-framed, glass French press. She carefully pushed down the plunger.

"You take cream? I have no refined sugar, just honey."

"Black is fine." George stood awkwardly by the kitchen door trying to keep a lid on his nervousness. "I'm so worried that I'll run out of time. Christmas is coming fast."

Amber poured the coffee into two thick, handmade clay mugs and handed one to George. "In my experience, time isn't a relevant thing in the spirit world."

"What do you think it means?"

Amber puzzled over it as she spoke. "I'm not sure. I'm still trying to digest all that you've told me. I will say that you're not alone. Ghosts are common here on Nantucket. There are a lot of theories as to why and what, but that's all they are, theories. Apart from the moors of England, Nantucket is among the most haunted places on record."

"Really? Not Auschwitz or Hiroshima?"

"I'm sure those places rank highly, but ghosts don't seem to correlate with the way in which people die so much as with environmental conditions. Nantucket has its own moors, very similar to England."

"Moors?"

"Swampy, marshy areas, covered with gnarly wooden underbrush."

"Ghosts are supposed to like that?"

Amber suppressed a giggle. "It's not a question of liking. We can't think of ghosts as if they are people. That's for the movies."

"But they were people."

"*Were* is the operative word. As ghosts, they may not have actual thought."

"Do they get stupid when they die?"

"Once dead, they are an essence of what once was. Not living and thinking. They are an impression, left in a space from a past time. Emotional residue."

"This all sounds a little ..."

Even in his current state of desperation, George was hesitant to out-and-out disagree with people, so he let his statement dangle. Amber was more than smart enough to catch his meaning.

She asked, "Ever hear of Kirlian photography?"

She led George into her impressive wood-paneled den stacked high with shelves of books and magazines. None of it was clutter. Everything was perfectly organized.

She stepped over to a shelf, piled with issues of National Geographic. She ran her finger down the bound edges until she found what she wanted. She withdrew an issue and sat on her couch, inviting George to sit beside her. She opened the magazine and flipped through pages as she spoke. George noted how she ran her hand down, flattening, caressing each page she turned, regarding it with special care.

"Life is just the arrangement of molecules in changing patterns," she said. "Some patterns take longer to fade. Look at a bright light, then close your eyes. You can still see the pattern it made on your retina. There is something about these moors and the air around them that's conducive to lingering patterns. Things aren't disturbed here. There's a way to photograph an object to see the electrical field it generates, the aura."

"Aura? I've been the 'New Age,' wacko route already."

Amber handled the insult with dignity. "How 'New Age' is National Geographic? This isn't some wild theory. This is scientific fact. We all generate an aura. They're as individual as fingerprints."

She turned to a photo of a maple leaf. One of the points was missing. A jagged glow of light perfectly outlined where the missing point would've been.

The photo excited George. Finally, he was seeing some concrete confirmation of a world beyond. He took it as validation—vindication even.

She continued, "I've seen photos of amputees who have been missing limbs for years. The auras around where their limbs once were are always exact. Just like that leaf."

George gently took the magazine from her and immersed himself in the pages. As he did, his face grew more troubled.

"This is all very interesting," he said, "but how does it explain Rebecca?"

Amber's lips tightened and flattened out as she prepared herself for the unpleasant truth.

"It doesn't," she said.

George continued staring at the pages, avoiding her eyes as the very vindication he'd just felt dissolved into condemnation.

"Not fully," she continued. "Stories of personified

ghosts with names and such are usually the embellished tales of legend or fiction horror stories for the movies. I haven't seen one stand up to scientific scrutiny."

There it was, George's worst horror realized. Even ghost believers thought he was nuts. His last road of promise was another dead-end. *Now what?*

Amber saw the distress on his face.

George spoke with a flat, pensive voice. "What are you telling me?"

"It's nothing to get alarmed about, just something to consider."

"What is?"

"Even those ghosts in the classic ghost stories and B horror movies, well ... they come into our world. They don't bring us back to theirs."

Panic time! "So I'm just nuts, right?"

"Not at all. I'm just saying that there must be another component. A ghost sighting may well have been the spring board but ... the rest ... Is there a family history—"

George didn't let her finish. He sprang to his feet.

"I'm not crazy! Rebecca is more than residue, more than some imprint. She's not some fantasy or delusion!"

"I'm not saying she is. You're jumping to conclusions. I'm just saying there are other avenues to investigate. I'm not an expert. Here, let me give you the name of somebody who is."

She fished through a bowl of business cards and came out with one to hand George. He took it and read it: DR. EUGENE PANTONE – Psychologist.

George crushed the card into his pocket and stormed out with not so much as a thank you or a goodbye.

George wandered the streets. His steps were powered by anger and fear. He found himself in front of Mitchell's Book Corner once again. He slowly opened the door. Inside, Walter steeled himself against possible attack as he watched George walk in.

This time, George didn't go to The Nantucket Room. He passed that by and headed for the Psych and Self Help section.

George walked down the section's aisle as if it were his last mile. With tear-brimmed eyes, he searched through the titles. He stopped and withdrew a book titled *Understanding Schizophrenia.* In solemn defeat, he brought the book to Walter at the cash register. Walter took the book with self-satisfaction at knowing that he had called it right about this guy. George saw the judgmental glare in the cashier's eyes as he waited for his purchase to be bagged.

Once he was back outside in the cold night, George decided that he couldn't face going back to his room, not yet. Too much accusatory night lay in front of him. He came up with a classic answer he had learned from growing up in Irish Boston. He headed for a bar.

He settled into a corner table at The Brotherhood of Thieves. He went Irish all the way: Jameson Irish Whiskey with a Guinness chaser. After the first one, he just started dropping the shot glass straight into the pint of stout. By the fourth one, the waitress began to get concerned. As he ordered another, she asked, "Are you driving yourself anyplace?"

What a set-up! His inner self cackled. He said, "Only crazy!"

With the warmth of five rounds in him, George stumbled to the end of Straight Wharf. He wasn't sure whether he'd stop walking when he reached the end. A devil, deep inside, mocked him and egged him on, delighting in his destruction.

Maybe this is the end? he thought. *So what?*

At the edge of the wharf was a black void. He stopped at it. He stared into the blackness and spoke out loud with a small and quivering voice.

"Rebecca, were you ever real?"

With a throbbing head, he made his way back to the Quahog B&B. He filled his tub with hot water, as hammers seemed to strike his hung-over brain. He watched the water flow in and shimmer around the porcelain.

Lost in thought, it became overfilled before he knew it. He knelt down beside it and turned off the faucet. He watched the delicate ripples. Steam waltzed across the surface. He thought about Rebecca lying in there, the last place he'd seen her.

In a burst of passion, he thrust his head under the water and tried to hold it there. He could hear the comfort of life's absence calling him. As if he were nearing the end of a race, someone said, "Just a little further, a few more steps. One big breath will end it."

His body twitched and spasmed in protest. Finally, he burst from the water and fell to the cold, tile floor, gasping for air. As his lungs replenished themselves, he curled up in a fetal position on the bathroom floor. His eyes were slits of fatigue. As his body relaxed from the stress, his eyes slowly closed, and he drifted off to sleep.

In bright cold sunshine, a man stares through a spyglass from the bow of a ratty schooner. He shouts back behind him without turning around or

taking his eye from the glass. "Black Baller on the Rose and Crown!"

George snapped awake in that same spot on his bathroom floor.

THIRTY-SIX

Morning dawned with the same bleakness of the day before. The sky was a mottled collection of gray, shaded patches. The thick, damp air carried a penetrating cold that reached every part of George as he shuffled zombie-like into town. He looked like a shell-shocked war victim with hollowed-out, vacant eyes. His brain was corroded by rancid fears and self-hating doubts.

As a last resort, he dragged himself to the address on that business card, Dr. Pantone's office. He must have stood in front of the place for hours, terrified that someone would see him there, or worse yet, Doctor Pantone would spot him through the window and come out to retrieve him like a lost sheep. Finally, fear got the best of him. He walked away.

George slowly ambled along Main Street. He turned on Centre and stopped. Across the street, in front of the high, white-columned meetinghouse that sat next to the Pacific National Bank, there was a bustle of activity. The meeting that Bolgers had pitched to him was going on.

George crossed the street for a better look. A poster in front of the building proclaimed all the wonders of Bolgers' redevelopment plan. Beside Bolgers' smiling face was an artist's rendition of his

Surfside project, complete with upscale chain stores and lots of parking, surrounded by layered tiers of high-priced, nautically themed condominiums. A banner on top read TOWN MEETING: DISCUSSION OF REDEVELOPMENT PROJECT.

As George studied it, a new strength trickled into his veins, a strength born of anger that he was yet to understand.

Inside the hall, Bolgers was already droning on to a group that varied from the disinterested, to the angry, to the excited.

"Redevelopment is the only way to keep our economy strong," Bolgers said. "We must look to the future. We must march into it, armed with the charms of our past, to be sure, but always looking forward, not back."

Bolgers' eyes shifted as he noticed George step into the room. He was relieved to see Harry Beal in full uniform, standing beside the seated group, leaning one foot against the wall behind him and listening with his arms crossed. As he spoke, Bolgers continued to watch George.

"Seaport towns all along the coast have been going through the renaissance that was so kind to us a few decades ago. We enjoyed a luxurious time of little competition. Not even Martha's Vineyard had our historical charm, and it was almost as hard to get to."

A few people chuckled. A studious-looking citizen stood up to speak.

He said, "We've got more millionaires buying homes in the moors than they have in Beverly Hills. Those property values—"

Bolgers didn't even let him finish. "Should we just become a playground for the rich? That won't help us as a town. We need to compete."

"With who?" a voice shouted from the group.

"With all the other towns! Now there is nearly a

glut of such towns. Newburyport has been completely renovated, Portland, Maine—the list is long, all going after the same tourist dollar. Since these places aren't islands, travelers need to give up little in the way of familiar comforts such as their favorite restaurant franchises and so on. We have to keep pace in order to remain viable."

George shot up to speak. "Nantucket's not about the future. It's not even about today. Nantucket's treasure is its past. It may be the only place left where you can't get a Big Mac, or a Whopper, or Taco Bell. There is no mall, no multiplex cinema. Don't you see? These aren't Nantucket's weaknesses. They are her strengths."

Bolgers grasped at straws. "I don't think you've been recognized to speak."

George shot back, "It's a town meeting! Anybody can speak."

"Ladies and gentlemen, this man is an off-island coof who I took under my wing. I only recently suspected his treachery. Now it's confirmed."

In the crowd, Betty Bolgers slowly put her hand to her lips.

George stood his ground. He spoke directly to the crowd, surging with the new confidence that Rebecca and his subsequent search for her was in the process of giving him. "His project will bring new people and new money, that's true. But what will you have lost?"

Another guy popped up to speak. "Bolgers tried to push this through without us even getting a chance to vote!"

Another man talked to George from his chair. "As Mayor, Bolgers got that Surfside project land through eminent domain. He already started construction. It's too late."

George barked, "It's never too late!"

Bolgers fumed helplessly as he saw his neat little meeting come apart before his eyes.

Walter, the bookstore proprietor, stepped over to Harry Beal, pointing out George. "He's a trouble-maker," Walt said. "He tried to mess up Mitchell's."

"He's making pretty good sense now," Harry said.

Bolgers worked on damage control. "There are plenty of real estate firms that would love to get a foothold on this island. The very reason for that is because it is the gold mine of which I speak. Don't let this outsider, who's obviously been sent here by one such firm, unravel your future. This man has no stake in Nantucket."

George exploded, "I have more of a stake here than you can possibly imagine!" He looked at the crowd. "More of a stake than any of you can know!" He focused his rage back at Bolgers. "Don't you fucking dare question my stake."

The crowd gasped at the "F" word. It wasn't the time or place. The wind drained from George's sails as he realized this. Bolgers relaxed. He knew he had the upper hand again.

Bolgers said, "Sir, your language betrays your true nature and your true intent at this meeting. Officer Beal, I want this troublemaker removed from these proceedings."

Beal remained at his spot against the wall, smirking at the stupidity of Bolgers' demand but knowing that he'd probably have to comply.

George continued, "Unfortunately, that language is an apt description of what you want to do to these people and to Nantucket."

Bolgers' face burned red as he bellowed, "I want him removed, not just from this hall, but from the island itself!"

Beal continued to lean against the wall, trying to resist obeying Bolgers for as long as possible. Walter remained beside him. Now another man joined them, the man who had told George he'd *"catch his death,"* back when George first wandered up Main Street in a crazed state after just losing Rebecca.

Beal and Walter both nodded to the man who wasted no pleasantries in getting to his point.

"Harry, that guy's nuts. He had a seizure on Main Street. I thought he'd kill someone."

With an exasperated sense of resignation, Beal looked at the two men, then at Bolgers and then at George. He pushed himself off the wall with his foot. "Well, I guess four out of five doctors agree."

Harry made his way toward George who was continuing to speak, fighting through a rush of emotion that came from thinking about his stake here. "I only came here a short time ago, that's true, but I discovered such a ... I've experienced ..." George had no words to describe his plight. "I ... In my heart I know ..."

Betty Bolgers shifted her concern from her husband to this poor wretch who she'd tried to help at the Atheneum. Harry Beal arrived at George's side. He gave him a friendly slap on the shoulder. "My bench warmer friend," Beal said.

George froze as he looked at Beal and sensed the trouble he was in.

"Let's you and me take a little walk," Beal said.

"Am I under arrest?"

"Do you want to be?"

Beal walked George through the crowd to the door. As he did, mixed applause rang out. It was impossible to tell how much of it was in support of George and how much of it was in support of his being dragged out. The two men didn't speak again until Beal got him outside. Harry did the talking.

"You seem like a nice enough guy. I don't know what beef you have with Bolgers, but he's not in the habit of losing. The first morning ferry leaves at seven o'clock. Best thing you could do is be on it."

"You running me out of town like in the Old West?"

"Not running, just advising."

"Threatening."

"Don't turn this into 'good guys/bad guys.' Bolgers has got my butt in a sling, just like everybody else. You'll be doing us both a favor if you're on that ferry."

George had a million arguments he wanted to put forth about this being a free country and just as many accusing statements about Bolgers owning the cops, owning Beal—about Beal being a sellout, a whore, and other things. But none of those broad, black-and-white pontifications seemed to fit the more delicate and nuanced reality.

Still, he wondered, as he walked off in silent compliance, if fear was the only thing that stopped his tongue.

George's sleep that night was a fitful rage of self-reproach, fear, and indecision. Was there a physical threat involved here? Did Bolgers own this cop? *Am I a dead man if I stay? What's my life worth if I go? Could I ever look myself in the mirror again if I go?*

He awoke long before dawn, just staring up at the darkness. As morning started to break, he forced himself from bed and stepped over to the window. He could see the ferry's smoke stack just over the rooftops. It had spent the night there and was now coming to life, preparing for its morning departure.

George stole a look at the clock—five forty-five—

still plenty of time to make that ferry. The sun hadn't yet climbed above the horizon but was announcing itself with a brightening of the eastern sky. Elsewhere in the heavens, stars were taking their leave.

George turned from the window and grabbed his duffle bag. *Live to fight another day,* he thought.

He began stuffing his wrinkled clothes inside. Then came the books he'd bought. It was hard to cram it all in. He lifted the duffle to the bed so he wouldn't strain his back trying to zip it. As he did, the top book, a large soft cover, fell out onto the floor. It was a book he'd bought at Mitchell's but hadn't opened yet, titled *Nantucket: Then and Now.*

As he picked up the book, its pages fanned open. Something made him stop and flip through those pages before stuffing it back in his duffle.

Each page married a recent Nantucket photo with one of the exact same location from the late 1800s. A few were from even earlier times.

He stopped on a page that warranted closer inspection. The modern photo was of a pretty little cottage in the Nantucket seaside village of Siasconset. The other photo was hand-painted from a pre-Mathew Brady daguerreotype of the same cottage. In this old photo, a woman stood out front. The woman was Rebecca. The caption read *The Earliest Photo Record – A young lady in front of her cottage – Siasconset.*

He had found her!

His hand caressed the page as he let himself drink in the meaning.

As the seven o'clock ferry was just casting off for Hyannis, George was just off the foot of the wharf, at Young's, renting another moped.

THIRTY-SEVEN

George sped along the Siasconset road. Determination defeated any feelings of cold or fears of the trip. His mission was once again clear to him.

The craggy, windswept moors rolled on both sides of him and stretched to the horizon. Gnarled, weather-beaten trees twisted their arthritic fingers away from the prevailing wind. In their frozen torment, they looked like snapshots of a hurricane.

He finally reached the Siasconset bluff. He stared down at the raging sea a hundred feet below him. His heart raced as he felt her close by.

He left the moped against a wooden post and walked along a narrow grassy path, strewn with two tire-width lanes of tiny white shells. His feet crunched loudly on the little shells. He preferred the silence of the grass between the shell strips. None of that mattered in reality, because just below those cottages, the sea roared like a lion. The wind practically sang an aria as it blew through the Lilliputian paths and grassy, wooden-walled alleyways. Nobody could hear feet crunching on the shells but him, or so he thought.

The cottages on each side of the path were ragtag shacks of weathered wood. Hundreds of years ago, they'd been built from pieces of sunken ships and driftwood found on the beach. They were shelter for hearty fishermen who spent months out here away from town, fishing off the bluffs, before whaling was even a sparkle in someone's eye.

George walked cautiously along the little pathway between the empty dwellings. Somehow, the volume of sea and wind only served to accentuate the silence of this seeming ghost town. Something told George that danger might lurk behind any corner.

He spun quickly at the sound of loud banging. Relief came as he saw that the sound came from a wooden bench swing that had been hung on a second floor porch. It must have given enjoyment to the summer people on warm afternoons, catching the pre-sunset breeze. Now abandoned, it dangled by only one of its chains as the wind batted it around in playful torment, like a cat with its prey.

Uneasiness grew. It was the feeling again of being alone in a place meant for the enjoyment of many. Every footstep he took felt like an announcement, as if he might awaken some sleeping giant. Dry leaves made a delicate tingling sound as the wind chased them along the seashell path before him.

George stopped with a quick breath as he saw Rebecca's house about a hundred yards off. His heart told him that everything had been leading to this moment. Now, mixed with the sea's roar was another sound, an unnerving, low growl. At first, George wasn't sure whether it was just another nuance in the base sound of ocean. In the next instant, he knew it wasn't.

He twisted back to see a Rottweiler slowly keeping pace with him from about twenty feet behind. It looked like a Doberman on steroids. Its shoulders were massive boulders of muscle. George knew on a visceral level that the growl hadn't been to scare him off.

This dog was about stalking and stealth. George was prey. The growl was an accident, a failure of predatory technique. The beast wanted to be discovered only when its teeth were in George's neck, but bloodlust excited it so much that it had betrayed itself with unwanted sound.

George turned to face the dog as he stepped back slowly. The dog didn't charge but matched him step for step. Hairs on the beast's back stood straight up. Its mouth retracted to show drool-drenched teeth.

George was at a loss.

"Okay, boy. Good dog."

Even through his terror, he felt stupid for saying it. He knew that if he ran, the monster would give chase. That would be no contest.

Maybe I could just walk slowly backwards for the whole hundred yards to Rebecca's?

He brushed that thought away as soon as he had it. The two foes locked eyes as they continued this slow dance. Death was so close that George could taste it.

All of a sudden, the dog shifted mood. Something new had entered his brain. He trotted off down a grass alleyway between two cottages and was gone. George blew out a huge sigh of relief as he turned his attention back to the wonderful sight of Rebecca's cottage. It was still about a hundred yards away. That backing up session with the dog hadn't bought him much ground. He walked towards it slowly, carefully, as if he were on a tightrope.

Suddenly, the dog reappeared about half way between George and his goal of Rebecca's cottage. The animal hadn't become distracted—it had just figured out how to outflank him.

George froze in his tracks. Again, the dog didn't charge. He merely stood there waiting. Steam puffed from his nostrils and circled his massive head. He seemed to be challenging George—as if the animal were saying, *"Is what you want important enough to get by me?"*

George took a few steps forward. The dog didn't move. He merely smiled with that lecherous, tongue-laden grin that dogs get when they know a feast is on the way. George could see the bloodlust in his eyes.

Maybe going forward isn't such a good idea? he thought. The dog was now a good one hundred and fifty feet away.

George stole a look back at his moped, about fifty or sixty feet back. In that quick glance George took behind him, the dog pranced about thirty feet closer and then stopped when George turned back.

The dog stood still with a *"What? I didn't move"* face.

It was a game now—like Red Light, Green Light, when George was a kid. He thought hard about it. The beast was still more than a hundred feet away. The moped was less than half that. Could he make it to the moped before being devoured? Would he just end up like the slow antelope running at the rear of the herd with the lion stretching up to embrace its rump? He had to try. It was his only shot.

George spun and burst down the shell path for his bike. The Rottweiler gave instant chase, closing fast. George switched a few inches over to the grass for better traction. Fear pushed his feet faster than he ever thought they could go. His heart nearly exploded from his chest. The dog still narrowed the gap. George focused on the nearing moped. Even if he reached it, could he hop on and fire it up in time? The dog closed faster. The moped was still about twenty feet off. The dog had narrowed his distance to sixty. Both creatures poured on a final speed burst, like distance runners with the finish line in sight.

George reached it! He grabbed the handlebars, twisted the bike up into position, and jumped in the saddle, all in one quick action. The dog was five feet away. George revved the engine. It roared to life.

The dog lunged a millisecond too late. The moped whined as it shot forward. The dog gave chase, snapping at the tires and trying to get a purchase on George's leg. As George's speed picked up, the dog dropped back, knowing he lacked the endurance to catch the machine.

George continued his full-speed flight for nearly a mile of straight road. Then he stopped and spun around, confident the dog was gone. To his shock, George saw the dog where he'd left him. He stood defiantly in the middle of the road about three quarters of a mile back.

Suddenly, George's fear for his safety dissolved into thoughts of Rebecca. For the first time, he was sure that there was something that he would die for. He twisted his wrist on the throttle and gunned the moped back into battle. Like a jousting knight, he aimed straight for his enemy.

The Rottweiler stood his ground, panting out dragon-like clouds of steam from his nostrils.

The moped gained speed. George saw his target growing larger, closer, but still not moving. The beast dared him to press on.

George quickly closed the gap, his eyes locked on his foe. At the last twenty feet, he gunned the machine again drawing whatever speed was left. He opened his mouth and roared a battle cry. The beast bared his teeth and brought out a growl from the depths of his being, but the sound was drowned out by the whine of the overtaxed engine.

Ten feet left. The dog's eyes became confused. *What is this monster I'm fighting?* he must have thought.

Five feet left. Confusion turned to fear. The dog leapt from the path of the screaming moped.

George roared past, and like a bull hungry for the red, spun his bike around to face the dog again. The rear tire spat pebbles and minced shells. The two warriors locked eyes again, but the dog's fight was gone. His eyes were full of more question than power, with tinges of doubt, fear, and regret.

George held the stare. The dog tilted his head in "RCA Dog" fashion. After a moment, a silent agreement or acknowledgement was made. George didn't understand it, but he felt it in his gut. The dog trotted off without looking back. He headed in the opposite direction from Rebecca's cottage. George watched him until he was a tiny black dot.

Savoring the victory and shaking out some of his fear, George refocused his attention on Rebecca. Now that he knew the exact location of the cottage, he could ride his moped right up to it. The sun had long since started its long slide for the horizon. The little village became edged in the orange glow of late day. George rode his moped slowly through the delicate tiny cottages. The raging sea was showing orange glints as the sun began its final descent. The wind stole the day's warmth. The cold began to penetrate.

When he got to Rebecca's cottage, George gently laid down the moped and approached the structure with slow reverence. He carefully extended his hand to touch the side.

The house was obviously empty. Storm shutters were nailed across the windows to save them from the season.

George tried the door. He knew it would be securely locked. He circled the house, looking for something, but he didn't know what. Some sign of her perhaps? Some clue as to what happened to her or where he should go next? Anything to have this trip not have been in vain.

In the back, he found a white wooden trellis. It climbed the weathered wooden shingles to a second floor porch. A storm shutter had come loose up there and was banging around in the wind. A way in!

George looked at the thick wooded vines that snaked through the lattice. Roses! The season had done in the flower. Only the thorns remained. It would be a painful climb, but he wouldn't let that stop him now.

He grabbed on and started the trek upwards. Thorns pricked and scraped him the whole way, but his mission was too important to let that stop him.

Just before reaching the porch, a vine piece gave way beneath his feet. He slipped and fell to the frozen turf. Sprawled face down, he painfully lifted his head and realized that he was staring at a pair of official-looking feet.

Harry Beal towered over him.

"Should have caught that ferry," Beal said.

"It's not what you think."

"Oh, I'm sure. You were just here to read the meter."

Part
Three

THIRTY-EIGHT

The door of Nantucket's jail cell slammed in George's face. Harry Beal locked it from the other side.

"You don't believe any of it?"

"I've seen it all on *Tales from the Crypt,*" Beal said.

George had spilled his guts about everything on his ride back to town in the rear of Beal's squad car. Harry had reminded him of his Miranda rights several times, but it didn't stop him. Lawyers were scarce on Nantucket after Labor Day, but Beal assured him he'd find one. Still George didn't shut up.

Now, as Beal locked the jail cell door, George was still going.

"It's the truth! How could I make something like that up?"

"Nuts can be pretty creative."

"I'm no nut!"

"Don't worry," Beal assured him, "you get another shot. I'm having a shrink come in. We'll see if he believes you."

Fear welled up in George's heart. "I thought you were talking lawyer before."

"You got that right, if I charge you."

"You're not?"

"We'll see. For now, you got a problem talking to a shrink?"

George swallowed hard. "Of course not."

Harry left George in his cage and stepped through the doorway to his tiny office. A mountain of clutter covered the top of his wooden desk. On a note-filled corkboard was a calendar with the monthly picture theme of Andrew Wyeth paintings.

Harry sat down at his desk and opened the top drawer. Inside were two neat rows of what looked like whale's teeth. He took one out and started to scratch on its side with a nail. He stopped for a moment and looked around at his bleak surroundings. He opened the drawer again, staring in behind the teeth at a half-full fifth of gin.

Should he or shouldn't he?

That was an easy-ass question. A better question was would he or wouldn't he?

Tonight he wouldn't. Most nights he hadn't, most nights for years now. He slid the drawer shut again. He was proud each time he made that decision, but he still kept that emergency stash for those times when the night closed in on him and he no longer felt welcome in his own skin. He scratched a little harder with the nail, trying to hurry past the memories that spilled out of that drawer each time he opened it.

Harry wasn't a Nantucket native. He'd been a summer kid who'd come with his well-to-do parents for more years than he could remember. Though he'd lived here full time for decades, since his twenties, he'd never be a Nantucketer. He'd always be an outsider, a coof.

He liked it that way.

He was never a joiner, never wanted to belong to any group. That's why, no matter how much he drank or how much he wanted to stop, he never became a 'friend of Bill's.'

He didn't need them anyway. He was doing fine on his own—fine, he told himself, as long as he kept his own record of days sober and days not.

He could never think of that stuff without thinking of the other stuff, the worse stuff. His crisis had come the same year the '60s died—1970, the year of Kent State and unrestrained Nixon, the year Harry turned eighteen.

Drinking wasn't the problem. Drinking was just a byproduct of his problem's solution. The solution was Bolgers.

Sometimes the cure was worse than the disease. So many times, Harry had wished for a "do over."

Back in the jail cell, George sat on his cot, leaning against a chipped cinderblock wall that had endured too many paint jobs. Moonlight was the only soft comfort, falling through the barred window with gentle fingers of silvery blue, caressing George as he drifted off into quasi-sleep. George noticed that the window was gone.

Now the moonlight was falling through a grate on the ceiling. The whole room was in motion, rocking and creaking back and forth. It suddenly wasn't a room at all. It was not anything George could recognize. He heard the slosh of waves. The dark figure of a man leaned over the grate to peer down at George.

"Weather's easing," the man said.

A gruff voice ground from the distance. "Just let him rot there!" it said. "I'll not waste a ration on him."

George popped into full wakefulness. He tried to

process what he just experienced. It was more than the panic attacks he'd been having in Boston.

A dream? Maybe. Maybe not?

He hadn't had these kinds of blurred lines between dream and reality until he had come to Nantucket. He looked up at the ceiling—no grate. Moonlight once again fell softly through the window bars. He was reluctant to risk sleep again, but fatigue finally forced him to go there.

Morning came with brightness and noise as Harry Beal burst in with jingling keys and a funny kind of sunny disposition. It wasn't often that Harry had guests, and he was going to milk it for all it was worth. He poked a paper bag through the bars at George.

"What's this?" George asked, as he wiped the sleep webs from his eyes.

"Breakfast!" Beal said. "A croissant and cappuccino."

Beal took in George's surprised expression. "This IS yuppified Nantucket," Beal said. "I do have to make concessions. Plain, stale bread and dented tin cups of water are hard to find here."

George smiled as he took the bag. "I guess I'll just have to sacrifice."

The two men caught each other's eyes. Though Beal doubted George's story, his eyes held little to no judgment. George even sensed an unspoken respect and kinship between them. He was greatly relieved at this. He decided that perhaps he could relax a bit.

A knock came at the outer door. A muffled voice shouted through it, "Anyone home in there?"

Harry looked back at George. "That would be your head doctor."

George watched Harry go through his office to answer the door. His comfort quickly evaporated as he remembered why he was here, what he was up against, and what was at stake.

Harry answered the door and led Doctor Pantone inside.

When they were introduced, George remembered clearly that he was the man whose business card Amber had given him. He remembered standing outside on the street in front of Pantone's office and not mustering the courage to go in, the courage to face the reality of his condition.

One possible reality, he tried to remind himself.

With the sly smile of a half-intended joke, Harry Beal said, "I'll just leave you two alone."

With that, Beal was gone, back in his office.

THIRTY-NINE

Harry leaned back in his chair and surveyed the clutter that once was his desktop. He rested his feet on the windowsill near the radiator and lifted the whale's tooth again. He continued his work on it with the nail. It was a way for him to lose himself in what he, at one time, had the audacity to consider a future in: art.

Unfortunately, as he loosened himself up enough to do it, he also often unleashed the pent-up venom.

Why did it have to happen? How would it have gone if Bolgers hadn't stuck his nose in? What would his life be like now? What if I just tell him to go fuck himself?

In that long ago summer of 1970, Harry renounced everything those in his parents' world stood for. It was a typical story for back then, but the depth of Harry's integrity strengthened the resolve of his belief. His rejection of parental values and his embracing of progressive politics was stronger and more thought-out than most.

Back home, he could blend in with others of like mind, but on Nantucket, at least in the insolated circles his parents traveled in, he was an outcast.

He liked being an outcast, always would. He preferred watching the world from enough distance to give him a critical perspective on it rather than being among the throngs of participants whose very participation kept them from seeing the forest for the trees. He reveled in his rejection by the world that he was forced to chart his summers through.

Everything changed when he met Emily. Emily—what a name. Emily Dickinson, Emily Post, Harry could think of no Emilys who fit his radical-left visions of what a person should be. No Harrys either, for that matter, but he was sure that there must be some Harrys somewhere.

He'd started to notice Emily a few years before as she traveled in the same high-priced circles. He befriended her a year later.

He liked the way her humor challenged every presumption of the status quo. He thought her friendship might save him from summers of boredom and alienation, but he was seventeen by then. She was fifteen, just a kid. Still they grew close, to her parents' terror. Maybe their terror was part of the attraction for Harry?

When Harry came back that next summer of 1971, Emily had bloomed. The girl was gone, replaced by the most beautiful woman Harry had ever seen. It was two years after Woodstock. Sex had been reinvented, along with the rest of young life.

By August, Emily was pregnant. At eighteen, he was legally adult for such things. Emily was sixteen. Jailbait, they used to say. Harry had never even thought about it. The rightness he'd felt in her arms blotted out anybody's idea of wrong.

In that instant, everything changed. Nothing would ever be the same.

Harry was shocked out of his anger-infused memory by Dr. Pantone stepping in from the room that contained the cell. He continued to work on the tooth as Pantone sat down across from him.

"Isn't scrimshaw politically incorrect these

days?" Pantone asked.

With resignation, Harry laid the tooth on his cluttered desk so he could better address Pantone.

"They're plastic. I get them from a place in Cleveland. I just draw on them and sell them to tourists."

Pantone saw the hints of painful memory around Beal's eyes. He noticed the Andrew Wyeth calendar on the wall. To Pantone's mind, regular-Joe, salt-of-the-earth types like Beal ought to have Playboy pictures on their calendars.

"Are you a budding artist?" Pantone asked.

"Already gone to seed, more like."

"There's always time. Follow your bliss, as they say."

"I'm not the patient. How's our mystery guest in the cell?"

"Standard stuff. Why waste your taxpayer's money on me?

"Standard stuff? Maybe in your world, Doc—not here."

Pantone puzzled at this. He kept listening but with heightened interest.

"The Christmas Stroll is coming. I'll need the cell. But with that loony story of his, I'm not releasing him until I get an official okay from you."

"What loony story?"

Beal told him everything. George had withheld it from Pantone for fear of his psychosis or schizophrenia being professionally confirmed.

When Pantone heard it, he couldn't wait to re-interview George. He turned on his heels and hurried toward the cell room with Beal trailing behind.

FORTY

As they entered, George sprang from his cot in surprise. Beal let Pantone into the cell and left them. Pantone calmed George down and sat on the cot with him. He explained what Beal had filled him in on.

George's face darkened as he listened. He felt the warm sweat of self-loathing guilt pulsate on his scalp and slide down his back. He kept his eyes on the floor, hoping for salvation there. When Pantone finished, he waited. The pressure for George to respond grew heavier by the second. Finally he broke.

"It was just supposed to be a relaxing weekend."

"Relaxing from what?"

"All the normal stuff."

"Explain normal," Pantone said.

"Pressures of work, relationships, city life, you know—normal."

George wondered whether saying normal enough would make it true.

Pantone took a slightly different tack. "What happened?"

"I met this woman."

"Sounds normal so far."

"Not a regular alive woman."

George saw Pantone's eyes widen with new interest and realized that he was over the cliff now. It would all come out. No way to stop it.

"Not a dead woman either! I'm not some sicko ... Not exactly a dead woman ... she was alive."

"Can't be dead unless you've been alive," Pantone said.

"She was alive a hundred and fifty years ago ... give or take."

"A ghost?"

"I don't know. I went to see a woman who said she wasn't."

"Amber Baskin. She said you might call me. I didn't realize that it was you who she meant."

George's red flag of paranoia went up.

Am I being talked about? Who else is part of this dragnet?

He knew it was wiser not to voice these thoughts right now so he kept them to himself. His brain was on fire. "I must be cracking up!"

Pantone gave him a long silent stare before responding. In that time, he watched George's body language, his face, his eyes. He tried to get a true sense of George's mental state. Then he spoke. "Do you know about regression therapy?"

"Is that where they make you go back to being a baby or something?"

"Hardly. Some folks believe that this is not their first time here, that they have unfinished work."

"You mean on Nantucket?"

"In life. Sometimes we have to go back before our births in order to fix problems that span between lives."

This guy's not going to call me crazy. He's crazy, himself. As George thought this, his confidence trickled back. "I've already gone the fruitcake route. I thought you were a real doctor."

Pantone took no offense at this. With comforting tones, he merely explained himself. "Doctors don't have to subscribe to one set of beliefs or treatment options. We all have our specialties. This is one of mine."

Pantone waited for a response. Finally, he added, "What do you have to lose?"

"Is this going to help me find Rebecca? That's all I care about."

"Sometimes we have to let go of our expectations in order to achieve them," Pantone said.

Pantone moved from the cot and pulled up a spindly wooden chair that was also in the cell. He sat across from George, nearly knee to knee.

George tried to avoid eye contact.

Pantone slowly reached across and touched George's shoulder.

Emboldened by the comfort of Pantone's hand, George carefully looked up until he met the doctor's eyes.

As Pantone spoke, there was a new authority in his voice. Not an intimidating authority like George was used to, but a kind, knowing wisdom.

Pantone said, "Now ... just relax ... and breathe normally."

George sucked in and out as if he was wearing an oxygen mask.

"Not quite," Pantone said, as he waited patiently for George to slow his breathing. Then he continued, "Let your eyes close."

Pantone watched patiently as George closed his eyes.

"Breathe in on my count of three. One ... Let the new air fill your lungs. It's fresh, cleansing air, calming air ... Two ... Feel your lungs sending this calming air throughout your body ... into your fingers ... your toes ..."

FORTY-ONE

Harry sat at his desk, working more on his scrimshaw as he waited for Pantone to reemerge.

Bolgers barged in. He was the last person Harry wanted to see. Bolgers motioned to the cell room with a dramatic flourish. "What's he being charged with?"

Harry put down his scrimshaw. "I don't know. You have any ideas?"

"He was found breaking and entering, for Christ sake!"

"Wasn't for his sake, and the guy hadn't broken, and he hadn't entered."

"That was his intent."

"I start arresting for intent, there'll be no one left to sell Frappuccinos to. Besides, the homeowners are summer people. I haven't even been able to contact them yet."

"Did you try?"

"Try—what a good idea. Why didn't I think of that?"

"You didn't even ..."

"Of course I tried. I've left messages on all of their phones. I'm waiting to hear. They'd have to press charges."

"I'll press them," Bolgers bellowed.

"And charge him with what? Messing up your

speech?"

"I'm the goddamned Mayor!"

"Can't charge him with that."

"You best remember who appointed you to this job."

"I know. The goddamned Mayor!"

"I'm not taking any more of your BULLSHIT! I can send you back to face the music anytime."

"I'm not sure there's any music left to face."

"If you want to find out, be my guest." Bolgers spun and stormed from Harry's office.

Harry went back to his scrimshaw, digging the nail fiercely, working out his anger.

There's probably nothing to face, he thought. *I've been Bolgers' fucking prisoner all this time for nothing.*

His mind burned with memories of the most beautiful feeling of his life being ripped from him, then dirtied and sullied. A first love always runs more deeply. It's born of innocence, with lust and love playfully intertwined.

He still thought often about Emily, tried to picture what she'd look like today, wondered how things went for her when it all turned bad and they were separated.

Emily's father had hated Harry from the start. There was the normal dislike a man has for his daughter's first love, but there was more, too. Something ugly, forged in the depths of her father's subconscious. It came out of repressed jealousies that were too dark to acknowledge. Added to that, Harry's long hair and outspoken views were the stuff of every father's nightmare back then.

When Emily showed up crying and pregnant one hot night of an August dog day, her father's pent-up rage went nuclear. There was a warrant out for Harry's arrest on statutory rape charges. Bolgers stepped in with enough money and connections to make it go away. Ravaged by fear and guilt, Harry went along with the arrangements. He never fell fully out of love with Emily, though he'd never seen her again.

He tortured himself often with wondering—who she was with now, what became of their child? He never even knew if it went to term. Did she miscarry or abort? Or was there a child of his, living, unknown to him, somewhere in the world?

Sometimes he let these thoughts eat away at him, along with thoughts of where his own life would've carried him had it not been for this debacle. Instead of living under Bolgers' thumb, he could have gone anywhere, done anything. The world had been wide open to him. All in one night, that wide-open world closed down.

Since then, the only weapon left in his quiver was his humor. It kept him sane, kept him from killing Bolgers or himself, or both. His humor had acquired a dark, cynical edge over the years, but maybe that was just wisdom?

Harry picked up his coffee mug and walked toward the jail room so he could check on Pantone's progress. He stopped on his way as another thought occurred to him. He took a sharp left and opened the door to what should have been a small closet. Inside, a plump, fortyish woman sat at an old-style phone switchboard with a police radio on top. She waved to Harry without turning as she talked to a friend on her headset.

He called to her, "Millie?"

She hurried off the phone. "Got to go. Duty calls."

She spun around in her chair to face Harry.

"Get Sam on the radio. Tell him to take my rounds today."

"He's probably home. I'm better off just calling him," she said.

"Use carrier pigeon if you want, long as you tell him."

"What's up?"

"So nosey," Beal said.

"Comes with the job."

"I just think things might get more interesting around here."

"You're giving me goose bumps," she said.

Harry left her to her tiny cubbyhole and sauntered toward the jail room door again.

FORTY-TWO

When he saw Harry, Pantone put an index finger to his lips, requesting silence.

George sat on the cot with his eyes closed as Pantone continued to speak in a gentle, hypnotic tone. "You're walking down a winding, stone staircase. The stones feel cool and comforting to the touch. Each step is darker, cooler, more relaxing. We're going deeper and deeper and ... deeper ... stepping down through last week, now ... through last year ... all remaining tension turns to liquid ... feel it running out of your fingers and toes ... Step down further now ... down through five years ... ten. You are free and safe to go as far as you need. When you are there ... tell me what you see."

Harry looked on skeptically as George just sat there with his eyes closed.

Pantone watched George carefully.

Finally, as Harry was preparing to pronounce the whole thing stupid, George said something.

"Mountains."

Both men watched George with renewed interest. A moment went by before he spoke again.

"Mountains of water ... waves."

George saw it all in sharp detail. Wave-tops boiled and spewed white froth that mixed with the wind and swirled skyward towards a purple-gray muddle of clouds. A decrepit two-masted schooner with reefed-in sails battled through swelling mounds of foam-marbled waves. Rain sliced in sideways on the boat.

George saw it all like a movie in his mind and tried his best to describe it.

"A boat ... with sails that have been tied down so only little patches still show. It's a bad storm. The boat! It's a schooner!"

George realized that he knew that because Rebecca had taught him. In fact, this boat looked just like the one they had talked about.

The wrecker! It was the same boat! George knew it in his bones.

Pantone's voice eased into the scene as a calm, steady guide. "Can you go closer to the boat? Can you board it?"

Suddenly, like in a film jump cut, George was on deck. He felt the rain stinging his face. He heard the wind howling through the rigging. It sounded like rosin bows drawn across mistuned violins.

On the quarterdeck, a stocky, bearded man paced frantically, aided by a brass-topped walking stick. It was hard to tell in the rain-swept dark, but he looked familiar.

George took a few steps closer. He looked like Bolgers. It *was* Bolgers—Bolgers the First! George recognized him from that memorial plaque with the relief image of his face that he had seen on his first Nantucket day.

As he described the things he saw, Pantone gently led him deeper until he was living what he saw, living and still describing it to Pantone as it happened.

"I'm studying Bolgers. He is tougher than the Bolgers I know, stronger and meaner. I watch as he slaps and screams at a terrified young boy who

mans the wheel.

"'Keep that goddamned heading!' he says, 'You've more to fear from me than the weather, you worthless lubber!'

"I'm realizing that this bully of a man doesn't inspire an ounce of fear in me. He inspires only anger and contempt. Here, I'm a different man, a man with courage. Bolgers is captain of this ratty little schooner. These realizations feel more like memories.

"I take a few steps toward Bolgers. I watch Bolgers crane his neck up to the main mast crosstrees and mouth a curse. I look up to the crosstrees, barely visible through the storm. In the edging flash of lightning, I see what Bolgers is cursing. Another teenaged boy is clinging to life up there. He seems frozen in place. Frozen maybe in fear, or maybe pain."

George's voice rose an octave in excitement.

"I know who I am! I know what to do! I'm First Mate of this tub! I've been summoned by Bolgers, and I'm on my way to receive orders.

"I walk briskly and stop sharply at the quarterdeck lip, as is custom for the mate on a sailing ship. I call to Bolgers.

"'Sir?'

"Bolgers points up to the crosstrees as he barks to me. 'Get another man aloft to unfoul that throat halyard! Someone who's worth a damn this time! We've got to reef in another two points.'

"I hear myself reply sharply. 'Aye aye, sir!'"

As George sat on the jail cell cot reliving and recounting these things, he felt like he was along for the ride, inside this new persona. As Pantone brought him still deeper, he realized that it wasn't a new persona at all, but a very old one. He felt less and less along for the ride and more like this was a part of him. Was him! He wasn't just watching it. He was living it.

"Responding to Bolgers' order, I run forward through the driving rain. I stop at the main mast and look up at the poor boy stuck up there about ninety feet above deck. Instead of calling for another man to go aloft, as I'd been ordered, I hop to the shrouds and climb up the ratlines myself.

"I have no hesitation. I have fear but ... for me ... here, fear isn't something to be stopped by or controlled by. It's just something to work through.

"As I make the long climb, I feel new muscles I was never aware of. Working them feels good. Wind drives the rain like needles through my face. As I near the crosstrees, I'm ninety feet above the deck. I can feel the wild arc of the mast as the boat rolls with the sea. It swings through the rain like a giant metronome.

"I reach my goal and pull myself up, wedging my feet against the white crosstrees to brace my body against the slippery mast. From there, I see the problem. The throat block is twisted around its own halyard line, and it's slapping uselessly against the mast about fifteen feet below me.

"I lean across to the frozen crewman. His name is Owen. He is sixteen. Owen holds a large iron hook in his left hand. A thick hemp line is tied to it. I inspect the knot and then shout so he can hear me over the wind.

"'No good! You need a working clove hitch, or the hook won't take the weight.'

"The storm is wild, scary, and dangerous but I'm ... calm, confident. I'm more worried about this poor boy. I want to calm his fears. Even though I have to shout to be heard over the wind, I keep a patient, instructive tone.

"I say, 'Hold the standing end. Take your right hand and ...'

"I stop when I see that Owen is twisting his right hand away to conceal it. I notice the boy's ashen, pain-stricken face. 'Show me,' I say.

"With great reluctance, Owen holds out his right arm for me to inspect. The wrist is bent at an unnatural angle. Purplish red bruising and swelling surrounds the joint. He must be in awful pain, but he is trying to hide it. His face and voice register mostly embarrassment. His eyes plead an apology as he talks.

"'Misjudged that damned wind,' he says.

"I survey the situation and weigh my options. Fear and guilt are in Owen's voice now. 'Sorry,' he says.

"I look at him. My heart nearly breaks for the poor kid. 'Sit tight,' I say.

"I ease myself out along the crosstree to get a better look at that slapping and twisted lower throat halyard block. Then I return to Owen.

"'I'll climb down the mast to free that throat halyard! Then, I'll be back for you!'

"Owen shouts through his pain, 'You'll get yourself killed that way! Let them send up a boatswain's chair!'

"'No time! We've got to reef in!' I say.

"I carefully bend down and grab onto the upper block of the halyard lines that lead down against the mast. Holding tight to the block, I roll off the crosstrees and let my feet swing to the mast. I must look like a mountaineer ready to repel down a sheer cliff. I shout back up to Owen. 'Don't worry! I'll be back. I promise!'

"Owen looks down at me. I see doubt in his eyes.

"While still holding the block tightly with my right hand, I grab for the swinging halyard with my left. After a few swipes, I get a hold of it. Still clutching the block, I pull on the halyard to make sure it is fast and can hold my weight. Then, quick as I can, I bring both hands to the halyard. I start to lower myself *hand by hand, step by step, down along the mast. After a few steps, my feet slip outward around the rain-slicked mast.*

" 'Mother of GOD!'

"I hit it crotch first! My head gets that hot, moldy nausea that women will never know.

"After a few failed attempts, I regain my footing and continue down. I finally reach the twisted block, climb below it and place my feet on the gaff boom collar. This will be a good work platform. I reach up, squinting from the rain, and untwist the block. With that done, I free up the halyard line. I shout to the men on deck below, 'Reef away!'

"Breathing a sigh of relief, I look back up to the crosstrees, fifteen feet above me. Grabbing the halyard line, I put my feet against the mast and try to climb back up the way I came—no good. I slip and crash against the mast, taking it full body this time. After two more failed attempts, I concede that gravity is not on my side. I need to go back up to get Owen, but I need to do it by getting down to the deck first so I can re-climb the ratlines.

"Then, the gaff boom collar I'm standing on lurches hard enough to nearly knock me off. The crew below has started to reef in the sail! The gaff I'm on starts lowering in short jerks. I shimmy out along the gaff boom until I reach the brail, about halfway out. As the gaff boom sinks, the stationary brail appears to be rising from my perspective.

"As it comes up, I grab the brail line and swing my legs up, wrapping them around the line, like a kid playing monkey on a playground jungle gym. Hand over hand, I lower myself down past the sail to the end of the lower boom. I stand up tall on the boom's end, waiting for the sail to fall to its new reef point. I hold up my hand to the deck crew, ready to signal them a reef stop point. They look up at me, waiting for my signal, from about ten feet below me.

" 'Avast!' I shout. 'Make her fast, men.'

"There is no doubt as to who is in charge of these men. They may fear Bolgers' wrath, but they respect and obey ME!"

As George sat on his cot with Pantone, he was completely enthralled with this person he was riding inside of. He was almost in love with him. At the same time that his heart danced, it also ached.

How could the pittance of a man I am have been such a hero? What happened to me? How could I have failed my former self so thoroughly? If he met me, he'd probably beat the shit out of me.

George tortured himself with these thoughts, making his trance lighten.

Pantone came to the rescue, gently leading him deeper until his hypnotically induced adventure continued.

"The ceaseless, wind-driven rain continues its assault on us as I hop from the boom end to the deckhouse transom and then to the deck. No sooner do my feet slosh to the deck but Bolgers breaks through the crowd of crewmen.

"He is enraged by ... jealousy, I think. He resents that I get along with the crew. He thinks it undermines his authority somehow. He swings his walking stick down. Crashing its brass top into the midship rail, he screams, 'I said send a bloody MAN up there! My first mate stays on deck!'

"The more he screams, the more I let it roll off my back. That's my secret weapon—lack of anger, lack of intimidation. It makes the crew love me and Bolgers hate me all the more. I respond to him in almost a singsong voice. 'Right you are, sir. I'll be back in just a moment.'

"I spin to the ratlines, climb upon them and head back up for that poor crew boy, Owen.

"In a rage, Bolgers grabs at my feet, screaming the worst epithets he can think of. It is no use. I'm

already on my way, out of his reach. Bolgers is left with a hostile crew who has just seen his authority successfully thwarted, once again.

"My arms start to ache this time, re-climbing that ninety feet. At the top, the crosstrees seem to be swinging even more wildly. I finally get to Owen and look down upon his wretched, weather-battered form.

"I shout through the wind, 'Can you stand?'

"'Not sure,' he answers.

"After an instant's thought, I turn away from the boy and bend to my knees.

"'Climb on my back!' I shout. 'I'll carry you.'

"Owen is afraid of this prospect, but his confidence in me wins out. The boy winces from his pain and suppresses his need to scream as he climbs upon my back.

"From over my shoulder, Owen asks timidly, 'Can you sneak me past the captain?'

"With a slight chuckle, I say, 'Don't worry about him.'

"Carrying Owen's extra weight, I make my way down the storm-ravaged ratlines to the rail, fearing that my knees will give out at any moment. At the rail, I slowly spin Owen in to the waiting arms of grateful crewmen. They gently peel Owen off my back and bring him to the deck. Then I jump to the deck myself just as Bolgers breaks through the crowd again, screaming his usual screams.

"'You men back to your posts!'

"Bolgers extends his walking stick and pokes me in the chest with it.

"'You think you can ignore me!' Bolgers bellows. 'Make a fool out of ME!'

"I explain. 'He has a broken wrist, sir!'

"Bolgers' rage explodes. 'Make it a matched set, then!'

"Bolgers bashes Owen's good wrist with the brass end of his walking stick. After a short scream,

Owen crumples in place to the deck, unconscious from the pain.

"Bolgers and I lock eyes. I burn red with rage. I can't control it. I backhand Bolgers hard on the face. He staggers back as blood squirts from his nose. Bolgers straightens himself, clutching his blood-spattered face.

"'You mutinous fool!' Bolgers bellows.

"A long moment of heavy silence ensues as we both stand our ground, but neither of us advances. The crew looks on anxiously. Some are hungry for blood—others are hungry for justice, a thing they think can only come from mutiny.

"It feels like we're standing there forever. Tension grows. The crew looks between us like they are watching a tennis match. I'm on the edge of mutiny, but I can't follow through. It would be a betrayal of my commitment as first mate. I think my crew will stand up for Owen and for me, but they don't. They just watch, like children waiting to be led.

"Why don't they come to my defense? Aren't we a team?

"Finally, it is Bolgers who breaks the standoff.

"'Take him below and put him in irons!'

"The crew looks around to each other with bewildered, disappointed faces. None of them can meet my eyes. I know I've disappointed them by not taking over the ship, but the duty I've sworn myself to is too important to throw away in anger.

"They've disappointed me, too. If they had stood with me in solidarity, there'd be no need for mutiny. Bolgers would be contained.

"My heart breaks as two of my most trusted crew, good friends of mine, Second Mate Hollings and Boatswain Gordon, reluctantly take hold of me and lead me below. I offer no resistance."

From his present-day spot on the jail cell cot with Pantone sitting beside him, George could feel his past-life counterpart's range of emotions. This man who'd stood up for his crew so many times wanted the crew to stand up for him this time. The poor guy also knew that, as their leader, it was his call to make. Perhaps it was he who had failed them? Along with all of this was his burning contempt for Bolgers the First. What was the manly thing to do—let his anger drive him to mutiny? Or endure the job he'd agreed to do?

Which was weakness? Which was strength?

George could feel all of these thoughts as if they were his own. He knew that at one time they were.

He could see their remnants in his present life. These questions had always haunted him. *Action or inaction? Confrontation or compliance?*

With a sinking heart, George knew he'd always chosen the safest of the two. He dwelt on how many times his choice had been wrong. His worries were lifting him out of his hypnotic state.

He could hear Pantone's voice again. "Take a long ... cleansing breath ... clear your mind of any clutter ... step deeper ...

George again reached the level where he could continue to describe his experiences.

"I am back on the schooner, but this time I'm alone, chained against the wall of the empty cargo hold. I look up to the grated hatch cover overhead. Its hard square holes are softened by the moonlight. Hollings sticks his head over the grate to speak down to me. 'Sorry, sir,' he says.

"'Sir's a title reserved for captains,' I say.

"'It's you what deserves the title,' Hollings says.

"He's silent for a minute. It's awkward. Then he says, 'Weather's easing.'

"I know he's at a loss for words. He feels bad.

"I hear Bolgers voice booming from the back-ground.

"'Just let him rot there! I'll not waste a ration on him.'

"Hollings looks off to make sure that Bolgers can't see him. Then he turns back to me and says, 'I know you ain't used to fo'c'sle rations, but it was the best I could do. The men was glad to give some up for you.'

"I reply, 'That a tribute to me or a comment on the poor quality of food?'

"Hollings grins as he pulls a stained, oily satchel from his pants and pushes it in through a grate hole, letting it fall down to me.

"Though it falls nearly out of reach, I manage to grab it. I bite down on the piece of salt pork and almost vomit as I taste the rot. Weevils crawl out from inside it. I see a rat foraging in the corner, and I toss it to him. 'Have yourself a party!' I say.

"The next morning I'm carried on deck and tied to hatch cover that leans up against the main mast for this purpose. I'm to get ten lashes with the cat and a week's demotion from First Mate. Hollings will hold the position. It's Hollings, too, who holds the cat, ready to do the honors."

"Can you describe the cat?" George heard Pantone ask through the fog of the world he was reliving.

"It's a stick with nine long strips of leather. At the end of them strips is embedded glass so's it will rip into the skin better.

"Bolgers is gleeful. He almost sings it when he says, 'Let's see how tough you are once the flesh is off your back!'

"The first lash burns across me, and I can feel some blood start to trickle, but the strips only fell across me lightly. I could tell. I know for sure when I hear Bolgers bluster out at Hollings. 'Manly strokes, Mister Hollings,' he says, 'unless you want to be next.'

"I know Hollings doesn't want to do this. We are friends. His next blow is much worse. His fear of Bolgers is stronger than his loyalty to me.

"By the tenth, I'm ready to faint, but I won't give Bolgers the satisfaction. When they untie me and try and help me below, I shake them off, staring old man Bolgers straight in the eyes. 'I'll stand on my own, thank you,' I say.

"Bolgers gives me his most hateful stare, but behind it, I can see a kernel of fear. I'll take that little kernel as my victory."

George could feel himself drifting back into his body. He became aware of Pantone and the jail cell again. In that netherworld between both realities, he could still feel all of the emotions and pain that inhabited his former incarnation, but he was no longer feeling them from inside. During this transition period, he had the fleeting perspective of distance.

He thought, *If only that past George could know how loved and respected he was by his crew. If only he could see himself in as good a light as others saw him.*

As he came more fully into his present life, George tried to apply that lesson to himself. It was a weak construct, destined to weather many storms of self-loathing, but perhaps it would stand? Perhaps it would strengthen?

He could hear Pantone talking him back to reality. "Four ... you are stepping back up now ... Three ... you are relaxed and at peace ... Two ... you can fully remember all that you've seen ... One ... and open your eyes."

George became fully conscious. "Was this a dream? A hallucination?"

Pantone stood up and stretched his back as he replied, "Are you any kind of expert on schooner construction or sailing?"

"No."

"Then it would have been a pretty neat trick to have hallucinated all that stuff accurately."

"Do you know if it's accurate?"

"You can bet I'll find out."

"What about Rebecca? I'm running out of time."

"Time may not be what you expect it to be."

"But I'm on a mission."

"And that mission has brought you here. Relax and go with it."

George tried to let himself settle in with that thought. "Will you be back tomorrow?"

"You can bet the farm on it."

As Pantone opened the cell door, George stood and took a step toward him. Pantone stepped outside the cell and closed the door behind him. He saw the desperation in George's eyes.

"Don't worry," he said. "We're on the right track. We'll pick it up tomorrow."

"In the morning?"

"I've got some research to do, about schooners. Look for me around lunch time."

Feeling unsettled but hopeful, George watched him leave. When he sat down again on the cot, he saw that the day was gone. Looking at the darkened window as he leaned against the wall, George realized that he'd dreamed about that moment in the cargo hold with Hollings talking down to him before Pantone ever showed up.

He hadn't understood the dream when he had it. He thought back to so many other times when confusing dreams had tortured his sleep—violent, scary dreams. He thought about the panic attacks. Was he to live out their realities in future hypnotic sessions? The idea frightened and excited him at the same time.

FORTY-THREE

The next morning came up bright and shiny. Harry Beal popped in with a smiling face. Following him was Betty Bolgers, carrying an oversized picnic basket that was decorated with Christmas ribbons. She greeted George with a warm smile.

George glowed at her kindness, happy for the mothering comfort she would bring.

"From the Atheneum, right?"

Betty nodded affirmatively.

Harry darkened the morning by saying, "This is Mrs. Betty Bolgers."

George's happiness was betrayed by the very mention of Bolgers. He now watched her with suspicion.

Harry saw the change in George and tried to mitigate it. "Mrs. Bolgers has always been our kind-hearted benefactor."

"It's nothing, really," she said. "The world is hard enough already. Why not ease things where you can?"

"Spoken like a true politician," Beal said.

"Oh, my husband's the politician in the family."

George and Harry both grimaced at that one.

"And that's why we need more of them like you," Harry said.

Betty blushed a bit. She was flattered by the

comment and not in disagreement about it. Still, she felt honor-bound to defend her husband. "Oh, his bark is worse than his bite."

"Tell that to those who've been bitten," Beal said.

George smiled as he listened to the exchange.

"I suppose," Betty said, "he does have a tendency to make people feel trapped sometimes."

"Like a spider," Beal said.

Without them realizing it, their banter had taken a dark turn revealing true pain in both of them. Harry saved the day with a quick subject change.

"So, Betty, what do you have for us today?"

Betty flushed with relief and with gratitude to Harry for providing the subject change. "It's nothing really. I was baking my cranberry biscuits, and I thought, *'Why not make a few extra?'* Once the production line is going, it's hard to stop."

Harry and George laughed with her warmly. Betty turned to George, in the cell. "I do remember you from the Atheneum."

"Me, too," George said.

"You remember you, too?" she kidded.

It was an old joke. The kind a relative might make at a family gathering where people laugh through obligation. But, somehow, coming from her, it seemed fresh. George's laugh was real.

Maybe it was because of the tentative way in which she offered her joke out, as if she were venturing onto unfamiliar, treacherous ground. It hinted at an inner spark of cheeky humor that had long been deadened by decades of oppressive judgment.

As Harry opened the cell door, Betty sat on a stool and pulled back the cloth cover of her basket, revealing a half dozen beautiful biscuits that looked like they had rubies trapped inside of them. They were still steaming. A hand-packed ramekin of butter sat on top.

George envisioned her hand-packing that butter with tender care. He thought about all the times when Betty's beautiful kindness must have been squashed by life with Bolgers. He wished he could save her from it. This desire was made all the more acute because, for George now, both of the Bolgers that he knew had become a combination of the two. They were intertwined. Amalgamated Bolgers.

Harry, George, and Betty sat on their stools in a knee-to-knee huddle, like naughty school kids sharing something out of sight from their teacher. They laughed at stories and giggled at jokes until nothing was left in the basket but crumbs.

As Betty finally stood up and brushed herself off, preparing to leave, George marveled at her resilient love of life. No matter how long it stayed locked in a cage, George realized that she could still call it out at will. He thought about how he had lost that resilience through the trials of a much shorter and less daunting life than hers. He felt like his own excuses had been laid bare. It was time for him to stop wallowing in victim-hood and reclaim his own resilient charms.

The three said their goodbyes, and Betty left.

When she was gone, Harry said, "Another tragedy of marriage."

George added, "A damsel in distress." George thought about Rebecca.

FORTY-FOUR

Sunshine streamed through the multi-pane windows of The Even Keel Café. The sounds of plates, silverware, and voices were at a near crescendo, but it all added to the character of the place. Pantone sat across from Amber Baskin. His lips flirted with the heat of his steaming French roast coffee. Amber watched him over her cup of herbal tea.

"That's the high test. You'll be wired all day," she said.

"Actually it's a popular misconception. Dark roast coffees taste richer so people think they have more caffeine, but since the roast is longer, more of the caffeine burns off, so there's less."

"You doctor types just know everything."

Pantone grinned with slight embarrassment. "Okay, okay, I'm not the best at making small talk with ladies over breakfast."

"You're a regular James Bond."

"Maybe not Bond, but I am doing some good detective work."

"Spill it."

"I've been in the Atheneum all morning."

"Oooo, danger. I hope you wore your Kevlar vest."

Pantone chuckled as he continued, "I researched everything he talked about, and it all checks out, schooner construction and outfitting, reefing in for a storm. Bolgers' great grandfather did captain a schooner."

Amber put down her tea. "So we're not saying nut here?"

"Were we ever?"

"No, I guess not."

"I can't wait for the next session. It's like I'm living a real life movie."

"He's living it. You're watching it."

"It's both."

Amber saw how animated and excited Pantone was.

"I'd recheck your facts on that caffeine thing if I was you."

"You tea drinkers are never any fun."

FORTY-FIVE

Pantone was nearly as excited as George was. He sat with him in the jail cell and led him slowly, deeply into another episode of his past existence.

George tried to shelve his excitement enough to concentrate and let the magic work. Finally, he could see it. He was once again inside this hero of a man he once was.

"I'm on the schooner again. Four drunk and hung-over men are lying on the deck in front of me. I've just doused them with a bucket of water. Hollings and Gordon are with me. They're laughing. I make a little speech to the drunk men.

"'Good morning gentlemen,' I say. 'Welcome to our delightful cruise. We'll be sailing the sparkling waters from the tip of Provincetown down to Block Island and Montauk.'

"These guys have been ... what's the word? Shanghaied. Bolgers has thugs who work for a share of the profits. They roam the bars for drunks, preferably coof drunks. Sometimes they get the guy drunk in the first place. Once these poor fellows are in a stupor, the thugs drag them aboard where they become our crew. There's all kinds of ways we get a hold of them. We mostly sail with the same crew, but every trip, a few desert us, and we've got to pick up

a handful this way.

"One of the victims, Pickering is his name, he is scrawny and weak, a desk man. He's terrified. He pleads for us to take him back to shore. He says he's got a good bank job and a wife in Salem.

"I've got no sympathy. He was brought down by one of Bolgers' whores. They work just like the thugs. Maybe we should send him back to his wife? She'd give him worse than we can dish out. He's practically going to cry. The seasoned crew only laughs at him. I do, too."

The shock of this realization snapped George out of his trance. For his whole life, he'd been like this Pickering character. His past persona was like the guys who tortured him through school. How could he process this without hating either his current self or his past self?

Pantone told him not to judge, just to watch and accept. He told him that acceptance was the doorway to wisdom.

"You get that from *Dr. Phil* or the back of a cereal box?" George surprised himself by striking out so vehemently. It wasn't in his nature.

"Sometimes a platitude can exist because it is valid."

Pantone said it with no trace of anger or defensiveness. For some reason, that word "platitude" jabbed at George. It caught in a fold of his brain and just wouldn't go away, like a stubborn piece of food that gets caught in your teeth. He couldn't understand it, but as he puzzled over it, Pantone gently guided him down into a trance once again.

"The men are assembled amidships. I'm teaching the green ones what's expected of them, what we do. I'm good at it. Hollings and Gordon roll out a medium-sized cannon. I tell the group, 'This cannon's

for saving lives. Not taking them. It's called a Lyle gun. We load a special padded ball into it, so as not to cause too much damage. A long hemp line gets attached to the ball. A "line" means rope to all you coofs and lubbers.'

"That always gets me a laugh, at least from the seasoned crew. I explain how we shoot the padded ball out so it wraps around the yardarm or bowsprit of some ship in trouble. Then I tell them, 'Here's the fun part!'

"I show'm the breeches buoy. It's a big, round life preserver with a wide leather strap connected across the inside and hanging down like a big diaper. I demonstrate by stepping into it and pulling it up around my waist. I explain how we connect this to the line we shoot over to the ship by a block and tackle pulley system. One of us, usually me, pulls himself over to the ship and rescues whoever's on board, one by one, before it sinks. I tell them they'll all have a chance at it, and I watch their jaws drop in terror. That's one of the fun parts for me."

Pantone started to bring George back to the surface of reality. When he was done, George sat there confused and disappointed.

"I barely got started. Why am I out?"

"You seemed to enjoy toying with people back then."

"All in good fun."

"How do you feel when people toy with you today?"

"That is what I was talking about before. You said not to judge."

"Perhaps I'm bringing this up too soon?" Pantone explained, "I want you in a place where you don't make judgments, but you do make connections."

George thought long and hard about this. He hated being toyed with, being teased, and put down. His hatred of the instigator had long been his best defense.

"So, I was an asshole back then?"

"That sounds like a judgment," Pantone said.

"What else would you call it?"

"I don't think naming it is the big lesson here."

"What is?" George asked.

"It's not so simple a question."

"Can you explain it?"

Pantone took a deep breath as he decided how best to articulate his thoughts and how much he wanted to reveal. "Your past incarnation seems to scorn weakness. You and I know that weakness is a condition more than a choice. As such, it shouldn't be so harshly judged. Today, you scorn those who lack your weakness. I'm sure you do so for protective reasons, but nevertheless, it's also a judgment, and it keeps you from your recovery. Whole people are a mix of everything. The more of everything you embrace, the better it all works."

George grew antsy and defensive as he listened. Pantone was opening the doors to caves that he'd rather not visit.

"I just want to find Rebecca. That's what I need to do."

"It would be a pity if you found her but were unprepared for her."

"Unprepared? How?"

"Look at the divorce rates. Love can't always sustain things over the long haul. You have to be good to and for each other."

"More *Dr. Phil*?"

Pantone held in his resentment and changed the subject.

"Let's settle down now," Pantone said. "We'll leave analytical talk for another day. Let's clear our minds of the clutter and step down ..."

Soon George was completely under once again.

"I'm in a tiny space in the forward part of the boat. It's called the forecastle, pronounced FOLK-sill or fo'c's'le. It's V-shaped. Not enough room for two people but I'm in here with six. It's hot. We're sweating, but so used to it, we hardly notice. The smell of stale sweat is sickening. Sun rays stream in through a tiny grate overhead. The boat's roll makes the rays slice across us in a continual, rhythmic pattern, like little square searchlights.

"I'm sitting in the middle, at a tiny, knife-scarred wooden table. I'm the center of attention. The new crew—those green, shanghaied men—is mixing with some of the seasoned crew. That scrawny guy, Pickering, is there. He looks like he's thrown up a few times. His nerves, anger, fear, and depression are all worsened with the roll of the boat. I call to him.

"'Pickering! Fresh air and a view of the horizon will cure what ails you.'

"Hollings chimes in, 'That and a musket ball!'

"The men laugh. I do, too, but there is ... tenderness beneath it. I watch Pickering climb topside. I feel bad for him. Part of me still thinks about him while I'm talking to the other guys.

"A greenhorn asks, 'Where are we headed?'

"'Most likely the Rose 'n' Crown,' I say.

"'Rose and Crown? Sounds like a pub,' he says.

"The guys are laughing. Me, too, but then I turn serious.

"'Rose 'n' Crown is no laughing matter,' I say. 'Of all the shoals around Nantucket, Rose 'n' Crown's the worst. She claims the most ships. Old Bolgers knows he just has to drift around in the area and wait. Sooner or a later, a ship will run itself aground and be ripe for the picking.'

"The men are shocked when I tell'm. They think they're on for some kind of rescue mission. That's what I showed'm on deck with the Lyle gun and breeches buoy. Even Bolgers presents himself that *way to better his image in town. Nantucket Life Savers, he calls us. There's a real group like that, started over in Surfside, but that ain't us. Bolgers just paid'm off enough to use the name. That way he can plunder with impunity, even look like he's doing the world a service. Any 'service' is to himself.*

"What we are is wreckers. We plunder wrecks— stranded and sinking ships—for all the goods they carry. Sometimes we buy them goods off the victims for pennies on the dollar in exchange for their safety.

"If it was up to Bolgers, he'd leave them all there to drown. More than once he says 'I'm not paid a penny for human cargo.' I'd like to shove those words down his throat someday. I've pushed him into rescue missions. He's hated me for it, but he always takes the credit when we get back."

Pantone could see the anger that was building inside his subject. George seethed with hatred. Soon the toxic levels would be too high. Pantone decided to keep him under but redirect him.

"Take a deep cleansing breath now. Match your breathing to the beating of your heart. Feel the rhythm of your body and let yourself slowly synchronize with it."

Once he saw that George had calmed a bit, Pantone gave him a slight suggestion. "It feels so stuffy in here, so hot. Let's climb up on deck. Feel that crisp sea breeze. Smell the salt in it ... Tell me what you see ..."

"I climb up through the fo'c's'le hatch onto the foredeck, near the bow. The day has gotten late and a stiff cold wind is cat's pawing across the water. Pickering is there, looking off from the starboard rail. I can see the pain on his face. I feel bad for him. I step over to him.

"'Come on,' I say. 'You're in with us now. You'll like it if you let yourself.' Pickering doesn't respond

to me. He only smirks, as his eyes get glassy.

"Hollings climbs up through the hatch now. I hope I can keep things private with Pickering. That's what he needs. I tell Pickering, 'You're part of the crew now … part of us … like every plank is part of a good ship.'

"Pickering doesn't look at me. He keeps looking at the water as he says, 'Is that an old sailor's platitude?'

"I never heard that word before. I feel a bit stupid. Hollings laughs at the word. I snap at him. I tell him not to show his ignorance. I know I'm on thin ice. Hollings challenges me, 'Okay, what does it mean then?'

"I don't want to bullshit about it, but now it's a point of pride. I don't know what to say. I know a platter is like a kind of plate, but it seems stupid to take a chance on saying it. Pickering saves me from embarrassment by explaining that a platitude is like an old saying that people have. He says they're usually something romanticized. He says there's plenty of them that sailors have, like when they talk about their boats like they were women, something living."

Pantone saw a shift in George, a deepening of his emotions.

"I tell him they are something living. They're not merely things to get us around. A ship is built from living things that don't just die. They keep on living. Every ship has her own peculiar nature. She tests the quality of a man. She punishes, rewards, forgives. She talks to you. She tells you what she needs by the sound of the wind through her rigging or by the luff of her sails, by the strain of her masts or the creak of her hull."

As George continued to speak, Pantone became

mesmerized himself. George had drifted deeper than Pantone could ever have brought him. The core beliefs of his former incarnation were coming up through him, filling him with all the emotion of a life experience he'd never before realized. George's tone changed from wistfully romantic to somber.

"When she dies ... founders on those shoals and starts to break up ... you can hear her screams. She screams like an animal caught in a trap. There's fear and pain in every splinter of it. She pleads with you to save her or to put her out of her misery. Those who've heard it will always know. They'll never forget it."

George fell silent. His glassy eyes remained focused on some fixed point of significance in the private world his brain was creating for him. Pantone watched him with growing concern. He worried that George had somehow slipped beyond his grasp. He was afraid to shake him or even touch him. He started calling to him gently.

"George?"

No response. No change of focus or expression.

"George? George is that what you told Pickering?"

Still no change.

"GEORGE—WERE YOU TALKING TO PICKERING?"

Finally, George's eyes refocused. Still in the trance, he said, *"Yes ... Pickering ... They've all gone below now except for the dog watch. I'm alone with the stars."*

Pantone breathed a sigh of relief. "George, we're stepping up now, up the winding staircase of years ..." He worked on him gently through that long road back to his present self.

Once George had come back fully, he slumped in

his seat, completely drained from the experience.

Pantone checked his vital signs. "I thought I lost you there for a second."

"I remember," George said.

Pantone stopped what he was doing. "What do you remember?"

"Ships ... They do die like that. It was like all of my rescue experiences were ganged up together. I saw them all at once. Experienced them, I should say."

George went on to tell Pantone all about the daring and tragic rescues he had performed, about getting as close as they could to sinking ships in the middle of storms and shooting that padded canon ball over, then, with freezing fingers, tying the breeches buoy onto the line. How, trusting with his life that it was secure enough, he would pull himself over to the ailing ship as both vessels bobbed wildly out of sync with each other in the storm tossed, confused sea. Then, one by one, he'd save as many as possible.

He talked of babies dying in his arms, of having to knock out one woman whose panic kept her from getting on the buoy with him, then carrying her dead weight across to safety, only to lose her to frostbite the next morning. Every trip was a cheat of death, and every time he went, not just willingly, but he fought to go. He needed to be the one doing the saving, making the difference. He needed to be the caretaker, the protecting father.

When George was finished, Pantone was completely spent just from listening to him. "I thought you said you were just wreckers."

"That's why I had to fight to go," George said. "Bolgers would just as soon let them all die if there were no loot to plunder. That goddamned plaque by the bank, it's a fucking lie!"

"Maybe it should be your face on there?" Pantone said gently as he prepared to leave.

"You're going?"

"If I'm this drained," Pantone said, "you've got to be completely wiped."

Pantone bid George goodnight and slipped out of the cell. George lay back on his cot and tried to sleep. He thought about those painful cries of the sinking ships. He could remember the way the wood seemed to call to him. He then remembered the planking of the stairs at the Quahog B&B and the way that every creak had made him feel. It all started to make sense to him.

FORTY-SIX

Even with his great fatigue, it was hard for George to shake off the excitement of what was happening. After about an hour, sleep did find him as he stretched out on the jail cell cot. Unfortunately, the sleep was short-lived.

George was shocked into wakefulness by the sound of a wastebasket thrown against the bars. He sprang to his feet. There, before him, separated by the bars, was a sneering and seething Bolgers.

"These bars ... Are they like your father's were at MacLean?"

"MacLean?"

"The mental institution. Wasn't that your Dad's part-time address?"

"You fucking ..."

George lunged for Bolgers through the bars. Bolgers jumped back out of reach like a kid teasing a dog at the end of his leash.

"Temper, temper. Don't make it any easier for me to put you in there. That would take all the sport out of it."

"You slimy piece of shit! You don't have the power to—"

"On the contrary. Your family history, combined with your documented episodes and delusions while here on Nantucket, should make it a slam dunk as they say."

"It's still a free country!"

"Not when you're a danger to yourself and others. You've no family to vouch for you—I've checked into that. As Mayor, my duty and my power to accomplish that duty are quite clear."

In a rage, George reached frantically through the bars at Bolgers, like that dog on the leash, too angry to understand his restrictions. Bolgers merely laughed.

"If you had half a pair of balls, you'd come closer to this cage," George shouted.

"I've nothing to prove to you. Only to the Massachusetts Court. That should be a cakewalk. It's not so hard when the Mayor himself is signing the commitment papers."

"You try it! I'll go to the press. I'll expose you for what you are!"

"Well then, I'll just add paranoia to the diagnosis. After that, you can have your fifteen minutes of fame. You can spew all of the 'black helicopter' theories you like. It'll all just strengthen my case."

"You FUCKing ..."

"You have a nice night now."

Bolgers left as if he didn't even hear the screams and curses that George flung behind him.

A few minutes after Bolgers was gone, Harry Beal stepped in timidly to check on George.

"Did you hear any of that?" George barked.

"I heard it. Hyannis probably heard it. Boston, maybe."

"He can't do any of that shit. He's a fucking buffoon."

George liked how "fuck" had risen from his self-talk to his actual talk. It was a power usually first appreciated by teenagers. He didn't mind being a late bloomer.

Harry hemmed and hawed a bit before answer-

ing. "Bolgers doesn't have much in the way of respect ... but he does have power. If I was you, I'd be
thinking in terms of a quick getaway."

"Whose side are you on?"

"I'm Sweden."

"More like Vichy France, I think."

That hit Harry like a knife. He thought of the
many times he'd promised himself that he would
stand up to Bolgers and then caved. Each individual failure, each ripple of self-doubt, now joined
with other ripples until they became a tsunami.
George could hear the flutter in Beal's voice as he
spoke.

"Look, I'll be happy to let you out in time to
catch the first morning ferry. In fact, I'll drive you
there myself. I don't care if it IS my ass."

"No thanks," George said. "I've got to see this
through."

"See WHAT through? Maybe he's right? Maybe
you ARE crazy?"

"I don't know what I'm chasing here. I do know
that, if I let myself get scared off, I'll have put myself in a worse place than that bozo could ever put
me."

Harry looked at him with admiration and a bit of
envy—envy because he wished that he'd been the
one who'd made the definitive stand against Bolgers.

FORTY-SEVEN

George sat up into the morning light as Pantone was let into his cell. Harry quietly left them alone without speaking one word.

"I'm on a tighter deadline than I thought, Doc."

"I know. Harry told me."

Pantone looked over to the closed door that led to Harry's office. He held that gaze as he spoke. "Officer Beal's a good man, you know."

"I know. I don't think he knows."

"That's the tragedy sometimes."

Pantone looked back at George.

"Well, I guess we shouldn't waste time," Pantone said as he took a seat with George.

"Is there a way to speed things up? Get me to Rebecca faster?"

"You mean go through the abridged version of your past life?"

"Something like that. I feel a real urgency. Time might be running out."

"Yes, in both lives. You're being shown what you need to know. I'm not controlling it. Some deep part of you is."

Pantone started the slow processes of leading George down to where he needed to be. When the time was finally right and George had arrived at the depth of his being, Pantone again said, "Tell me what you see."

"Apple trees. I'm in an orchard on a hillside near the four windmills, overlooking Nantucket town. I take the hand of ... the hand of Rebecca! She's here! She's with me!"

The excitement started to lift George from his trance. Pantone gently guided him back to a deeper level, calming his excitement just enough for George to stay there and keep describing the event.

"We're running together through the high grass. We stop to look down over the town. Rebecca says to me, 'I so love it up here above the stench of tar, coal soot, and whale blubber.'

"'I'd not realized your distaste for the trappings of modern life,' I tell her.

"We start to walk along the crest of the hill toward the apple trees. The windmills swish and rattle and creak as their blades spin. They're like ramshackle Ferris wheels almost out of control. They are beautiful and fearsome at the same time.

"She says, 'The oil industry has crowded out the world that God meant for us to have.'

"I tell her, 'The oil is from God. He made the whale. It brings Nantucket fame and fortune.'

"'And why then,' she says, 'have you not gone into the hunt?'

"'I'm not a killer of things bigger than my finger,' I say. 'Need a bug squashed, I'm your man.'

"We both chuckle but I wonder if I've come off too weak, afraid of the whale. I don't dare look at her eyes, not yet. We're on a date, a rantum scoot of sorts."

Pantone risked disrupting George's state to ask, "A what?"

"A rantum scoot. It's an old Nantucket phrase—it means playing around, free form, having fun."

Pantone was glad that George wasn't so fully in his hypnotic state that he couldn't answer. He didn't want to lose him again, and he wanted George to be able to view Rebecca with enough perspective to know some things his former self might not have known.

George continued to speak:

"I know we're on a date, but I'm not sure how much we know each other. We're making small talk. I'm uncomfortable with small talk. She's ... beautiful. I wish I knew how I was coming across. I do know! I can see us both together! We're falling in love!"

Pantone smiled at himself for having made the right decision.

"I'm beside her again. I take her hand more tightly. I feel more confident. I want to turn her to me and kiss her. She breaks free and runs ahead.

" 'We need apples!' she yells.

"My moment is ruined. I walk after her, barely keeping up.

" 'It's September. They'll still be green,' I say.

" 'The younger the better!' she calls back to me, 'Before age drains them of character.'

"The more playful, strong, and witty she is, the more I fall in love with her. I finally catch up to her as she's climbing one of the apple trees.

"I playfully scold her, 'Hasn't the Bible taught you about the wickedness of apple-picking women?'

" 'Has age drained your character?' she asks. 'Have you forgotten how to climb?'

" 'A schooner's rigging has kept me current on that score,' I tell her.

"I feel bad when I think of the schooner—of Bol-

gers and all the tragedies that being with Rebecca has let me forget. The schooner is an unwanted intrusion, but it's something worse, too. I brush it from my mind.

"She's already halfway up the tree. I bound up past her like a big brother might.

"I call down to her. 'Hurry up slow poke!'

"'So that's what has become of chivalry?' she jokes. 'Climb right past a lady. Some hero you are.'

"I put on a funny exaggerated formality and say, 'A thousand pardons, Madame. Please give me your delicate hand.'

"Going with the joke, she holds out her hand in an exaggerated, ladylike way. I take hold of her and pull her up to me. She sits on the branch just below mine. She reaches up and plucks an almost ripe apple. I watch her chomp down on it. The juice runs out the sides of her mouth and down her chin. It's the sexiest thing I've ever seen. I'm nervous with the silence. I try and make conversation.

"'Riper than I thought,' I say. 'It's going to be an early winter.'

"She takes another bite. This time she notices the dribble on her chin. She laughs at it. I laugh, too. As the laughing stops, we are staring deeply into each other's eyes. I'm overcome with passion for her. My throat closes. I have no words to speak. Her eyes tell me she shares the feelings. From them, I get the confidence to reach down to her.

"Seeing no protest, I reach further, hoping to brave a kiss. To steady myself, I place my hand beside her on the branch where she sits. My added weight is too much for it. Just before our lips make contact, the branch snaps. Rebecca falls about three feet and lands on a lower, thicker branch. She loses her balance and starts to slip from there. This time it will be a long fall to the ground.

"I quickly loop my legs around my branch and stretch down to grab her and bring her up to me.

Once she is secure, I settle us both on the thicker branch. I can see she is rattled and short of breath, but she is relieved.

"She says, 'Well, I suppose you are my hero after all.'

"We sit there quietly for a moment while we catch our breath. I'm bursting with love for her or lust or both. I can't tell the difference.

"She says, 'It seems that God himself has offered his opinion on your advances.'

"'Perhaps it was an opinion on your eating his apples?' I reply."

Pantone watched George laugh at his own cleverness. Then, as George continued, his tone darkened.

"I can see something distant in her eyes, something bad. I fear that she's having second thoughts about me. I have to know. I press my luck and lean in again to kiss her.

"She stops me short by saying, 'I sail for England in two days.'

"I feel like I've been kicked in the stomach. I can only eke out one word. 'Why?'

"She tells me, 'That school I've talked about—the wayward children. I've a chance to bring a group here. They can start a new life in Nantucket.'

"I'm desperate. I grab at any straw. 'And your father will put up with that? You traipsing around the globe?'

"'He'll be gone on a whale hunt for the next three years. He can hardly object. In fact, I sail with him as far as The Azores. That's where he'll turn south and I'll continue on to England.'

"I can't hide my hurt from her. She sees it in my eyes.

"She says, 'Relax. I'll take a fast packet home

with the children. With luck, I'll be back by Christmas.'"

Pantone could see that George was in distress. Tears streamed from the corners of his eyes. Pantone brought him out of his state as quickly as he could safely do so.

When George returned to his fully wakened state, he exploded with rage.

"Why did you bring me out? I've lost her! She's lost! Put me back under."

"I'm starting to worry about you in these sessions."

"I don't care!"

"I am a doctor. My patient's safety has to be my primary concern. I seem to remember taking an oath like that. I think we've done all of the sessions that I can—"

"One more day!" George cut in. "Just put me under one more time."

Harry Beal stepped into the room just in time to hear George's pleading.

Beal said, "If I don't get you on a boat by tomorrow morning, Bolgers will own your ass. It'll be too late for me to help you."

"What's Bolgers' beef?" Pantone asked.

"Our off-islander here embarrassed him, screwed up his little show. Bolgers is like a pit bull when he goes after someone."

"There may be more to his anger than even Bolgers knows," Pantone said. "What can he really do, though?"

"There's the B&E thing," Beal said. "Bolgers is already talking to the 'Staties.'"

"The State Police? Do they have the jurisdiction to interfere?" Pantone asked.

"Who knows? I never underestimate his power to make shit happen. If I try and stop him after the ball really gets rolling, MY butt will be in a sling."

George fired back, "Forget about your butt for once!"

Beal looked truly hurt. "I'm trying to save YOUR butt."

"I'll take care of my own." George spun to Pantone. "I need one more day!"

"We have come a long way down this road to just turn back," Pantone said.

Harry looked at both of them as he thought about it. "If I go head-to-head with Bolgers, I'm done here on Nantucket. I'll have to move to Florida or some shit."

Pantone and George looked back at Beal. They were now united about continuing. Beal saw the new courage on George's face. He thought about how he'd dismissed George as a loser early on. Shame flooded over Beal as he reflected on his own failures of nerve when it came to Bolgers.

Finally, Beal said, "Okay, one more day."

Beal turned and went back to his office. Pantone and George turned to each other, silently sharing the victory.

FORTY-EIGHT

George was up with the sun, eager for this last effort. He knew that he was on the right track now but still had no idea what he could do with what he discovered. How could he use it to help Rebecca?

It was an hour before Pantone came through the door, one of the longest hours George had ever spent. They dispensed quickly with pleasantries and got right into the session. George felt the ease with which he could now travel down this familiar road. He reached his former plateau, the one he'd spent most sessions in, and sank right past it, going deeper. Soon he was on Bolgers' schooner again, trying to warm his fingers over a wood-barrel fire on the portside deck, amidships.

He spoke to Pantone:

"It's frigid cold. I can't get myself warm. There's a hole in my heart that I've carried for months now, since I last saw Rebecca. It's taken a toll on me. I feel less sure of myself, less able to stand up to Bolgers. Bolgers senses it. He's running me extra hard, trying to break me while he has the chance. It's been working, though I'm still putting up a fight.

"Hollings comes up on deck. His pea coat is wrapped around three layers of clothes, but he's still doing that stiff, funny dance to keep warm. Even

when his mouth is closed, steam puffs from his nostrils like he's some great dragon. It comes out of my nose, too. Snow starts to swirl around haphazardly and disappear into the dark green waves.

"Hollings says, 'We're barely into December, and it feels like mid-January!'

"I just stare into the waves. I'm in no mood for conversation. Still I say, 'The Gulf Stream usually keeps snow from these waters. The Labrador Current must be forcing it down, keeping it south.'

"Hollings says, 'Aye, it's a bad sign.'

"Then Bolgers screams from the quarterdeck. 'All hands! All hands!'

"Crewmen scramble up on deck. Hollings smiles at me and says, 'Old Bolgers is taking your job.'

"I tell him, 'I've no will for shouting, these days.'

"'So I've noticed,' he says.

"We both cross to the starboard side to see what's exciting Bolgers so much. We're coming up on a three-masted schooner. She's twice the size of us. She's waterlogged, sunk up to her gunwales. She's sitting on a reef. She'll sink no further.

"It's not so terrible an area as the Rose 'n' Crown, but still it's a spot ripe for the plunder. I watch for Bolgers' hand-sign. When I get it, I yell to the crew, relaying his orders.

"'Drop your headsails!' I say.

"Once that's done, I shout, 'Brace up the fore! Brace up the main!'

"This is to spill the wind from the sails so's we can slide to a stop right alongside the wreck. We'll need no breeches buoy here. The water's deep enough for our keel, and the waves are slight, so we can come right up to the rail. As we get close, I notice that there's not a soul aboard. It's eerily still and quiet.

"Perhaps they've all abandoned ship? I think. I hope so. One lifeboat still rocks in its portside davits. Maybe the crew all fit in the other one on the star-

board side? Those davits are empty. I take relief from that.

"As we slide to a stop, Bolgers hops over to the swamped ship's deck. He splashes into an inch of seawater. He is happy that there are no people to deal or dicker with. Whatever he finds will be his free and clear. Once he looks in the hold, he's ready to dance a jig. He sticks his head out and yells to us. 'Christmas has come early men! Come on over and feast your eyes.'

"Hollings, Gordon, and even Pickering beat me across to the doomed boat. I just don't have the enthusiasm to move fast. When I finally get there and look down into the hold, I see crates stacked as high as the beams. All of them contain Irish whiskey. Normally, I might think of the party that lies ahead or of my share in the profit, once these are offloaded and sold in town. Today, I only think of the labor involved with transferring those crates to our boat. My depressed mood has drained the strength from my muscles.

"Hollings slaps me on the back. 'Come on, Samson,' he says. 'We've got a day of hard work ahead of us.'

"I'm sure he meant Samson both ways. For the strength I've always had and the way I've let a woman sap it. I'm not sure why I've let it hit me so hard. I ask myself that question a lot. I've always been independent. I've never needed anybody. I've not even lost her. She said it wasn't good-bye. She'd probably be back by Christmas. It's the first time I've felt need, felt less than whole by myself. I hate the feeling. If this is love, I should toss love over the side right now. Watch it sink to the bottom and be done with it. Hollings is right. There's work to do. It is time to put a cork in this female-styled self-pity and get to it.

"I help the men form a fire line of sorts. We pass the whiskey crates along from inside the swamped

ship's hold, over the rail to our deck and then into our hold. The work feels good on my tired arms. I feel my strength coming back and along with it some of my old self-assured attitude. I smile to myself as I think of the age-old battle men fight between women and whiskey. It's always been a choice that defines the kind of man you'll be. The two things can never live together in harmony. Now here I am at that battle's nexus passing the whiskey between my hands while I ponder my desire for this woman. Right now, I hope the whiskey wins out so I can return to being the man I used to be.

"By the time the booty is transferred, we are all dead tired. Now our schooner is weighted down far beyond safe levels. She's riding so low in the water that the small wavelets of this calm sea state are licking and oozing through the scuppers. Any kind of sea worth mentioning will wash right through us.

"The work has taken most of the day. The sun is far to the west and radiating little to no heat. Bolgers assembles us on deck. Feeling like the great benefactor, he pulls out two bottles of whiskey from a crate, telling us that we've earned sharing the bottles as a bonus for our good work. I suppose we're all expected to get down on our knees to him now in thanks.

"Bolgers uncorks the first bottle and swills a full quarter of it before passing it along. As he watches it circulate, he uncorks the second bottle and takes healthy hits off of that, consuming nearly half. Sharing two bottles between us has been redefined. The last men to drink will have nothing left but spit and fumes.

"Once I would've fought Bolgers on this, but what's the point? These blokes wouldn't appreciate it anyway.

"Finally, we set full sail and plow through the water on a slow crawl for Nantucket. We are barely making two or three knots. We could walk faster. I'm *near the quarterdeck where I can hear and relay orders from Bolgers. Hollings is at the bowsprit staring forward on watch. He has a spyglass that he uses off and on for closer inspection.*

"We've been under sail about an hour when I see Hollings snap the spyglass to his face. He calls back to us. 'Black Baller on the Rose 'n' Crown!' he shouts.

"I call back to Bolgers' relaying the message. 'Black Baller on the Rose 'n' Crown, sir!'

"'I heard! I heard!' he spits.

"'Shall we change course?' I ask.

"'Nonsense! We're full to our scuppers. We're heading home.'

"'But a Black Baller is a passenger vessel,' I argue.

"'Precisely my point!' Bolgers bellows. 'I'm paid for cargo. I'm paid not a penny for human life.'

"'They could be drowning!' I shout.

"Bolgers acts disgusted, like I'm saying something so stupid, a green hand should know it.

"He says, 'You know as well as I that they'll not sink past their scuppers on those shoals. That's why they got goddamned caught on them.'

"'The right thing is to go to them,' I argue.

"'Stop being an old lady,' he says, grinning at what he sees as my weakness. 'We'll go home, unload, and then, in the morning, we'll check on them.' He sneers triumphantly at me. 'Don't worry your pretty little head about it,' he says.

"I want to rip his face off. I want to take over the boat. I look around at the other crewmembers nearby. They're pretending not to have listened. They don't care. I'd be alone if I tried to fight Bolgers. In my self-pitying state what good would I be?

"I keep quiet. We go to Nantucket. In the hours it takes to sludge through the water to town, night falls completely. Along with the dark, comes a bitter cold. The wind picks up, slicing us to the bone. It's the

coldest night I can remember.

"In the morning, we have to chip the ice off the bow and stern lines just to shove off. The still waters of the inner harbor are crusted with the ice. Saltwater almost never freezes. Even icebergs and growlers are fresh water, broken off of glaciers. We heat water from the stove just to pour over the belayed halyard lines so we can raise sail.

"We make our way to the Rose 'n' Crown shoals. Hollings spots the Black Baller on the horizon. I join him at the bow to watch our approach. The sun is fully up now, and the sky is that crystal blue that only a cold day can give you.

"We watch the ship slowly grow closer. She looks none the worse for wear. Most of her sails seem to be furled, except for that foremast topsail, the one with that logo of theirs, the black ball in the middle of the white sail. The sail wasn't tied off. It hangs loose from the yardarm, like a curtain. A lone puff of wind rolls around slowly inside of its cheeks, billowing the sail up and out before spilling out the sides."

Suddenly the present-day George froze up and lifted from his hypnotic state. Seeing that black ball struck fear in his heart the same as that hockey puck had way back in the bar with Jim and Ray that night.

"What's wrong?" Pantone demanded.

"I'm done."

"Done!"

"All done. Time to go home now."

George's voice was weaker and smaller than it had ever been. He was scared to the bone. Pantone could never let it end like this.

"You're the one who demanded this day. You have to see it through."

"I've seen it. Time to go now."

"You can't quit a race right before the finish line."

"And you can't hypnotize a guy who doesn't want to be hypnotized."

"That sounds like a challenge," Pantone said.

George smirked as he started to get up and call for Harry Beal.

Pantone physically sat him back down on the bed. "Officer Beal is out. It's just you and me. We're locked in here together for a while."

Pantone could see the fear in George's eyes. Pantone reached out to touch his shoulder and comfort him.

"Look," Pantone started, "you're probably right about hypnotizing a guy against his will. So, why don't you let me try? If you don't really want to go under, you won't. If deep down you really do, I'll be there with you the whole way through."

George thought about it as he tried to gather his courage. He thought about how far he'd come, about Rebecca, the object of his mission. Could he let her down? The answer was obvious.

With a deep breath, George said, "Okay."

George closed his eyes. Pantone started slowly, carefully, trying to ease him back to the spot as safely as possible. He gently held George's hand the whole time.

After a long and slow descent, George arrived there. He started to describe it.

"Because of the shallow depth of the shoals, we can't get our schooner close enough for direct boarding. The water is relatively calm—there is no need for the breeches buoy so we take the long boat.

"Bolgers stands piously at the stern as eight of us row to the ship. Hollings, Gordon, and Pickering are among them. As we come alongside, I first see them. They look like ornaments on a sparse Christmas tree. I can't make out what they are at first. Perhaps my brain won't let me?"

Pantone saw George's face curdle with pain. Tears built in George's tightly clenched eyes. The doctor in Pantone started to worry, but they'd come too far now. He let things go on.

"They are children, lashed to the rigging and first yardarm. I see no movement in them. I hear no crying out. The silence is ominous.

"As we slide to a stop, I scramble up to the ship's deck, transfixed by those lashed figures the whole time. As soon as my feet hit the deck, I know the worst. Death permeates the air. The ship reeks of it. As much as I don't want to, I know I have to climb the ice-coated ratlines to reach those kids. I know in my heart that there will be no saving, just retrieving. My stomach sickens, putrefies, and shrivels inside me like a prune.

"I reach the first child, a boy of maybe eight or nine. His tears have frozen over his eyes, turning them to cloudy balls of ice. His little fingers are clutched around the shroud. I try to release them, but they are frozen so tightly and stiffly. I get a purchase under his index finger and pull hard. His finger snaps like a crisp piece of celery. The sound echoes around my head. My soul drops out through me."

Pantone studied George as he spoke. After the initial showing of pain, there were no overt flutters of emotion, just a nearly monotone retelling. He had retreated to some protective place in order to relive this. Maybe it was the same place he was driven to when it first occurred? Maybe it was the same place from which he had lived most of his present life?

George continued:

"I look around at the other children, tied or dangling from other spots in the rigging. I know they will all be the same. I instantly know what must have

happened. This isn't the result of some sadistic punishment or abuse.

"*When the boat started taking on water, with no rescue in sight, they must have thought that even if the boat sank deep enough to submerge the deck, in these shallow waters, it wouldn't sink all the way to the first yard. They figured the children would be safer in the rigging.*

"*I look down to the deck. The rest of the crew is fanning out in search of survivors. Bolgers saunters behind them, not caring one way or the other about survivors. I look around again at the frozen little souls tied to various spots around the masts, rigging, and yards. It's hard to look, but harder not to. The poor kids will have to wait for the sun to warm them enough for removal of their bodies.*

"*I start to climb down. When I hit the deck, I meet up with Hollings. We walk aft together. We break through the aft cabin door. This would be the captain's quarters. A lone lamp still flickers in there, generating scant warmth. A stove fire had recently burned. Though it is now out, its smell and warmth still fills the room. We see the Captain sitting motionless in his chair.*

"*It takes a moment for me to realize that his eyes are vacant, like black buttons, and the back of his head is gone. Brain matter clings to the wood paneling behind him. A hand musket dangles from his forefinger. Hollings and I stare at each other, silently acknowledging the guilt and trauma that must have driven him to this.*

"*In the silence, we hear a feeble tapping. We listen closer. There is a muffled voice. It comes from a hatch leading to a lower deck. I yell to Hollings.*

"'*Get a light over here!*'

"*I run to the hatch. Hollings follows me with that lamp from the captain's desk. I fling open the hatch cover. There, trapped in frigid, waist-deep water, is Rebecca!*"

George fluttered up into his present-day self just long enough to say, "She's wearing the same dress she wore when she first spoke to me at The Quahog."

Pantone knew instantly that he was referring to the present time. Then, just as quickly, George was back, again, in the 1840s.

"She must've dressed hastily when the ship hit. The top part of her front is undone. I see the top of some silk-like undergarment and ... the very tops of her ... The rose petal pouch she'd gotten from her mother, is hanging on a string from her neck. I can see it ... between the tops of ... her breasts."

Pantone could readily see arousal moving in to sit with George's terror. They were uneasy bench mates. A squeak of shock came from somewhere deep within George's lungs.

"Her eyes widen as she sees me. Maybe it's love, maybe just relief? She opens her mouth to talk but only shivers come out. I tell her not to try talking. My brain is on fire trying to figure the right course of action. I've saved many people in many situations, but suddenly I'm a novice.

"Though novice I may have become, I still must be the one in control. I reach in to pull her out but she's caught on something. She speaks to me apologetically, as if it were her fault almost. She says, 'My ankle ... I think it's broken. Something heavy is upon it.'

"I peer through the near black water and see nothing. Without a second's thought, I dive in, feeling her terrified body as I slide past her, forcing myself down to inspect the problem. My lungs are ready to explode as I survey it. Finally, I burst back up next to her, closer than if we were dancing.

"I tell her, 'A bureau or trunk of some sort has

tumbled onto your leg, keeping you from coming up.'

"She looks straight at me. Her eyes are shimmering pools of trust. She asks, 'The bureau, can you right it?'"

George rippled up to the present for an instant. "Right, not write!" Back under he went.

"*I just nod wildly to her, take a deep breath, and dive for the trunk. It won't budge. Trying to muscle it loose is a waste of time.*

"*From under the water, I can hear that the wind has changed, and waves are now battering the hull. I hear the groaning protests of the ship's frame, the wood's creaking calls of distress. There won't be much time. I spring for the water surface again and climb back out onto the cabin floor. I look down on Rebecca as I pant to replenish my lungs. She looks up at me. Her eyes plead for deliverance.*

"*She says again, 'Can you right it?'*

"*I scream to Hollings, 'Get a line over the cabin joists! I'll tie a clove hitch and we'll pull that trunk away!'*

"*Hollings snaps to it. 'Aye, Aye!' he says.*

"*As Hollings scrambles topside for a good length of line, Rebecca looks into my eyes. 'What of the children?' she asks.*

"*I haven't the heart to tell her. 'They're being taken off as we speak,' is all I say.*

"*Hollings returns with a thick length of halyard that will be perfect for the task. He tosses it over the thick beam that runs directly over the hatch hole. I grab the end and pull it through the beam. Then I dive quickly back into the hole and bring the end around the trunk. I surface with it, climb out, and proceed to tie my clove hitch. Hollings can see my hands shaking. He offers to tie the knot for me, but I push him away. For Rebecca, I must do it by myself.*

"*My fingers fumble on the knot like a green hand*

or landlubber, a coof, but I persist until it's fast.

"*Hollings and I both pull on the line. Slowly, the trunk starts to move. From the corner of my eye, I see Rebecca brighten as she feels herself being freed. The knot fails! The trunk falls back, trapping her even more painfully.*

"*Just then, at the worst of all times, the ship shifts from the force of the battering waves. It settles down deeper, sinking Rebecca to her chest. Sea-water pushes between her breasts ... Rose petals float loose and swirl around her. The ship lurches and sinks a little further. An iron batten falls across Rebecca's shoulders, bending her backwards. Fear and pain race through her eyes. She looks at me questioningly. It feels like an accusation. I dive across her.*

"*I pull on the batten as hard as I can. It won't move! I summon all of my last reserves of strength. Still nothing.*

"*She starts to sink further. My added weight is hurting her situation. I scramble back up to the floor and reach down to help free her from there. She has sunk so far that I can barely reach her. The water is up to her neck now.*

"*I wedge my legs around the hatch opening's frame and bend down toward her, like when we were in the apple tree. I strain every vertebra to the breaking point so I can reach her. Rebecca's gaze locks on me. Love and trust refuse to leave her eyes. I pull frantically on the batten.*

"*The ship is coming apart now. I can hear the groans and whines as complaining boards are split and ripped from the hull. Time is running out. The crumbling vessel sinks still further as she settles deeper into the shoal.*

"*Rebecca falls out of reach. Water swirls around and submerges her upturned face. She is now about three inches under the surface. Her eyes stay focused on me, but that love and trust turn to helpless fear and disappointment. Her eyes bulge with be-trayal.*

"I stretch down even further causing painful snaps in my back. Our faces are now about two feet apart, but I am helpless. She watches me for what seems like forever. Love slowly flows back into her eyes. Then she finally gives in to her lung's demand for breath. A bubble comes out of her mouth as water rushes in. I watch as her soul leaves her body. I watch those beautiful, loving eyes become emo-tionless, opaque disks. A last bubble escapes from her lungs. She passes from woman to corpse."

Pantone watched carefully as tears streamed down George's anguished face. Should he rescue George from his turmoil? No, he decided. George would never be whole if he didn't see this through. Pantone waited patiently for his subject to regain enough composure so that he could to continue. Finally, George started to speak again:

"I scream like an animal. I can't stop it. In a rage, I grab the gun from the dead captain's fingers and bound up on deck. I hear Bolgers barking at his crew before I get topside. He says, 'Let's get our asses off this wreck before it turns to flotsam!'

"I emerge on deck with the gun. Bolgers sees it and stops in his tracks. 'You'll hang if you ...' Bol-gers starts to say.

"I point the gun at him. That shuts him up. Rage pulsates through my body. I'm a hairsbreadth from pulling the trigger. My hand starts to shake. Self-hatred rolls across me. My hand shakes more and more violently. Bolgers stands there motionless, try-ing to hide his fear but afraid to make a move. Fi-nally, I turn the gun towards myself, put the barrel in my mouth and pull the trigger.

Pantone's rapt attention turned quickly to concern and then to fear as George fell silent. He ceased to breathe or function. Pantone sprung to him, checking vitals and screaming. "George! George!"

FORTY-NINE

The tiny jail cell was jammed with paramedics who were packing up to leave. George sat on the cot. His shirt was opened, and one sleeve was rolled up, hinting at the EMT work over he'd just received.

"You sure you don't want to come with us?" an EMT asked.

"No ... No, that's okay," George spoke in a sullen monotone.

The EMT studied George's face as he spoke. "We've gotten you stabilized so we can't force you to come with us, but it is our strong recommendation that you do. You should be checked out by a doctor."

Pantone stepped forward. "I AM a doctor."

With reluctance, the paramedics looked Pantone over and continued to pack up.

Beal and Pantone had been pushed to the fringes of activity when the paramedics first crowded around George to work on him. Beal had remained calm, leaning back with one foot against the wall. Pantone had been frantic, like a worrying parent. Now that the paramedics were readying to leave, he couldn't wait to talk with George. He pushed his way over. "George! What happened?"

It took all of his strength for George to lift his tired, defeated eyes and look at Pantone.

"Tell me what happened!" Pantone demanded.

As a paramedic closed his plastic case, he snapped sarcastically at Pantone, "Why don't you just ask him to sing and dance while you're at it?"

Pantone quieted as he realized that his excitement was eclipsing his sensitivity. He stood back with Beal and waited for the paramedics to clear out. They both watched George with concern, noticing that his pale cheeks had the slight flutter that indicated the presence of true, clinical shock.

As soon as the paramedics left, Pantone stepped over gingerly to George. He gently asked, "What happened?"

George looked at him as if he was just now noticing him in the room. He opened his mouth to speak, but no words came out. Finally, he eked out some syllables, but they were fractured by the flutter in his voice.

"She ... I ... It's over ... I'm going home now ... Time to go."

Harry saw that as his cue to step in. "The last ferry of the night leaves in one hour. You can be on it before Bolgers even knows you're gone."

Pantone tried to ignore Beal's words and hide his anger at him. He spoke directly to George. "You can't just walk off after this kind of experience. You need to process it."

George was starting to come around now. He was already "processing" more than he could bear. "I found out things I didn't want to know. I wish I'd never come here. This is why I don't take vacations. Let me just go home and forget."

Pantone couldn't drop it. "Why would you be shown things that you have no power to change? Nantucket's funny about time—"

"Stop it! It's probably been some crazy-assed delusion," George barked.

"Look at the way you can talk to me. Even in

your current attitude of defeat, you can stand up for yourself better than you could before. A delusion couldn't have done that for you. You've been shown an actual past. Maybe it's a past you can change?"

"You got a time machine up your sleeve?" George asked.

Harry Beal stepped over to them. He bent down and helped George to his feet as he spoke to Pantone. "Sorry, Doc, looks like you won't get rich writing a book on this one."

Beal helped George to the door. Pantone was at a loss for words. In his office, Beal picked up George's duffle bag for him, and they continued out to his squad car. Beal put George in the front passenger seat. As he rounded the hood to climb in the driver's side, he saw Pantone in the station doorway.

"Mind if I ride along in the squad car?" Pantone asked.

"Police cruiser," Beal said. "Got to have a squad to call it a squad car."

"Well, can I come?"

"Against the rules. If I let everybody ride, there'd be no room left for dangerous criminals."

Beal got in, planning to drive away before Pantone could respond. He knew Pantone was just angling for more time to convince George to stay. He wasn't going to fall for that bullshit.

Just as Beal put the car in gear, Bolgers' car rolled up, blocking him in. Bolgers slid out. Beal sprang from his driver's seat.

"Where are you taking this man?" Bolgers demanded.

"Gee, we thought we'd go on a picnic," Beal said.

"He's going nowhere!" Bolgers bellowed.

"Move your car," Beal said.

"If you dare interfere I'll—"

"You'll what? For years, I let you scare me with a

fucking ghost. You can't do shit."

Beal pushed past Bolgers. Bolgers grabbed Beal by the arm to pull him back. Beal spun and clocked Bolgers with a hard right hook. Bolgers went down. Beal slipped back into the squad car and banged Bolgers' car out of the way.

The ride through Nantucket's quiet, dusk-darkened streets felt long and silent. Both men had been through too much together to exchange small talk, and neither of them wanted to bring up anything of substance.

Finally, George said, "I'm sorry. I misjudged you before."

After a short, thought-filled silence, Beal replied, "No, you didn't."

They drove in more silence.

George said, "That won't end it you know. He'll be after you now."

"Screw him. He can't do me worse than I've done to myself all these years."

"Well, I want to thank you."

Beal said, "Maybe I should be thanking you?"

As they neared steamboat wharf, Beal's radio crackled to life. Millie's voice scratched through the tiny speaker. "We've got a disturbance at The Jared Coffin House. The pub."

Harry spoke through the plastic hand-mic. "I'm on it."

"Disturbance?" George questioned.

"Bar fight."

"And you said you didn't have a squad," George smiled slightly.

"Millie's not exactly a squad."

"Is she the whole rest of the force?"

"In summers, we've got a fleet. We could be *NYPD Blue*. After Labor Day, we go back to plain old N. P. D. That means a deputy in one more car and Millie on the switchboard. Not exactly *Super Cops*."

"You've got to get better movies to reference," George said.

Harry grinned as he nosed his car to a stop at the bottom of Broad Street. "There's your ferry. If you run, you'll still make it. I've got to head up the street and wreck someone's weekend."

George slid out and turned back for his duffle bag. Harry put out his hand. For an instant, George looked at it with surprise. Not many men had offered out their hands to George. It was a sign of respect he'd mostly learned to do without. There was a sincerity to it that touched him.

He leaned in and took Harry's hand. They locked eyes as they shook. George could feel the genuine affinity they shared.

"You make sure you catch that ferry now."

"And you go fight crime."

George leaned back out of the car and shut the door. As George watched Harry barrel up Broad Street with all of his cop lights flashing, the true depths of his traumatic ordeal opened up to him.

For all that he'd gone through, all of the emotional devastation, there was no self-pity in his heart. For as long as he could remember, self-pity had been his secret friend. It had also been the past-life George's undoing. Now it was gone, and he didn't even miss it. It was replaced by a fresh strength, a confidence that told him he could take whatever may come.

He grieved hard for Rebecca and for the man who he once was, the man his soul inhabited all those years ago. But this was a healthy grief, not one more thing to wallow in.

As George watched Harry's car come to a stop way off at the top of Broad Street, he remembered the ferry. He spun to see it, still more than a football field away. The giant steel tongue it had laid out for trucks and cars to drive across was slowly rising up to its seaworthy position. Crewmen were casting off the lines.

"Shit!"

George ran as fast as he could with his duffle. As he reached the ferry, it had already pulled away from the dock. He thought he might be able to make the jump and put on an extra burst of speed. At the last possible second, he realized that it was an impossible leap to make. He stopped short at the very edge of the dock. The bag flew past him. Its inertia almost dragged George into the sea, but he let it go just in time, saving himself. He watched his duffle sink into the ink-black sea.

A fisherman on his way to try his luck off the end of the pier had watched George almost go in the drink. He shook his head. "Jesus pal, if you fell in, they'd be fishing out an ice cube."

George smiled at the guy.

With no more words, the fisherman headed out toward his fishing spot beyond the glaring lights of the ferry landing.

George watched the ferry slowly disappear around Brant Point Light. He thought about what he'd been through since he'd first stepped off that fat boat for a long weekend. He thought about Rebecca, and his grief became too heavy to carry. He knew her request, his mission, was real and that he'd failed at it. He wanted to get off the island so he could start to heal, start to forget. Inside, he knew that there would be no forgetting and little or no healing.

He watched two Coast Guard vessels fire up and flash their lights as they readied themselves to chase the ferry. He knew who was behind that. *At least I won't have to worry about Bolgers for a little while.*

George wandered through town while deciding on his options. It all felt different to him somehow.

It was as if he'd lived here in his youth and now he was seeing it through older and wiser eyes. Tiny white lights shined warmly against the night from Christmas wreaths and trees done up in Victorian splendor. Many shops that would normally be closed for the season were open now for the Christmas Stroll, offering free warm apple cider. George took some to sip as he walked.

Somewhere off in the distance, carolers were singing. Their voices sounded young, innocent, pristine. The festive mood contrasted sharply with George's inner state. He began to doubt that he'd ever escape the torment of what he'd been shown. He fixated on the memory of Rebecca's eyes in those last, living seconds.

Now I know now why I was born hating myself, he thought. Suddenly he felt as if every bad image he'd ever had of himself was validated by what the hypnosis had shown him, every bad fortune was deserved. He quickly started to sink lower than he'd ever felt in his life, lower than when he first came here.

He stepped into an antique store and helped himself to more warm cider, hoping desperately to find something to at least distract him enough to ease his pain. He quickly looked over tables and tables of junk. He started to absentmindedly flick through a rack of old used clothes.

He stopped with utter shock. There, on the rack, was the billowing shirt that Rebecca had first bought him. He lifted the shirt with gentle reverence. It was threadbare from a century and a half's worth of wear, but it was the very same shirt. The faded mark of her lipstick smear was still on the chest closure.

George never considered for a moment that it might be some other shirt with some other stain, that this might be mere coincidence. No, he knew in his bones that a truth was operating beyond logic.

Soon, George was wearing that shirt, with no coat over it, strutting boldly down Straight Wharf toward the sea.

The temperature had dropped. Stray snowflakes swirled in the black sky. A fierce crosswind tore at the Christmas wreaths that were hung on the lampposts for the Christmas Stroll. The corner of George's shirt with the faded pink mark of Rebecca's lips slapped wildly against his chest. He was oblivious to the weather.

As he walked, the few passersby he encountered were alarmed at the sight of him. Most cut a wide arc around him. The combination of his determined face, his lack of proper clothes, and his unwavering direction towards the end of the wharf said only one thing to them—jumper, suicide. Most people didn't want to think about it, preferring the comfort of denial. Others didn't want to risk being attacked or being the one who became the last straw that pushed him over. George never even noticed the cold or the other people. In his mind, he was alone with the night, in his own world.

As he pushed on further, a lone fisherman called out to him, "Hey, buddy, think it over. Things aren't that bad!"

George passed him by with no acknowledgement. He came to the edge and stopped, his toes teetering over the side. His heart raced as he looked down into the black and beckoning waves. He became mesmerized by their rhythmic lift and fall. Plumes of steam billowed from his quickened breath and wrapped around his head. In this endless moment of decision, thoughts ransacked his brain. Did those waves hold an answer, a solution, or merely death? Did he have the courage to find out? He knew that everything had led to this moment. His heart skipped as he saw rose petals floating on the water's undulating surface. His breathing fell in sync with the pulsing of the waves.

In the warm glow of lights outside of The Jared Coffin House, Harry Beal was letting two drunk kids talk their way out of a night in jail. His radio crackled. He reached in and grabbed his hand-mic.

"Go."

Millie's static-riddled voice said, "We have a potential jumper at the end of Straight Wharf."

"Shit!" Beal said mostly to himself as he waved off the kids and jumped in to his cruiser. Then he realized who that jumper just might be. "SHIT!"

He gunned the car into action with sirens and lights blazing. He did a quick three-point turn and headed down towards the water.

George stood on the brink of decision. The waves almost licked at his toes. He could hear Harry's siren in the distance but getting closer. There wasn't much more time to think. He looked out and saw the two Coast Guard vessels returning in the distance. Whatever he'd do, he'd have to do fast.

His eyes darted up to the bobbing sterns of pleasure boats tied in to slips nearby him. One boat's stern read LEAP OF FAITH. Another read NOW OR NEVER.

With a breath of brave commitment, George dove into the black waves. Onlookers screamed.

A woman yelled, "Call 911! Call 911!"

A man responded, "Call the morgue. He's dead already."

Harry sped his car up to the end of the wharf. He barely got it in park before spilling out onto the gravel and running, only to find that he was too late. He stared into the empty waves with heart-break in his eyes.

FIFTY

The water felt bracingly cold on George's already freezing body. The darkness embraced him as he breaststroked deeper. This would be the solution to his mission or the end of his suffering. He knew now that either would be preferable to living with the guilt of his failure.

He could slowly see his water world lighten from black to gray. His brain felt like it was collapsing in on him. The water's lightening continued. George started to see brightness.

Was this the universal doorway to death? Was it some waterlogged version of that thing all death survivors describe, that bright light they move forward to? These questions flickered through George's brain as it chilled. Along with them was a welcoming feeling of comfort, of being embraced by and cared for by something much bigger.

As the water continued to lighten, George no longer felt the cold. Color began to bleed into the gray of his world, tints of dark blue and green. It was day! Sunlight was penetrating through to him.

Suddenly he realized that his world had a ceiling, a rippling and undulating water surface about ten feet above him. He noticed something else— floating on that surface was the dark hull of a large boat or ship. George instinctually swam up toward it. Long before he got there, he knew what he would find.

His head broke the surface into the frigid air. There it was, Bolgers' schooner. Before George could have another thought, he was on the boat's strange and familiar deck. He was dry. He was sharing eyes and brain with the George of that time. For this miracle moment, they were one. He wasn't just reliving this life through trance so he could describe it and remember it. He was there fully as if the time that followed this moment hadn't happened yet.

George noticed that the boat was riding heavy in the water, nearly down to her scuppers. He saw Hollings at the bow, looking through his spyglass. George recognized him instantly, as if he'd only seen him five minutes before. Hollings shouted back to the crew.

"Black Baller on the Rose 'n' Crown!"

George snapped his head back to see Bolgers on the quarterdeck. He shouted to him, relaying the information.

"I heard. I heard," Bolgers sneered.

"Shall we change course?" George found himself asking.

"Nonsense! We're full to the scuppers. We're heading home."

"But a Black Baller is a passenger vessel."

"Precisely my point," Bolgers said. "I'm paid for cargo. I'm paid not a penny for human life."

"They could be drowning!" George shouted.

This was it: the crossroads of George's existence, his crisis of decision. He turned boldly to the helmsman standing next to Bolgers at the wheel. It was Pickering.

"Set a course for the Rose 'n' Crown!" George barked.

Bolgers' face went comical at the idea of his authority being challenged. "In what delirium are you?" Bolgers asked.

George focused his eyes on Pickering's frail, fear-filled face. "That'll be two points starboard, old Pick."

This was Pickering's own crisis of decision. Taken aboard under protest and forced to live the kind of "man's life" he'd thought he'd successfully avoided, would he now show courage or compliance?

Bolgers was so sure of his control that he spoke in a singsong voice to George, as if he were explaining an adult situation to a small child. "First of all, my dear boy, our boat is too heavily laden. We'd get stuck on the shoals ourselves."

"Very well!" George shouted. George dipped into the after cabin and quickly came back with his arms full of Irish Whiskey bottles that Bolgers had had them scavenge from that last ship. "Let's lighten it up some!" George tossed them all over the side. His crewmen looked on with sorrow and grief as they watched the bottles sink.

Bolgers' comic mood turned deadly. "You'll pay for that!"

George tossed more bottles overboard. "Two points starboard, Pick."

Bolgers slammed Pickering in the shoulder as he screamed, "Nantucket! Follow MY orders!"

George's eyes softened at Pickering, along with his voice. "Follow your heart."

Pickering hung motionless in a short moment of indecision. He started to look back and forth between both of them as he weighed his choices. Then a smile bloomed on his face, a brave, triumphant one. He spun the wheel to bring the boat around toward the Rose 'n' Crown. George jumped victoriously to the top of the aft hatch. He looked around at the wide-eyed faces of his gathered crew, newly enthused with the lust for mutiny. "It's our boat now!"

George turned forward to make sure that Hollings and those manning the headsails knew. As he did, Bolgers came up behind him and swung his brass-topped walking stick down hard on the back of his head. George teetered and fell to one knee. Blood splattered on his shoulder. As if it were one smooth, continuous motion, Bolgers brought his stick back up with full force, bashing it into George's face, exploding his nose. The upward blow brought George back up to near-standing position before he tipped backwards, falling to the deck, taking it full on the spine. The horrified crew looked on helplessly.

Bolgers stepped over to George, who still rolled on the deck in blood-drenched agony. "Any other man who thinks he is good enough to try me will get worse." For emphasis, Bolgers began to kick George in the stomach. With all of his last remaining strength, George grabbed Bolgers' kicking foot and twisted it hard enough to break his ankle.

Bolgers spun, screaming in pain. His body slammed down on the deck. His walking stick clattered across the planking.

George dragged himself to his feet. Standing over Bolgers, he saw hope mixing with the fear in his crew's eyes. In that instant, Bolgers withdrew a dagger from his boot and thrust it into George's thigh. As George staggered back, pulling out the dagger and tossing it over the side, Bolgers got to his feet, pulling a belaying pin from the rail. He bashed it into George's ribcage.

Wincing with pain, George exploded upon him with quick combination punches that drove Bolgers back against the main mast boom. Bolgers reached up and grabbed the block and tackle that hung from the boom's aft end and slammed it hard on the side of George's head, bringing even more blood. George staggered back.

Bolgers clamored across the deck to retrieve his walking stick. He quickly grabbed it and returned, swinging it to deal George the final deathblow. He missed.

As George twisted away from the swing, he booted Bolgers in the butt, sending him to the rail. George grabbed the block and tackle, quickly uncoiling some of its line, giving it room to swing. He swung it hard across to Bolgers, catching him on the forehead and sending him over the stern rail to the sea.

The crew cheered as they ran for the stern rail to look over. They saw Bolgers floating face down. The block had split his skull. His bloating brain was mixing with seawater. The men cheered wildly but quickly sobered into silence as they pondered their fates.

Hollings said, "There's a noose waiting in the town square for mutineers."

The silence was heavy. Finally, Hollings spoke again, "Anybody see a mutiny?"

Pickering chirped up, "I sure didn't!"

"I think Old Bolgers might've slipped," Hollings said.

The whole crew mumbled in agreement.

"Slipped."

"Yeah, he slipped."

By the time they reached the Rose 'n' Crown, the sunlight glowed orange and slanted in from a low, western angle. The Black Baller's signature foresail with the single, large black dot in the middle billowed and rolled slowly in the gathering breeze. A brisk chop shattered the water surface. The sea swirled in eddies around the shallow shoal ridges and rushed around the dying ship's hull.

George turned to his crew and shouted, "We'll

get no closer tonight. Ready the breeches buoy."

Hollings said, "Old Bolgers was right about one thing. In the morning calm, we probably could've slid right up alongside."

"Wouldn't have been worth it," George replied.

They pulled out the Lyle gun, set up the line and crotch arrangement and waited as George loaded the gun, lined up his aim and shot. He hit his mark the first time. The men watched as the padded ball sailed over the lowest yard of the Black Baller and looped around several times to make itself fast.

Hollings jumped up and put his weight on the line to test its safety.

"Secure enough for my first trip over," George said. "I'll secure it fully once I'm there."

The crew dragged out the breeches buoy and George slipped into it as the men attached it to the line. As soon as they were done, George pushed himself off and flew out over the spitting waves, pulling himself toward the ship. The line dipped and rose violently as it spanned between the motionless ship, stuck solidly on the shoal, and the rolling, bobbing schooner riding the waves. George was careful to control the line, taking up slack and paying out to make it taut and thereby keep himself from falling to the sea.

Still groggy and injured from his fight with Bolgers, George could feel the ache of his arms and shoulders grow stronger with each pull he made toward the ship. It was a good pain. George knew there was a natural, purity to it. It was functional pain, pain that told him he was living.

He watched as the ship got closer and closer. Before he knew it, he was leaping onto the Black Baller's yardarm and securing the breeches buoy rig so it would dependably hold himself, his crew, and all survivors as they brought them across to Bolgers' schooner. He tied each knot with confidence and speed, then scrambled down the ratlines to the ship's rail and jumped upon the deck. On his way, he looked around the rigging to make sure that no children had been secured there yet.

The ship's captain wove through the worried passengers to greet George. "Thank God, you've come. We were about to secure the children aloft so the sea wouldn't drown them as we sunk further."

"What about the lifeboats?"

"Not nearly enough," the captain said, "and the waves would bash them to kindling against these shoals."

George looked at him with silent sorrow, knowing how that alternative had once played out. He felt the sad irony of the captain's best of intentions yielding the worst of results. He put a comforting hand on the captain's shoulder. "They'll be safe and warm now," George said.

He saw gratitude in the captain's eyes. He then quickly left him in search of Rebecca. He found her on the crowded deck. Her face bloomed with relief and passion as she first saw him. They burst into each other's arms. Forgetting all of the social dictums, their kisses raced over each other's faces. Their love consumed them.

"I'm here for you," his hoarse voice croaked.

She noticed his beaten face. "How many bar fights before you found me?"

"A story for another time—I need to get you off."

"The children first," she said.

"They are being taken off as we speak."

Since George had arrived at the ship, his crew had been busy. They pulled the breeches buoy back to the schooner, and a few of them had used it to come, one by one, to the ship. Then they had removed the contraption from the yardarm, lowering it to the deck where they could more easily get the victims in and transported back to the schooner.

George watched Hollings help two terrified children over to the breeches buoy. Pickering stepped up.

"I'll take them," Pickering said as he slipped his legs in.

George laughed at the sight. "Pickering! You've become a true old salt, I see."

"Better than a banker's life," Pickering called back.

George and Hollings helped send them off.

Rebecca waited until last, preferring to stay with George until the end. By the time he could leave with her, the sun had long gone, and the evening's first stars were showing their faces. The wind had changed and steepened waves now battered the ship's overstressed hull.

George looked over to Rebecca. "You're next, my love."

"Is it safe?"

"It's been child-tested."

George saw the fear in her eyes. "I'll be with you. What happens will happen to us both." Just then, the deck shifted as twisting, splitting wood cried out in pain. George lost his light tone. "We've no time to lose."

He swept her up in his arms and stepped into the breeches buoy, pulling it up around him and placing her on his lap. They headed out over the worsening sea toward the schooner. As Rebecca looked down at the waves spitting far beneath her feet, she grabbed onto George with all of her might. She felt the strength of his grip around her, and she let it inspire comfort.

As they were about halfway across the bobbing and twisting snake of a line, a spine tingling snap rung out from the ship and it settled another ten feet into the sea, bringing their line that much closer to the water. Rebecca screamed and grabbed on even tighter.

"Don't worry, my love. She'll sink no further."

"How do you know?"

"I just do."

Now it was an uphill climb to the schooner. With his crew's help, pulling at their end, George got himself and Rebecca safely aboard.

In the captain's cabin of Bolgers' schooner that night, whale oil lamps cast a warm glow as everybody huddled to stave off the bitter cold. George watched the orange light flicker in Rebecca's glistening eyes. She reached a hand across to him. He took it in his. Hollings sat wedged in the corner, slowly playing his fiddle. The music heightened the romance of the moment. Bottles of Irish whiskey, from Bolgers' plunder, were passed around liberally. Everyone took warming swigs.

Pickering leaned in toward George. "There are platitudes about the kind of men who inspire others to follow them." Pickering fell silent as if he were searching for the right words to say. "I'm better at numbers than words," he finally added.

George took the whiskey and drank, handing it to Pickering. "Let the booze do your talking."

Pickering smiled warmly as he took it, knowing that his message had gotten through. Rebecca and George watched the men as laughs and whiskey flowed freely. Rebecca looked lovingly into George's eyes. "The children are well asleep. Care to brave the cold topside with me?"

George didn't have to think twice.

The cold blasted against George and Rebecca as

they climbed out on deck. They cuddled tightly under his warm pea coat.

"Oooo, colder than I'd realized," she said.

"We're on the lee side of the island now. Out on the Rose 'n' Crown, it's twenty or thirty degrees colder."

They pressed more tightly together for warmth as well as romance. They watched the moon as it drew a silver river across the black sea. They listened as warm laughs and music still drifted up from below deck. The steam of their breath glowed blue in the moonlight. They kissed long and hard. As they did, something fluttered in George's brain. Something unwelcome.

He tried to ignore it but couldn't. It was the only thing that could destroy the beauty of the moment. Suddenly, present-day George was a few feet down the deck, watching his earlier incarnation with Rebecca. Then there was a final tug.

FIFTY-ONE

Waves rolled in with crashing strength on the sands of Surfside Beach. Tucked inside the curl of a wave rolled George. He was spit out unceremoniously onto the sand. It was daytime, a gray, cloud-blotted December day.

Shocked, saddened, and disoriented, George dragged himself to his feet. The bitter cold drove in through his wet clothes and gave him an uncontrolled shiver. He was wearing the things he'd first dove in with, that faded puffy shirt and his own pants.

He looked around in a desperate attempt to get his bearings. He recognized Surfside Beach but what time was he in? He looked over to where Bolgers' construction site had scarred the present day sand, but it wasn't there.

Am I still in some past? he thought. Then he saw a small plane angle in for its final approach to Nantucket's airport. He was back in the present.

He tried unsuccessfully to control his shiver as he looked out to the waves, trying to process all that had happened. Through all of his bone weary cold, he knew that he'd never felt so good and alive inside his present-day skin. He had succeeded in his mission. He'd answered her call, her distress signal across oceans of time. He knew he'd carry it in his heart forever. But along with it was his sad sense of loss. He now had knowledge of bliss in a world he could never again touch. He wondered if all things in his life to come would be measured against this yardstick. Would anything ever measure up?

He walked to town in a daze, slipping back and forth between joy and personal loss. He realized that the pants he was wearing were his modern ones and that he at least still had his wallet, frozen and waterlogged though it was.

It was already late night by the time he'd gotten back to town. No more ferries until morning. He dragged himself up Broad Street as far as The Brotherhood of Thieves and stepped inside searching for warmth and humanity. George leaned across the bar with still wet hair and a visible shudder to his body. He could barely hold himself up on his arms because of his extreme physical and emotional fatigue.

Behind him, bar patrons drunkenly sang Christmas carols. Bob McKenzie, the bartender, sauntered over with fatigue-laden feet.

"Jesus, pal, you could use a drink," Bob said.

"Just coffee, please. Strong and hot," George said.

Bob studied him as the slurred Christmas songs permeated the background. He looked at the shirt. "Pretty cold to be out there playing pirate."

George had no answer.

"How 'bout some chowder? On the house." Bob ladled some thick, off-white, chunky chowder from a cast-iron cauldron behind the bar. Dumped it in a heavy porcelain bowl and slid it in front of George.

"Thanks."

Bob watched George's hand shake as he reached for the bowl and spoon. "Coffee's coming right up. I could put in a shot of Jameson, make it an Irish."

George barely listened. He looked up at the bartender. "What happened to the Bolgers construction site?"

Bob was confused. "What's a bowlers construction site?"

"Bolgers," George said. "Tristram Bolgers the Fourth. He's the Mayor."

Bob's confusion heightened. "Harry Beal is Mayor."

After an instant of shock, George smiled warmly.

Bob continued, "Maybe you're thinking of Martha's Vineyard or something? There's been no new construction here for years."

A few stools down from George, a wizened, old, white-haired man listened to their conversation. He added his two bits. "Town ordinance forbids it. That's what keeps this place so special."

Bob added, "We cling to the past around here."

"That I know," George said.

As Bob left, George stared into his chowder and let the depth of his adventure sink in. Reality would be forever changed here. Bolgers the Fourth never even got the chance to exist because of what had happened to Bolgers the First.

Wearing a coat he'd just bought from that used clothing store, George was first in line for the next day's earliest ferry. He savored the thick sea air of this last Nantucket morning. He breathed it in slowly and let it settle in his lungs before trading it back out for more. He watched the lazy spiral of seagulls, which hung around hoping for the odd crumb-throwing tourist. That was a scarce hope for this time of year, and they knew it.

George watched the ferry slowly round Brant Point Light. It wouldn't be long now. He looked around at everything as if it were for the last time. Home was only ninety or so miles from here, and he knew that someday he would return to Nantucket, but he also knew that the return trip would be different. He knew that the experience of any future return would be lost to that netherworld between remembering this trip and experiencing the new one. In that moment, George wondered if he really would ever return to Nantucket. Perhaps it was best to preserve memories by not trying to revisit them?

The fat boat drifted into its dock and started to open its huge mouth. Inside her labyrinth lower bay, eighteen-wheeler trucks belched to life, filling the rafters with exhaust smoke as their engines rumbled up to idle. They were Nantucket's lifelines, the only way to get the thousands of supplies for their restaurants and stores.

The number of walk-off passengers was small. Once the last person straggled ashore, George stepped aboard. He headed straight for the top deck where he could best survey all of Nantucket as he left it. He watched from the stern as the ferry slid out and away from the town that had revealed to him so many things.

Nantucket had been as much a state of mind to him as a physical place. Now it was hard for him to believe that he was drifting away from it. He watched Brant Point Light, so close he could almost touch it, as the fat boat lumbered around it.

Before long, Nantucket was a distant smudge of gray on the horizon. As George watched from the stern, a bank of fog rolled in. Nantucket disappeared into it in much the same way she had first appeared.

"Good bye," George said, slowly and to himself.

He stayed there for a few minutes in case Nantucket might briefly reappear. Each gray second that ticked by made it that much less likely. Finally, he forced himself to look away, to look ahead instead of back.

As he made his way forward to the bow, he thought about Boston and the life waiting for him there. It was the first time that he could remember fully contemplating those things since he first saw Rebecca. He reached the bow and peered through the white chalky fog. Hyannis had yet to show its face. When it did, this trip would all really be over. George felt excited about moving on. He knew that he'd never fall back into his old ways, his old self.

He started to make out the gray form of the Kennedy Compound. Hyannis Harbor would not be far behind. The fog began to lift. The ferry's engines cut, slowing her to a drift. With that, the wind died. As they nudged into the berth, George noticed a slightly miniature replica of Brant Point Light in someone's back yard. He was glad for the reminder.

FIFTY-TWO

The next morning George was on the Red Line subway. This was a ride he'd taken every day for years. His body and bones knew every rattle, every squeal of the brakes. Nantucket seemed more and more like a distant dream, with features that were melting like ice cream in the hot sun. He started to worry whether or not Nantucket's hold could last.

He noticed a political ad on the subway car's entryway glass. It contained the photo of a strong, smart looking, gray-haired woman. The banner read:

ELISABETH WINTHROP for State Representative
COMMONWEALTH of MASSACHUSETTS

George studied the poster. He stood and stepped over for closer inspection. It was Betty Bolgers, only she'd never become a Bolgers, was never beaten down, never lost her spark of hope.

Nantucket was strong in George again. It was his guiding light. He knew it always would be.

George strutted from the elevator onto his old office floor. It must've been that he was walking so much straighter, but the cubicles all seemed lower and smaller. It was like revisiting your old grammar school and trying to imagine yourself sitting in your old desk.

Sheehan waited triumphantly for him at the end of the row. His arms were crossed impassively. So anxious to spew his abuse, Sheehan started barking as soon as he figured George was in earshot.

"Well, back in time for the Christmas party, I see. Ours is for *employees*. For you, they throw an excellent party at the *Unemployment* office." Sheehan relished accenting the employment/unemployment part. When he finished, he laughed at his own joke. His laugh became thinner and slightly more nervous as he saw no fear in George's eyes, no slowing down.

Sheehan tried again. "In case you're too stupid to understand that, YOU'RE FIRED!! You've been fired for WEEKS! Since before THANKSGIVING!!"

George arrived leisurely in front of Sheehan and stared at him as if he were some oddity that he was watching in a museum.

George spoke matter-of-factly. "Do you know that, when you yell, those little purple spider veins in your nose start to glow?"

"Where do you get the balls to ... Do you remember who I am?"

"Don't YOU remember?"

Laughs came from some of the cubicles. Jim gleefully popped his head over his divider but quickly shot it down again before Sheehan could see him.

"WHO'S LAUGHING?" Sheehan demanded.

"Maybe," George said with calm strength, "we should take you into a dark closest and see if we can't still read a memo off that thing?"

Sheehan fumed but was afraid that he was in a losing game. He tried to backpedal. "Where I come from, bosses command a certain respect."

"That may be true, but here on Earth, we have to earn our respect."

"Maybe I should just call security and have them show you the door?"

"Thanks, but I've seen the door."

The whole cubicle clad room was laughing now in short bursts of irrepressible joy. Sheehan exploded. "I'm calling security! I'm calling security right now!"

"No you're not. You're still standing here babbling like a blithering idiot."

The laughter blossomed.

Sheehan spun around in a nearly complete circle, screaming at all the cubicles. His body vibrated with rage as he did. "Who's laughing? WHO'S LAUGHING?" Sheehan's face went from red to purple. He opened his mouth again but closed it quickly since no good words could come to him. He spun and stormed into his office, slamming the door.

Jim stuck his head over the top of his cubicle and let out all of his pent-up laughter. As he caught his breath, he said, "Wow! You're my own personal hero."

George tossed off a confident "Thanks."

"Drinks at the Black Rose tonight?" George asked.

Still in shock, Jim said, "Sure, anything. I'm at your command."

The office staff all slowly raised their heads above their cubicles to watch George strut off toward the elevator in victory. They were awestruck.

As the elevator doors opened in the lobby, George stepped out into a glassed-in, palatial atrium. At the wall of windows closest to the door was a huge Christmas tree fit for Rockefeller Center or The White House lawn. On a high ladder, a woman was hanging the last few ornaments. On the back of her shirt were the words NANTUCKET CHARMS.

George walked over to the base of the tree as she was on her way down the ladder. When she got near the bottom, he called up to her. "Are you from Nantucket?"

She hit the floor and turned to him as she answered. "No. The company started there. We decorate in that old Nantucket, Victorian-style."

She was facing him fully now. George's whole body shivered. Here in front of him was today's incarnation of Rebecca. There was no mistaking her. Joy flooded his eyes to the point where she became slightly concerned.

"Are you okay?" she asked.

"I'm very okay. More okay than I can tell you."

They stared at each other in awkward but enticing silence.

She asked, "Have we met before?"

"Have you ever been to Nantucket?"

"No, but I've always wanted to go. Pretty stupid to say that when it's not even a hundred miles away. I mean, why not just go, right?"

George could feel her strong attraction to him and sense the school-girl shyness in her voice. He knew it came from a cosmic history that he could never explain to her. He was bursting with his already formed love for her, ready to take up where he left off.

"Perhaps we could go there together sometime?" George said.

"Hold it, soldier. Maybe we should start with coffee first?"

"I know a great place right around the corner."

She twisted her lips for a moment as she thought about it. The Nantucket invite seemed creepy for someone she just met but something about him seemed safe and familiar and exciting all at the same time. How could she pass that up?

Twisting one foot around girlishly, she said, "I'm due a break right about now."

He offered out his arm.

She took it, and they walked off, together.

ABOUT THE AUTHOR

Though Jack Comeau has made his living as an Emmy Award-winning Lighting Designer for TV and Film, he has stayed close to his seagoing roots. His grandfather was a Grand Banks fisherman from Nova Scotia. Jack has spent years crewing old New England schooners much like the one that appears in this, his first novel, *Distress Signal*.

jackcomeau.com
www.facebook.com/distresssignalnovel

THE ARTIST

Neil Borrell has long made his living directing major, national, network television in New York City but that is certainly not where his talents end. Neil is also a very accomplished artist, working mostly in the pen and ink medium. Among his favorite subjects are the tiny seacoast villages that that speckle Cape Cod, Martha's Vineyard, and Nantucket.

Neil's artwork on the cover of my novel, Distress Signal, does so much more than depict a famous Nantucket landmark that is the first thing seen by all visitors arriving by boat. He has captured the exact mood and tone that I've tried to convey with my words. I can only hope I've done it as well.

- Jack Comeau

THE ART

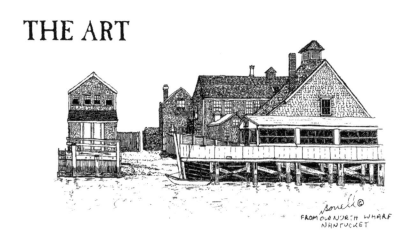

FROM OLD NORTH WHARF
NANTUCKET

OLD NORTH WHARF
NANTUCKET

Nantucket drawings by Neil Borrell

neil@borrellcompany.com
www.neilink.com

OLD NORTH WHARF
NANTUCKET

STEAMBOAT WHARF
NANTUCKET 6-75

Distress Signal
Jack Comeau

Also available in eBook Format

Made in the USA
Columbia, SC
12 October 2020